FIND ME GONE

FIND ME
GONE

a novel

SARAH MEULEMAN

HARPER

An Imprint of HarperCollinsPublishers

Originally published as *De Zes Levens Van Sophie* in Belgium in 2015 by Lebowski Publishers.

FIRST U.S. EDITION PUBLISHED 2018.

Designed by Jamie Lynn Kerner

Library of Congress Cataloging-in-Publication Data has been applied for.

ISBN 978-0-06-283465-2 (pbk.)
ISBN 978-0-06-287070-4 (library edition)

18 19 20 21 22   LSC   10 9 8 7 6 5 4 3 2 1

For LJ

I am not one and simple, but complex and many.

—VIRGINIA WOOLF,
The Waves

In another moment down went Alice after it, never once considering how in the world she was going to get out again.

—LEWIS CARROLL,
Alice's Adventures in Wonderland

FIND ME GONE

PROLOGUE

NOBODY KNOWS.

The woods are deep and dark. I run between the trees, stumble over roots, twigs snapping underfoot. Faster, faster still. The air is cold, the silent water flashes past.

I should have held her tight and never let go. As she slept beside me, her breath on my skin, I should have told her nothing means more than the scent hidden in the hollow of her neck, the scent of close as can be. And then that other, even sweeter, forbidden scent.

A rustling behind me. I glance back. I cannot see him but I can almost feel his hands on me. He must be somewhere among the tree trunks, every one the same. Where is the house? Shouldn't there be a house somewhere with a door that swings open, a friendly face, someone who can help? I don't know which way to turn.

Branches clutch at my party dress, claw at tattered lace.

Shreds heavy with dirt, water, blood. I think of warm rooms, beds piled with cushions, the pink blanket we snuggled under. Our little nest, safe from all the others. Far from any danger. A trickle of blood on her delicate skin.

I trip and slam facedown in the dirt. A throbbing cheek, a bloody tooth. Footsteps thud closer. Keep still, stay small, don't breathe. If only I could disappear. Dive beneath the leaves and never come up. Climb the highest tree and never come down. Sink into the waves and never come back.

Her face, so beautiful, so brittle. The taste of bitter earth. Footsteps closing in on me, I know I can't escape. My feet are slow, my mind is tired. I think about her safe embrace as my voice urges soundless, helpless: "Come find me. I need you. *Soon it will be too late.*"

I

AGATHA

GONE BABY GONE

NEW YORK, 2014

THIS IS THE WAY. MORE A LURCH SIDEWAYS THAN A BOLD STEP forward, but it's a start. Hannah trudges up the stairs of the run-down New York warehouse, halter top clingy with sweat, cutoff jeans sticking to her thighs. Every step of the climb, her feet sink into the soft, stringy wood. It's like the whole place is melting. Now and then she stops and leans against a wall before cursing the stale air and hauling another box up to the fourth floor.

Get away. That was the whole idea. Away from the It girls and their perfect parties, the terminally smug players, the bar-flies and wallflowers, the DJs with their loved-up teen group-ies. A brand-new start, no frills. The glamorous life has had its day. This is now, Hannah thinks: an empty room, twelve feet by twenty on the wrong side of the river. *So real.*

It's late August and New York is simmering. The apartment

has no air-conditioning and tepid smog drifts in through the open window. She lugs the last box through the door of her humble abode and wanders over to the kitchen or what passes for one: a sink, a fridge, and a microwave. She fills a tumbler with cold water and gulps it down. Once-in-a-lifetime deal, the broker had said. A steal compared to the upgraded properties down the street. Properties without leaky faucets, cracked floors, and weeping walls, she now understands. But Hannah was sold as soon as she saw the windows. Typical Bushwick windows: a mosaic of little square panes set in black iron frames overlooking the factories, sheds, and workshops that make up much of the neighborhood.

The grit and grime of Bushwick, a district on the edge of Brooklyn. Up-and-coming, so they said, a mere twelve minutes on the L train from the spiffy streets of Greenwich Village and the life she has left behind. Hannah crouches in a corner, elbows on thighs, toes spread on sweating concrete. Compact, a girl of almost thirty with a mess of blond hair and a faceful of freckles. From this angle it looks pretty spacious, she thinks to herself. Who's she trying to kid? It's not a fraction of the airy apartment she called home only two weeks ago. Everything's different now. Empty.

Not voguishly empty like her old lounge on Cornelia Street, the sleek brand of minimalism the glossies fall over themselves to feature. A room so understated it screamed Quality, Luxury, Style. No, she has taken it into her head to inhabit this tragic void, to crouch on a concrete floor with cracks that skitter away in every direction.

I need a sofa, Hannah thinks. A sofa, a table, and a chair or two. She catches sight of herself in the mirror propped against the wall: wrists clamped under her chin, alert, a rabbit in a hole, safe for now but so far removed from everything that once felt good. The phone rings and she jumps.

"Hannah?" It's Bee, of course. "Hannah, are you there?" A tense voice from her recent past, the Manhattan life she gave up or, as her friends say, *chucked away*. Hannah knows exactly what's coming: pressure sweetly but insistently applied. Just leave me the fuck alone, she wants to say. But that's not who she is.

"Hear me out, Hannah. I don't know what's gotten into you but I want you to come this evening. It's the best party I've been working on in years: high profile, huge sponsors, A-listers. I need you to be there. I invited the friends and everyone's coming. They are dying to see you, Hannah, to see how you are. We miss you terribly."

It's classic Bee: always on the brink of catharsis, tending her little flock. But Hannah knows: Bee needs the flock more than it needs her. She's constantly rubbing layers of varnish on her perfect family. Hannah moving to Brooklyn is an unfortunate scratch that must be repaired—but it never will. Hannah stares in silence till the cracks in the concrete morph into a herd of elephants, trunks clumsily strung together.

"Hannah, he just doesn't get it. He's in shock."

"I'm not in the mood for talking, Bee. This is how it is. I'm here, he wants me back. Point taken."

"Hannah doll, I'm the last person to leap to Boy's defense, but he's going mad. You took your things and didn't say a word, what is the guy to think? He wants to see you. He cares about you, we all do. You needed a change, I get that, but do you really have to *chuck it all away*? You can't just wall yourself in like some crackpot recluse and forget about your friends. For God's sake, Hannah, what's *the plan*?"

The plan, there always needs to be a plan. The thought of defending her plan for the hundredth time makes her sick.

"Are you listening, Hannah? Okay, so you're going through a rough time. We all know about the horrible thing that happened. But babe, I care about you and I need you to think what's truly best for you. Think of yourself, Hannah."

Isn't that what she *is* doing? Thinking of herself for once? The gray herd in the floor dissolves into elephant gunk. She squeezes her eyes shut and hears her voice say: "Okay, Bee, you win. I'll be there."

"Attagirl! It will be spectacular. Fantastic. See you soonest."

The knot in Hannah's stomach tightens.

ONCE UPON A TIME IN BELGIUM

BACHTE-MARIA-LEERNE, 1996

THEY HAVE NEVER SEEN THE CAVE BEFORE, THOUGH THEY OFTEN come to the woods to play. It burrows into the hillside, hidden away among the undergrowth.

"No! Me first! We agreed!"

Cheeks flushed from running, Sophie fixes Hannah with an indignant glare. A sulky girl in a red T-shirt and dungarees, her hair scraped into pigtails. Hannah has told her so many times she's lost count: Those pigtails have got to go. Not that it makes any difference. Sophie does whatever she wants and now she is stamping her foot on the ground.

Hannah shrugs. "Okay then, you first. See if I care."

Sophie marches over and peers into the black mouth of the cave. Feeling her way along the damp rock with one hand, she edges inside. Chin up, back to the wall, a miniature special agent

Dana Scully caught up in her very own X-File. Hannah can't help laughing. All this fuss about a hole in the rock. Alien life-forms have better places to hang out than a Belgian wood. Sophie looks back: Shhh! Then she disappears into the dark and everything goes quiet.

Hannah leans her tall slender frame against a tree and ruffles her hair, bleached almost white by the summer sun. She looks much older than Sophie, but there is only a year between them. Hannah is twelve and Sophie still eleven, though the wild and willful way she acts sometimes you'd swear she was only nine.

Cradling their penknife in her hand, Hannah opens the blade and clicks it shut, as her eyes find the bark where they carved their initials. Last summer, Sophie brought the penknife to Hannah's house as a token of their friendship. At first, Hannah had been shocked, then Sophie explained how all the boys cherish their knives, how she had read about it in her books, so why shouldn't girls as well?

The penknife was in fact a pretty thing: shiny with a gracious black antelope painted on the handle. As Hannah folded her hand around it she suddenly sensed a mysterious sort of power; as she clicked the blade out of its sheath she felt a spark, a strength, right there, within her reach.

From then on the knife switched from Hannah's pocket to Sophie's and back again: a knife to share, their secret weapon. Carrying it around felt exciting and adventurous and although they never talked about it, they each knew the other felt exactly the same way.

Now Hannah hardly ever thinks about the knife anymore. The whole idea seems silly, awkward even. And who knows what

Sophie feels these days? She pushes it back in her pocket, zips her brand-new jacket up to her chin, and looks around. The sun has gone and a chill is descending. She'd rather not be here at all. There was a party at The Sloop, the last before the end of the school holidays, but Sophie insisted they come to the woods. What's keeping her? Dark clouds close in above the treetops. Oh great, now her new jacket will get wet. She picks her way through the bushes to the entrance of the cave.

"Come on, Sophie," she yells. "It's going to rain."

The first drops tap her on the shoulder. A sudden gust of wind sends the sorriest leaves spinning from their branches.

"Sophie? It's raining. Get a move on." Not a sound. Only the wind.

"That's it! I'm coming to get you."

Reluctantly, Hannah ventures into the shadows, trips over a stone, and steadies herself against the slick wall. The cave is deeper than she thought, growing darker with every step. No sign of Sophie. Up ahead she spots another opening, smaller but just wide enough for a young girl. She hesitates, glances back toward the mouth of the cave, a fading patch of light. Reaching the opening, she wriggles out of her brand-new jacket and squeezes through the gap, brushing the brown streaks from her top before putting her jacket back on.

"Sophie?"

No answer, only more trees. The rain is falling steadily now. At the edge of her vision a shadow flits beneath the branches.

"Sophie!"

Hannah hears rustling and walks toward the sound, feels her anger rising. Her new jacket is already wet. Much more of this and she won't be able to show it off at school; the fabric will wrinkle and it will barely be recognizable as the prized possession she saved up for months to buy.

"For God's sake, Sophie!"

Raindrops fall thick and fast. Hannah runs past trees and under branches, pushes her way through the bushes. The woods seem vast now, the houses of the village more distant than ever. She could scream and no one would hear. Suddenly Hannah thinks of the missing children, the four young girls the whole country has been searching for all summer.

She tries not to listen when her parents talk about the girls: It feels awkward, wrong, a horrible secret she's not supposed to be in on. But what if it's real? What if Sophie has been abducted or is lying somewhere among the fallen leaves, wounded and unconscious? What if she wants to cry for help but can't? What if she never comes back? Hannah feels a stab of panic deep inside.

"Sophie!"

A crow caws in reply. Then a scream pierces the air and a shape shoots through the leaves. Before Hannah can spin around, a sudden force hits her from behind, sends her sprawling. A figure looms over her, face streaked with brown, hands caked in mud. A wild-eyed warrior who has been crawling through the dirt, who gives a triumphant laugh and yells, "Scared, eh? Ha ha! Boy were you ever scared!"

"Damn it, Sophie!" Hannah gets up and shakes her clothes, brushing dirt and rotting leaves from her jacket with firm strokes. To Sophie, every stroke feels like a slap in the face. She sinks to the ground and squats motionless, a pose Hannah knows all too well: eyes blank, lips sealed, frozen. Wild and willful one moment, fragile the next. Hannah melts inside. "You really had me worried, Sophie," she whispers, laying a gentle hand on her shoulder. "Don't do that again, promise?"

Sophie shakes her head so hard that her pigtails brush against her cheeks. She opens her arms and Hannah surrenders to her warmth, to the perfect fit of two small bodies. Softly, Sophie runs a finger down the bridge of Hannah's nose.

The rain begins to ease off. The woods have shrunk to normal size and the houses are peeping through the trees again. Hannah takes off her jacket and holds it above their heads. Untouched by the raindrops, the girls laugh and together they walk back through the drizzle, out of the sodden wilderness toward the broad lane lined with houses and the safe smell of freshly mown lawns.

LITTLE WHITE DRESS

NEW YORK, 2014

AN EXTRAVAGANT EMBRACE, AS IF SHE HASN'T SEEN HANNAH IN years.

"Welcome, darling," Bee coos, clearly high as a kite and channeling every society hostess since time began. Queen Bee to her friends and her professional coterie: thrower of parties, outré fashion icon, incidental dealer, peacekeeper, and patron saint of gay clubbers. Tonight she's a flurry of feathers and pink chiffon, a plunging neckline and thigh-length split showcasing a brazen lack of lingerie. Bronzed skin oiled and shimmering, tacky tiara twinkling atop a jet-black wig. A flamingo, towering above the crowd on stilt-like legs and killer stilettos.

Top heavy, thinks Hannah and pictures Bee taking one careless step, teetering on those impossible heels and then . . . boom. Just like the toy soldiers she used to play with. Pretty men all in a row, a shiver of delight as they fell at the flick of a finger . . .

boom, boom, boom. But Bee never wavers. At least never in public.

"I'm so-o-o glad you came!"

I can still make a run for it, Hannah thinks but instead she stays put and does her best to smile, demure in her white cotton dress, narrow ribbon at the waist, hemline just above the knee. Salvaged from a Brooklyn thrift store, the kind of dress worn only by Bushwick hipster chicks and seven-year-olds on Sunday visits to Grandma's. By far the most comfortable thing she's worn in years but here, surrounded by fashionistas in spray-on designer outfits, she feels uneasy and out of place, a wayward communicant.

Bee moves through the crowd toward her sporting a professional, almost violent smile. Hannah knows it all too well: the toothpaste selling in your face over the top aggressive upward jerk of the lips that seems mandatory in LaLaLand but only makes her think of angry monkeys and hissing cats. When Bee stands before her, the violent smile suddenly softens. She looks down at Hannah from her stilts, shakes her head in a mixture of bewilderment and relief, gently puts her soft manicured hands around Hannah's shoulders, and observes her tenderly.

She bends over and whispers: "*Really* glad. I know it wasn't easy for you to show up here, babe." A moment of silence. Bee fumbles with the ribbon on the white dress, pulls it straight. "But we'll talk about that later, right? Drinks, real soon, just you and me?" Hannah nods. Bee winks, then makes a buoyant turn with layers of fluttering chiffon and effortlessly picks up the festive script where she left it off.

"Hey, have you met Roger?" Bee exclaims, lassoing the first

male within striking distance. "Roger, this is Hannah. We used to work together." Poor Roger musters a flustered nod and stammers a polite "Would you like a drink?"

"Yes, but I'll get it myself." Hannah turns on her heels and goes in search of booze. She can feel Bee's indignation prickling in the back of her neck but the obligatory excuses fall just out of earshot. Oh don't mind, Hannah, Roger. She's going through a rough patch. You know how it is with us girls.

What the roof terrace lacks in size it makes up for with its sweeping vista of Manhattan. Bee has swung a sponsorship deal with a niche fashion label and conjured up a circus theme. The partygoers are bathed in the warm glow of cotton-ball lights strung between Disney-red lampposts. Toyboy waiters in starched white shirts and dicky bows hover with trays of champagne. A human flamethrower spews tongues of fire and a bouncing DJ is lost in music that can barely be heard above the deafening chatter of beautiful rooftop people.

The evening is warm but not oppressive. Hannah homes in on a table laden with drinks and ladles a generous goblet full to the brim with punch. Chunks of stewed pear bob in a pool of red. Getting drunk is a minimum requirement tonight.

She scans the crowd and sees him nowhere. Boy. Not a word since the door of their Village apartment clicked shut behind her and her stack of boxes. He was too proud to reach out, she too cowardly to give him the chance. Hannah walks to the edge of the night and gazes out: the Chrysler Building, pleasure cruisers on the Hudson, two bridges twinkling. A world where the price of real estate soars according to the number of bridges you look down on.

There wasn't a drop of water to be seen from their place in the Village, but that didn't stop them divvying up the bridges: Manhattan Bridge for Boy, Brooklyn Bridge for Hannah, and the bridge to Williamsburg reserved for the little girl growing inside her. A girl. No way she could know, but somehow she just knew. Baby names bubbled to the surface on a daily basis, almost became an obsession. Every evening she would arrive home with a fresh roll call and try them out on poor, weary Boy. Excited but in deadly earnest she would begin.

"Okay, listen up." Pause for effect. "Iris?" Check response. "Leyla?" A sigh from Boy. "Ivy?" "Emma?" "Jane?" Then he would laugh, grab her by the waist, and steer her across to the huge bed where they would lie side by side, his hand resting just below her navel.

"We have six months yet. It'll come, you'll see."

Only it didn't come. Their baby never had a name, never even became a baby. Suddenly one evening as she rode the subway home from Union Square, their little girl was gone. "It happens," said the nurse. "More often than you'd think." As if that changes anything. She takes a bitter gulp.

"Hannah!" She turns to see Robin and Malick charging toward her, arms outstretched. The perfect couple, eight years and counting: Malick in a cobalt-blue suit, checked shirt, and canary-yellow braces, Robin in designer jeans and a stretch T-shirt, flaunting his gym-bunny credentials.

"You! Here!" Robin grins. "How ya doin', stranger?" Kisses and opening gambits. "So how's Bushwick treating you?"

"Fine." She nods. "Only just moved in, really. Still finding my feet."

"And your book? Already typing those little fingers to the bone?"

"Yeah, getting there."

"And don't you miss us?"

There it is again. The burning question. Don't you miss us? Yes, she misses everyone and everything: the soy-milk cappuccinos from Danny's, the documentary screenings at Malick's place. But at the same time, she doesn't. There's a mist between her and missing.

"Is this all the rage in Bushwick, Hannah?" Malick takes in her white dress with a wave of his arm. "Renounced our wardrobe too, have we?"

Robin delivers a swift elbow to the ribs: *Button it!*

"Don't get me wrong, babe. You wear it well. But for a party . . . ?"

She takes another gulp.

"Is it some kind of statement, Hannah? Have you come to teach us all a little lesson? Not good enough as we are?"

She raises a feeble smile as Malick hits his stride.

"You see, I've been racking my brain trying to understand. What makes a successful columnist, adored by a blond Adonis like Boy, decide to abandon her fabulous apartment and bid farewell to . . . well, just about everything. What's up, Hannah? Weren't we worthy of you? Or is this a classic case of self-castigation?"

He hooks his fat thumbs behind his braces and shoots her a self-satisfied stare. Not a trace of the Malick she has known for almost ten years.

In little more than a week, Boy had put the loss behind him.

Why don't we give it another try? As if their little girl were a cup that had slipped from her fingers and could be easily replaced.

Out of the corner of her eye she spots an older man standing by the bar. He looks hesitant, almost as out of place as she is, observing the crowd as if the party were playing on a distant screen. With one last swig, she drains her glass.

"Sorry, but there's someone I have to say hi to," she says, sounding bitchier than she meant to.

Dizzy from the punch, she edges her way through the heaving crowd toward the Observer. He must be in his fifties, his muscular frame sporting a crumpled shirt and tailored denims. There is something imperious in his bearing, elitist even. Deep-brown eyes set in a broad face, a wry smile on his lips. She wants to ask what half a century of manhood is doing on a roof full of thirty-somethings in the heart of the Village. Instead she looks up at him and smiles.

"I've come to talk to you."

Dull to the point of embarrassment. Like a woman overboard, clinging to a fellow victim in the hope that he can drag her drunken ass ashore.

"That's kind of you." His amused twinkle makes her cringe.

"What do you do?"

"I'm a photographer."

"Magazines? Exhibitions?"

"Both."

"Hey, good for you." The response of a moronic teenager. Oh well.

"Just got back from a sailing expedition across the Pacific."

Ah, that explains the deep tan, the etched wrinkles, and the fresh breeze that seems to waft around him. Airbrushed. Younger than she took him for, perhaps. Odd accent too. Not American, but not British either.

"So you photographed the ocean?"

"Not likely." He laughs. "Spent most of my time lazing around. Escaping the nightmares I shoot for a living, searching for the kind of idyll Captain Cook might have stumbled upon. Nature unspoiled."

"And did you find it?"

"No, can't say I did."

He's based in Johannesburg, he explains, but lives life on the road, Africa mainly, his lens trained on revolutions, genocide, and natural disasters. Hannah nods but the words spark no pictures in her mind. Revolution, genocide: to her these are abstract terms, almost innocent when spoken at an upbeat rooftop party. She feels desperately naïve.

"And what about you?"

Gulping punch from her refilled glass, she wonders what to say. *I write pieces for a top-notch fashion glossy read by everyone on this roof and I'm damn good at it.* Hannah, the success story: beautiful, talented, surfing her way through the fast life. Or the truth: *I've given it all up to write a biography and have yet to type a single letter.* The cool fabric of her dress ripples against her thighs. She opts for the truth but sputters: she sounds incoherent, almost angry. He looks fascinated, poised to ask a question, but she is already heading back to the punch bowl, glancing around as she ladles another glassful. Still no sign of Boy.

She kills time with the Observer. He's a good talker and something of a celebrity, shuttling between war-zone chaos and the sterile surroundings of the world's museums, where his horrific images prick polite consciences in cool white spaces.

"Check that out!" he says. She turns to see four men on stilts galumphing among the revelers. Dalí. *Watch out!* A clown slams into her. Smudged mascara, cigarette clamped between carmine-red lips: a clown from a horror flick, a mask that hides a twisted mind or a secret camera.

As a child she thought cameras were watching from the eyes of her teddy bears. Every night at bedtime, she would turn their faces to the wall, one by one, so they never saw what was happening. *They didn't, she did.* A cobra tattoo slithers up the DJ's neck.

Her stomach turns, her head spins. The Observer snakes an arm around her shoulder. "Are you okay?" It feels warm, safe. Yes. I'm okay.

"I should probably go."

"Why the rush?" he asks. "Just as things were getting cozy."

Then, among the swarm of happy faces, she spots the hopeless figure she was expecting. Ice-blue eyes, a shock of blond hair, the lean contours of a perfect body. Boy. His face tight with anguish. This is all wrong, she thinks. Get out. Now.

"Sure you're okay?" the Observer persists.

"Get me out of here," she says. He doesn't waste a second.

She lets herself be led through the crowd, beneath an arch of flickering circus letters, down stairs, past brooding doormen, along a narrow hallway rank with piss and vomit, through a doorway clogged with yakking, swaying smokers, and out into the street. Everything is a blur. She leans against a wall and feels the Observer's warm hand on her neck, gliding over her hips, under her dress. This will do, she thinks. Anything is better than Boy's sad eyes asking why she left and being forced to admit that she doesn't have a fucking clue.

Under the white communion dress his fingers caress her thighs and slide between. Something is missing. There's always something missing. She lets her head fall to one side and he kisses her neck. *Something wanting* as the English so elegantly put it. *Something wanting*. Her.

IF I WERE A BOY

BACHTE-MARIA-LEERNE, 1996

THE VILLAGE IS SLEEPING. AND EVERY BELGIAN VILLAGE SLEEPS the sleep of the dead. Shutters down, cats indoors, cars under lock and key. Sophie is spending the night at Hannah's, an all-mod-cons villa that wants to be a farmhouse: a central bay window, a wooden carport, and an arched front door with a lead knocker—features it shares with nearly every other house in Bachte. A Belgian, so they say, is born with mortar running through his veins, destined to build his own unique sanctuary on this earth. But somehow every pile of bricks in Bachte ends up looking exactly the same.

Sophie is wide awake, fretting about the bombshell Hannah dropped an hour or so ago. *Mum and Dad say this year they'll let me go to The Sloop on Fridays.* The Sloop: a bar the schoolkids flock to while their parents turn a blind eye. The kids that go there tell tall tales Sophie finds bizarre, speak a language she doesn't understand, and act like the adults they are so plainly not.

"Why?" she asked.

"'Cause," Hannah replied. "It's where everyone goes."

Everyone? Yeah, right. "Everyone" meaning "the boys of St. Barbara's High." Sophie knows the score: Hannah is crazy about boys because the boys are crazy about Hannah. She perks up at every zit-faced dork that glances her way.

"Whatever," she snapped. "Just don't expect me to come."

"Aw, come on, Sophie! Why not? We'll chat a little, drink a little. It'll be fun, you'll see."

The very thought makes Sophie shudder. The boys ignore her and she ignores them back. At parties they never ask her to dance. It's not that she doesn't want them to, it's just that it never happens. There's a message stamped on her forehead: *Leave well alone!* A warning that never fades. She tosses and turns in her nightie with the smiley Mickey Mouse.

"Hannah?"

The spare mattress is thin and she can feel the wooden floor beneath. Hannah is sleeping in her own soft bed, her breathing deep and regular. The moon peeps in through the half-open curtains and lights up the room. Sophie gazes up at the ceiling— elongated shadow puppets balance on the beams, contorting into the weirdest shapes.

"Hannah, can I ask you one more thing?" Not a sound.

"Are you awake, Hannah?"

She kicks off the covers, rolls onto her knees, and watches her best friend, this quiet, sleeping girl. Hannah is beautiful, so very beautiful. With her long white-blond hair and her full lips that gently quiver with each breath. That she knows what those lips feel like, taste like, is a secret neither of them will ever tell.

She follows the soft and perfect curve of Hannah's waist and hips under her cream-colored nightdress.

Then she looks down at her own scrawny body covered in a hysterical Mickey Mouse. The other day she perched on the edge of the bathtub, naked, to look at herself in the mirror. All she could see was her ribs poking out and skin so pale you could almost look right through. It made her cry. Hannah is firm and graceful. Someone who can give shelter.

Sophie leans over her sleeping friend, so close that she can smell her breath, the heavy, intimate air of the life in Hannah's body. She shuts her eyes and breathes Hannah's breath. She wants to slide under the sheets, rest her body next to Hannah's, press her face to Hannah's neck, her soft breasts, to merge, to melt into her. Maybe. One more time.

Quietly she crawls back under her own covers. She looks up at the posters of Brad Pitt and No Doubt on the walls. There is a wooden crucifix too and a photo of Hannah and Sophie taken at the hospital soon after Hannah's baby brother was born. Two toddlers in fluttering skirts, running, running hand in hand down an endless, endless hallway . . . She begins to doze and finally nods off.

When she opens her eyes, Hannah is already up and dressed, standing at the mirror fiddling with mascara. Her mother calls upstairs. It's time to fetch the croissants for breakfast.

"Get up, sleepyhead." Hannah grabs a cuddly toy from her desk and hurls it at Sophie—a threadbare panda clutching a soggy stick of bamboo.

"Eeuch!"

"Did you sleep tight?"

Sophie barely slept a wink but she keeps it to herself. She doesn't say that she knelt for hours at Hannah's bedside, watching her. There's no harm in it, of course there isn't, yet somehow it feels wrong.

"Yeah, I slept fine."

They stroll downstairs where Hannah's father is reading the paper and her little brother is stacking toy cars one on top of another. The radio is playing and the presenter promises new and shocking facts in the investigation of the missing girls. The kitchen table has been set for breakfast.

"Hi Dad," Hannah says and gives her father an affectionate peck on the cheek. So this is how things go when life is good. Sophie lingers by the door and raises her hand. Yes, I'm here too—*again*. Sophie envies Hannah for all kinds of reasons, her father above all. A quiet man, always so patient and kind. Deeply religious too, something she has a hard time making sense of. Sophie doesn't believe in God, even though he has been with her ever since the ice-cold water was dribbled over her tiny skull. She can't help thinking true believers are naïve. But in Hannah's house, the Lord has done nothing but good. The big, bad world outside never seems to intrude. In every room, a crucifix.

Hannah's mom is juicing oranges at the kitchen counter. Nine o'clock on a Sunday morning and there she stands in her tight jeans, juice drops whizzing perilously close to her spotless white blouse. She always looks immaculate, a warm lipsticked smile at the ready. "Now hurry down for those croissants, girls!"

They take the money, grab a shopping bag, and stroll through the village to the little bakery. The sole preserve of the crusty baker's wife on weekdays, now three young salesgirls are darting to and fro behind the counter among big iron racks of steaming pastries. The place is crammed with customers clutching numbered tickets, eager to get their hands on fresh bread, rolls, and homemade pies.

At last it's the girls' turn to order their croissants. Sophie looks on as Hannah's eyes zero in on the salesgirl's hand. It's the same drama every week: Hannah hoping feverishly that this time she can leave the shop with her dignity intact, sent on her way with nothing more than a grown-up "Have a nice day." No such luck. The girl's hand dips into the jar beside the cash register and, flashing the brightest of smiles, she holds out two lollipops.

It is Hannah's firm conviction that they are well past lollipop age, and besides candy makes you fat. Shamefaced, she stuffs the offending goodies in her pocket at lightning speed. Sophie doesn't understand what the fuss is about and is already relishing the prospect of two lollies instead of one. As soon as they are outside, she sticks the first in her mouth and, cheek bulging, delivers her weekly dose of consolation.

"Don't take it personally. She's only trying to be nice."

"*Nice?* Retarded, that's what it is. Is she blind or something?"

She glares angrily and storms off at full speed. Sophie tries to keep up, searching frantically for something to lighten the mood.

"Hey! First day of high school next week!" She pokes Hannah in the ribs but barely elicits a shrug. Sophie loves school; Hannah hates it. More often than not, Sophie ends up with a double helping of homework: Hannah's and her own. It never takes her long, so it's an easy enough way to make Hannah happy.

"It's going to be *awesome*." She tosses the lollipop stick into the bushes that line the sidewalk. Hannah takes a croissant from the paper bag and hands it to Sophie. Then she helps herself to one.

"No, it isn't!"

Maybe Hannah's right. Even though they are changing schools, how different can it be? Same old dark-green uniform—the ugliest color Sophie has ever seen—and another posse of hawk-eyed nuns to watch your every move, plus Sister Gregoria ruling the roost. Strictly but fairly the pupils say, with grudging respect.

"It feels more serious somehow," Sophie muses.

"Huh! Like we're not serious enough already?"

"Yesh, vewy, vewy see-wee-us!" Sophie replies with a chunk of croissant hanging half out of her mouth. Hannah laughs and her face brightens.

"The big difference is now I get to go to The Sloop every Friday!"

Sophie winces. The Sloop! That was what kept her awake all last night. She doesn't want to tag along with Hannah to that stupid bar. Not now, not soon, not ever. But she knows Hannah will go, with or without her.

Sophie chokes down the mouthful of croissant, tucks what's left in her coat pocket, and walks the rest of the way in silence, her fingers kneading the warm pastry into a ball. Without a word they turn onto the driveway, around the big house and through the back door into the kitchen where the table is always laid and fresh coffee awaits.

LOSING MY RELIGION

NEW YORK, 2014

THE HARSH GLARE OF MORNING GUSHES IN. HANNAH STANDS AT the sink, head pounding, and drinks as much water as she can stomach. It's too little, too late. Yesterday's heat lingers in the room. She refills a mug that reads KEEP CALM AND LOVE BEARS in black capitals beside a picture of a photogenic grizzly. A surprise gift from Boy, a memento of the night they spent huddled in their tent in Yellowstone Park while what sounded like a bear sniffed and rummaged for scraps nearby. Boy's cheek pressed firmly to hers, frightened but not really. The fear of a camper who has pitched her tent in a numbered spot—compartmentalized, theme-parked fear. Not like this at all.

She pulls on a pair of panties and walks over to the window. Her skin smells of sex, silt and sour. She takes a rubber band from her wrist and sweeps her hair back into a ponytail. The bright sunlight shows up the dirt on the glass. It's Sunday and

Bushwick's wide streets are deserted. The view from her window doesn't look like New York at all, more like an abandoned industrial lot on the edge of a Rust Belt town.

Life in Manhattan came with a nonstop parade of extras: people in nonspeaking parts, always in motion, shopping or toddling by, even on a Sunday. How she had hated those long, lonely Sundays as a girl in Bachte, trapped within four walls, Mom and Dad slumped on the couch. A cake after tea, a bath before bed. Counting the hours till she could go to sleep and wake up to a new day, a new beginning.

The Observer is curled up on the small mattress, sleeping like a baby. She remembers him pushing her through the door, undressing her without a moment's hesitation, not a hint of respect for the mystery of a stranger's body. Routine, she thought. But not for her.

Before Brooklyn she used to be picky about her men; now she has taken home the very first guy who smiled. She always wondered if she would be able to surrender to a random man— now she knows she can. It doesn't make her proud. It confuses her, at best. She feels nothing but indifference toward the sleeping creature on her mattress who has nothing to do with her and never will.

She crouches at the foot of the bed and studies his body. There's something toad-like about it: big, round, ponderous. *Toad*, the word sticks in her head.

The first man after Boy. She remembers how last night with every kiss, every act of so-called intimacy, she felt herself drifting a little further away from Boy and how she felt relieved by the sense of distance she has been yearning for ever since she closed the door of their home on Cornelia Street.

Now, in the rasping morning light, with the stingy smell of sex still hovering in the air, she realizes the Observer is nothing but a tool. An attraction to repel. The promise of distance approaching. Soon she'll be able to say: *I loved Boy once*. She tries to, whispers: "I loved Boy once." But the words sound silly, wrong.

He needs to go. Loudly she begins to poke around in one of her cardboard boxes for something to wear. She unearths a Bob Marley T-shirt and pulls it over her head before stepping into the cutoff jeans she has been wearing all week. He grunts, turns over on the mattress, and puts a hand over his ear.

She recalls snatches of their nighttime conversation and the sudden thought that struck her: The man is still a boy. Unchanged by time, the passing of his years, the wars, his children, his lovers; they might have left a scratch or two but the foundation stays the same. She can't tell whether this makes her hopeful or extremely sad.

Hannah redoes her ponytail, less hurriedly this time, and strolls over to her bag. He finally wakes up, heaves his toad body from the mattress and rubs his eyes, a boy of fifty.

"I have to leave in a sec," she lies. "Running late again."

He looks a little hazy, still connecting last night's dots.

"Oh. No time for breakfast? I know a nice little joint for coffee close by."

Close by. Things are looking up: He knows what part of town he's in. He can't have been that drunk after all. Perhaps he even remembers the things they said in the dark, words that meant everything and nothing, like so many nocturnal exchanges. Fragments of sentences resurface, the suave turns of phrase that come so easily to him.

"You're a panther. I try to net you and you keep slipping away from me with that lithe body of yours."

She rolled over, laid her head on his chest, and laughed.

"And you are a fantasist."

He ran a lazy hand down her back. "Aren't we all? Those so-called realists are just lousy at presentation."

Her cheek brushed his chest, a rasp of stubble made her wince.

"Besides, it takes one to know one." He threw her a knowing look, pleased with his platitude. Closing her eyes, she thought: This man has built himself a house of words, a semantic bastion. How lonely that must be.

"Sorry, breakfast is a no-go. I should have been out of here ten minutes ago. I was trying not to wake you."

The Observer stands up, takes a demonstrative look around the void, and frowns. "Do you actually *live* like this? Or have you just moved in?"

Ouch, thinks Hannah. Good question. One to which she has no answer. "A bit of both," she says for the sake of it. The man has a slow, deliberate way about him that's getting on her nerves. As if he is planning to take his time with her, here in her own home.

"Right then," she says briskly, with a schoolmarmish clap of her hands. "I'm off now but take your time and close the door behind you. Give it a good, hard tug. It doesn't always shut first time."

He gazes at her, reprising his amused expression. She blinks first. "Tug it good and hard, okay?"

As if he knows exactly what she's playing at. If only she knew herself. No, she doesn't have anywhere to be and no this is not how she lives. But she has to get out of here now. Get away. She stands fidgeting at the door.

"Not that there's anything worth stealing, but still."

Suddenly she is acutely aware of the emptiness around her, the air on her skin: She is someone standing in a room, someone about to do something but what? About to disappear.

"Shut tight, remember." She shoulders her backpack. "Good-bye."

Her voice is thick with movie melodrama, but why? *Casablanca* this clearly ain't. We'll always have . . . what exactly? He says nothing. She turns and walks away. The first man after Boy. Tomorrow he flies back to Johannesburg and then she'll be able to breathe again.

A FLYING START

BACHTE-MARIA-LEERNE, 1996

TODAY IT BEGINS, SOPHIE THINKS. BUT THEN SHE ALWAYS THINKS that. Perhaps it's because deep down she knows the *real* beginning is still a long way off. For now, every day is a flickering, the merest hint of what life can be. One long false start.

She swings her legs out of bed and looks at the chair where her uniform is ready and waiting. The blouse draped over the back, sleeves hanging on either side, the skirt spread on the seat, two long white socks dangling below: a flattened schoolgirl on a chair. Today Sophie wants to make a good impression and not stand out, behave like a regular pupil. Ironing the blouse was tricky—precision is not her strong point. Once she was sent out of class because she couldn't draw a straight line with a ruler. The teacher thought she was pulling her leg but she wasn't. She simply couldn't do it. No matter how she tried, her lines refused to come out straight. She was banished to the corridor, desk and all, where the cold draft made her ill and she ended up spending the next two weeks in bed with a fever. It didn't make any differ-ence. Her straight lines still come out crooked.

She pulls up her white socks to just above the knee, buttons her striped blouse all the way to the collar, and tugs at her skirt. It's still September but chilly enough for a sweater. She really should have taken a bath last night, but somehow she never got around to it. The comb catches in her hair but once she has scraped it into pigtails no one will notice. She remembers the penknife on her bedside table and slips it in the pocket of her skirt. She glances at the clock: eight a.m. In fifteen minutes Han-nah will arrive on her bike to pick her up.

Sophie opens the bedroom door. The house is a bungalow and all doors face the living room. In the kitchen, she opens the freezer, peels off a slice of frozen bread, and sticks it in the toaster. She waits until the bread pops up, takes a slice of cheese from the fridge, fills a tall glass with tap water, and sits at the kitchen table.

As quietly as possible she munches on her bread and cheese. The plate scrapes on the table. The knife clinks against the plate. Metal on porcelain. Rock, paper, scissors. It's a game Sophie likes. She and Hannah used to play it all the time but now Hannah thinks it's stupid.

When she has finished eating, she rinses the plate under the tap. Ten past eight, perfect timing. She decides not to wear a coat, grabs the backpack she left by the door last night, and heads out-side.

"Bye, Mom," she calls.

No one answers.

A FEW MINUTES LATER, HANNAH COMES CYCLING ALONG. CHIN UP, tall in the saddle, proud as a peacock in her new jacket, a perfect braid in her long flaxen hair. A purple backpack is strapped to the back of her bike. That's new too, Sophie thinks, clutching her old leather satchel. It's wrinkled and worn but she wouldn't trade it for the world.

Hannah thunders over the gravel in the driveway and brakes hard. "Hiya."

"Hi."

"All set?"

"Yup."

"Nervous?"

"Nervous, *moi*?"

They flutter their hands in unison and thrust their hips to the side with a haughty toss of the head. *"Pas du tout!"*

Giggling, they set off along the Kortrijkse Steenweg in the highest of spirits, babbling about the best route to take and the girls they will and won't see anymore. Not so much a conversation, as a torrent of words to dampen their impatience. They are dying to know whether they will be in the same class, who their homeroom teacher will be, and above all how they are going to find their feet in that enormous schoolyard.

St. Martin's High is a collection of buildings hemmed in by a wall seven feet tall. It has the air of a fortress, always on the brink of lockdown. Cars file past at a funereal pace, disgorging little groups of children before driving on. The new girls skip through the gate, the older ones dawdle or drag their feet.

A burly nun stationed at the portal keeps a close watch on all the girls, a cautionary glint in her eagle eye: *Nothing escapes my scrutiny.* For a moment Sophie worries the woman might somehow see under her coat, through the fabric of her skirt, and discover their knife. Hannah and Sophie always carry it to school: It's part

of the secret and the thrill. She looks at Hannah, who's busy fiddling with her brand-new jacket, flashing likable smiles at everyone. Five more steps, Sophie braces herself, whizzes through the
gate. Nothing happens.

They park their bikes in the underground racks and follow
the flagstones to the place where everyone is gathering. They
spot Veerle and Evelien, two friends from primary school.

"How was your holiday?" Hannah asks.

"Super." Veerle grins. "And yours?"

"Fab."

They chatter to one another, a safe little clump of four in
the vast schoolyard. A playground for girls whose playing days
are over. So what *are* we supposed to do in all this space? Sophie
wonders. A hand taps a microphone. "Good morning, girls. Attention, please." Beneath a gray stone arch, a young woman has
mounted a postage stamp of a stage. "Atten-shun!"

The girls crowd around, hundreds of them. When everyone
has assembled, the young woman backs down two steps to make
way for the principal, a huge nun in a blue habit and a cream-
colored wimple. She has a slight stoop, like nearly every nun
Sophie has ever seen. How do nuns get so crooked? she puzzles.
Is it all that devotion? Bowing and scraping to the Lord day
after day?

"Good morning, ladies," Sister Gregoria bellows and the
microphone howls in alarm. "Welcome to this brand-new school
year. And of course a very special welcome to our new arrivals."

Sophie turns to Hannah and beams: The new arrivals, *that's
us!* But Hannah is transfixed, breathless in the face of so much
nunliness.

"We wish these new additions to our flock many years of fruitful learning." *AdditionZ*. *FlocK*. Every word Sister Gregoria utters is enunciated down to the last letter. Just like Madonna, Sophie thinks. *Like a virgiN, touched for the very first TiMe*. She makes a mental note to articulate clearly from now on, no more swallowing her words. She looks around and sees hundreds of faces flushed with awe. Within these walls, Sister Gregoria is a star.

The principal reads a verse from a floppy Bible, so well-thumbed it's almost disintegrating. "Verily, verily, I say unto you, He that entereth not by the door into the sheepfold, but climbeth up some other way, the same is a thief and a robber."

Hannah is entranced. Sophie feels uneasy. What do sheep-folds and robbers have to do with anything? Sophie loves a good story but after six years at St. Martin's Elementary she's heard more than enough Bible tales. Besides, what would the Holy Shepherd have to say about the murderer Marc Dutroux, the Belgian child molester who was arrested only two weeks ago? For months the whole country had been looking for the girls that disappeared: Julie, Melissa, An, Eefje, Sabine, Laetitia—vanished without a trace.

Now everyone knows what happened to them and what Marc Dutroux has done, things worse than you could even imagine, and yet imagining is what everyone does. The inconceivable horror: two children in a dungeon hidden behind a bookshelf, beaten, raped, starving, crying for their lives. Sophie knows: The horror is on the mind of every schoolgirl here; girls patiently waiting with their shiny schoolbags in their pristine white socks and freshly ironed uniforms. Innocence revisited. Sophie feels the cold metal in her pocket: At least she has a knife so she can protect Hannah.

"We shall now begin reading out the classes," Sister Gregoria announces, tucking the scraps of sacred scripture into a fold of her habit. "When your name is called, please make your way to the front. I shall read the names in alphabetical order and that is the order in which you will line up. Is that clear?" Silence. No one dares reply. Of course they don't, you don't answer back to a star, the Queen, God Almighty.

The reading of the names begins. Valerie Anderson. Conny de Bleekere. Veerle de Buck. Vicky Courteyn. Hannah and Sophie are in the same class. When Hannah's name is called, she pinches Sophie's side as she passes to take her place in line.

DAMNED EDITORS

NEW YORK, 2014

SUCH A BRAVE THING TO DO." WHEN PEOPLE THINK A RADICAL life change is incomprehensible, brave is the word of choice, a tried and tested euphemism for irrational or downright dumb. Here's another: That sounds like it's going to be great! Going to be: great. Right now: major mistake.

A laptop balances on two sweaty knees. Hannah sits on the concrete floor of her apartment, legs stretched out in front of her. Her jeans are pinching at the waist and she opens a button. The empty white page on her screen fades to gray in the bright sunlight. The cursor flashes, nags. She knows the drill. For ten years she scoured the New York party scene for tasty rumors chasing down juicy quotes from boozed-up celebrities. Quotes that after a year or two she could dream up herself. That's exactly what she did toward the end, when she realized she could easily predict who would show up where, what label they would be wearing, and what kind of dirt they were likely to dish.

And so the fabrications began. Little things at first: a hand-bag, a dress, a hairstyle. Before long she added people, brand-new people to a scene. Then came conversations, entire scenarios. The lies she wrote gave a new edge to her job but, frankly, she'd have done anything to recapture the rush that had gradually worn off, the frisson of privilege, the thrill of the unknown.

Once it had been an honor to be an eager young reporter sharing the same pulsing dance floor with the Jennifer Lawrences and Channing Tatums of this world. Not anymore. The magic is gone. People get sick, they die. The little girl growing inside her. New York glamour is the new Santa Claus—she is no longer a believer. And so it came to pass that two months ago she found herself pacing anxiously in a corner office of the editorial depart-ment on the twenty-second floor.

She stalked up and down between half-empty bookcases, while models looked down disdainfully from glossy, logo-spattered prints on the wall. She spoke. She heard herself say the words. She saw Stella, editor-in-chief, smile at her from behind her big desk. "What has gotten into you, Hannah?" Stella, empress of the fashion world, in a tight tube skirt and an immaculate white blouse, shimmering scarf draped around her neck with studied nonchalance and her raven hair swept back into the ultimate chi-gnon. She sank back into her ergonomic office chair and crossed her killer legs. Hannah's words had dried up.

"And you are serious about this?"

A nod.

"I see." Stella heaved a sigh that said: I can fix this but I would much rather be investing my precious time and energy elsewhere.

"Hannah, dear." Another sigh. "You have scaled the dizzy heights to which just about every journalist aspires. You write a popular column that demands only that you attend parties and come up with two hundred words per issue. Your star is rising and you are paid generously for your services. You do good work and we are happy with you. So what exactly is the problem?"

Those dizzy heights, they were the problem: a soupçon of sparkling copy with an eye-catching selfie to match. What next, dear readers? Hannah draped in streamers atop a designer barstool? Hannah in a sexy tuxedo, rose clamped between her teeth? Hannah with a radiant glass of expensive champagne. No, this ends here: her tributes to the fake and frothy, the crazy life that comes with them, the endlessly polite receptions where every phony puts their most fabulous foot forward.

She thought all this and said nothing.

"Are you sure, Hannah?"

"I know that I want something else. Something more demanding."

"I can give you other assignments. We are more than just a society column, you know."

"I know."

"And that is an option you are willing to consider?"

"I can't see it satisfying me."

Stella shook her head and leaned across her desk. "So what *will* satisfy you, Hannah? Grinding out a tome about female writers that no one will read? I hardly need to tell you that the best you can hope for is a handful of flattering reviews, and that will be that."

They are more than just writers, Hannah thought. They

fought their battles, swam against the current, and then disappeared one day. Just like the twelve-year-old girl who vanished from a Belgian village. A girl she knew better than anyone. See you tomorrow, she had said that dark November night. But that little girl never came home, she was gone forever. *No, pull yourself together, Hannah. Not here, not now.*

"This is the kind of project that makes an ideal sideline. Start in your spare time, see how it pans out. With all due respect, Hannah, you have a modicum of celebrity and you are well on your way to more. But jump ship now and within a year you will be nobody."

Am I somebody? Hannah wondered. The cute girl waving her microphone on the dance floor, is that me? The barstool babe and her glass of bubbly, is that somebody I want to be?

"I want to give it a try, Stella."

"All right then, if that's what you want. I'll look around for a replacement."

"Yes, of course."

"They're lining up out there, Hannah. Droves of them ready to take your job."

What job? she wanted to say. It was only ever an experiment, an extended freelance gig, a joke that got out of hand.

"Thank you, Stella."

And she walked to the glass door with the view of the editorial office she would never see again, past desks piled high with magazines, the wall plastered with clippings and doodles, the coffee machine that spewed lukewarm cappuccino. She felt nothing.

Stella leaned in the doorway and watched her go. "If this

goes wrong, Hannah, then what you're doing right now is not just stupid, it's career suicide. It can be pretty damned bad out there, you know."

She shrugged. *Pretty damned bad* sounds good to me. You have no idea what I have been able to survive.

The cursor flashes, taunts, then finally starts to move.

VISITING AGATHA

TORQUAY, 1916

I̶T IS 1916 AND AGATHA CHRISTIE IS SITTING AT A STURDY MAHOG-
any table, since she prefers a nice firm surface on which to work.
She is wearing a long gray skirt, a striped blouse, a polka-dot
scarf, and court shoes with a low heel; she's tall enough as it is.
Her thick blond hair is pinned up in a bun: an elegant young
woman of twenty-six. She is sitting in the parlor at Ashfield, a
dignified old house in the South of England, the house where she
was born.

Out in the world, far beyond Ashfield's walls, the First World
War is raging. The British are becoming ever more deeply em-
broiled in the conflict. Wounded servicemen are being plucked
from continental battlefields and shipped across the Channel to
be patched up in sleepy seaside resorts. Torquay has been roused
from its slumber. The town hall has been converted into an infirmary, the vicarage into a sanatorium. People are worried. The
war is closing in.

But when Agatha sits down at her mahogany table to write, the misery evaporates. At the typewriter in the rambling house, she loses herself in language, in the endless string of stories that her imagination yields.

"I bet you couldn't." Agatha recalls her sister Madge's words. "I bet you couldn't write a detective story." Madge liked to tease and Agatha was all too easily baited. She has spent years in search of a story and now her fingers are finally moving across the keys of the black machine.

The intense interest aroused in the public by what was known at the time as "The Styles Case" has now somewhat subsided.

Agatha stops, hesitates, bites on the pencil she uses to jot down her thoughts in a thick notebook. While out walking, she told herself the whole story, every sentence, every last line of dialogue murmured to the wind because what isn't said out loud is so easily forgotten.

Gone now. All her words are gone. A rim of mud on the hem of her skirt is the only reminder of the torrent of words out there on the moors. The keys seem to laugh at her: *You can't do it, Agatha. You have nothing to tell the world. Nothing at all.* Pencil between her teeth, she bites back her tears, a bitter taste of graphite.

The years spent looking for a detective to call her own ended one day when a bus packed with Belgian refugees pulled up at the infirmary. Out stepped a peculiar little man with an egg-shaped head and a striking black moustache, head bowed to one side and a perplexed expression on his face. He lifted his head and, for a moment, their eyes met. She stood there, rooted to the spot in her long white apron with its red cross. Yes, she thought in a flurry of excitement and relief, he's just right.

Strictly speaking, volunteering for the Red Cross was something that she, a young woman from the upper echelons of society, need never have done. She could have avoided witnessing the soldiers' suffering, the death throes, the corpses. But something in her yearned to know, to feel, to understand. She took a basic training course and set to work as a nurse.

Her first operation was a soldier with a gunshot wound, lying unconscious. The bullet had narrowly missed his stomach. His upper body was sliced open. She fought back the urge to be violently sick. The flesh, the organs: fragile, pulsating, exposed. She turned deathly pale and Sister Anderson, an older nurse, took her out into the hallway.

"Listen to me, Agatha. Only one thing in that room can make you faint: the ether. That you can do nothing about. To everything else in life you will become accustomed."

Sister Anderson was right. When a few months later an amputated arm lay on the operating table and Agatha was ordered to scrub the place clean, she picked up the lifeless limb without batting an eyelid and carried it out to the furnace. Down the corridor she walked, holding a stranger's arm in her arms, an unwieldy joint of meat swaddled in bloody white cotton. A memory both abhorrent and thrilling.

Now, at her typewriter in the nurturing glow of the crackling hearth at Ashfield, she finally understands why. Horror longs to be described, language worships pain. Blood and paper, it's the ultimate love affair.

A BELGIAN DUNGEON

BACHTE-MARIA-LEERNE, 1996

Mr. Verhoeven asks if there are any questions. If anyone feels like talking about the recent *events*. Twenty-four
girls gaze back in silence. He is the first male teacher at St. Martin's High, and he is their homeroom teacher. A gray jacket hangs
from his shoulders, the matching trousers sag from his waist,
his rimless glasses look faintly ridiculous. It's as if he's wearing
a suit for the very first time and he's still learning how it's done.
The girls have him down as thirtyish. He towers above them but
barely takes up a splinter of the classroom. He teaches English,
and even though he is trying to be sympathetic, leaning forward
on his desk with his arms spread wide, he is met by twenty-four
uncomprehending girlish stares.

Questions? Does he mean why in God's name would anyone
do such a thing? Or does he mean how can we make sure that such
events never happen to us? Cycle there and back fast as you can

and don't stop for anyone. Every morning before school, Belgian mothers and fathers warn their children tenderly, insistently . . . Don't talk to strangers . . . *or else!*

Sophie sits perfectly still while beside her Hannah fiddles with her pencil case. The silence is excruciating. "It is clear that Marc Dutroux, the murderer we've all been hearing a lot about in the past few weeks, is a monster, a psychopath," Mr. Verhoeven continues. "We have all seen the pictures, we talk to each other about what has happened—which is good. But I realize there may still be things you want to ask. If so, remember that you can always come to me." He tries to pull off a trustworthy expression. The silence deepens.

For months the country had been in the grip of the missing girls and then, only three weeks ago, two of them were found hidden in the monster's house, alive. The TV showed images that sent a shockwave through the country: a twelve-year-old girl with tired eyes was picked up under her arms and held aloft, an indignity usually reserved for toddlers. She hung there in mid-air, like a rag doll, a human trophy. Cameras flashed, people applauded. The media rejoiced. *We have found the children! We have saved them! It could have been much worse!* There was a monster, but there were heroes too. Justice had prevailed.

Three days later relief gave way to shame, when the dead bodies of two other girls were carried out of a dungeon. Horrific images that did not make the papers or the TV news but were imagined by everyone and instantly ingrained in the national consciousness. Suddenly, every Belgian carried this wretched scene inside, this dirty, ugly reality of girls being abused in a cellar, unsafe in a stupid country that had failed to protect them, where they were only found after the monster, the murderer had told the police where to look.

Sophie felt it too: the shame, the failure, and this morning, on the third of September, things only got worse. The bodies of two more missing girls had been discovered. An and Eefje in a shallow grave by a warehouse near the town of Charleroi. An's father appeared on the news that morning, a man the nation had taken to their hearts in the weeks leading up to this moment, who always seemed to know exactly what to say. The media jostled around him. Over a year ago, his sixteen-year-old daughter had gone missing. Today he stared at the ground, his glasses were wet, no prompt card with keywords for this brush with the media. Only the words "We can stop looking now."

A pencil rolls from Hannah's desk and hits the floor. Everyone looks at her, grateful for the distraction from this interminable exercise in embarrassment.

"Sorry," she murmurs, and stuffs the pencil back in its case.

Was this planned, Sophie wonders? Did Sister Gregoria instruct her staff to open a dialogue? If so, it would be a first. Talking is not highly regarded at St. Martin's, which operates according to one clear principle: knowledge in exchange for respect. You receive an education, please your teachers, and obey them at all times. You address them politely and only when it is called for. Your teachers have no lives, no interests beyond their profession. They do not have first names, only surnames, and they most certainly are *not* your friend.

And into this well-oiled machine shambles Mr. Verhoeven and his outsize suit, determined to break through the fourth wall. *How dare he?*

On the blackboard is the conjugation of the verb *to do*, but even the compelling force of chalk letters seems to have been overruled by the issue Mr. Verhoeven has taken into his head to address. He is not aware of the etiquette. Could someone please explain it to him? In the classroom we talk about tenses and square roots, about continents and kings. You are our teacher. You are *not* our friend.

"So," he repeats, sliding a ring binder into the middle of his desk. "If any of you would like to talk, please remember that I am here for you." He flashes a friendly smile at a class of two dozen girls who would happily disappear under their desks if they could. He clears his throat and launches into the present continuous.

Of course the monster is the talk of the schoolyard. That's hardly a secret, but there is a strange eagerness in the children's words, a boundless appetite for picking apart what must have occurred in that awful dungeon. The facts are discussed from a distance, as if the tragedy were a new Stephen King novel or the latest Spielberg movie.

Only it isn't. No Spielberg ever had parents panicking, imposing early-evening curfews on their children, demanding to know their exact whereabouts every hour of the weekend. Spielberg never sparked the sentimental expressions of parental relief when Mom and Dad arrive late at night to pick up their offspring from a party and drive them safely home.

Hannah saw it last night, the troubled, teary look on her mother's face as she sat on the bed and tucked the covers under her chin, just like she used to when Hannah was six. "I love you," her mother whispered in a tone she had never used before. The emotional charge of recent weeks, crackling in every newspaper report, smoldering in every news bulletin, festering in every new revelation was there in her mother's eyes. As if Hannah herself had crawled out of the monster's den, as if Hannah had been hoisted into the air and dangled in front of the cameras, as if she were the survivor.

Although it feels wrong, Hannah and Sophie participate in the endless schoolyard reconstructions, caught up in the momentum of the story. Now and then one of the girls supplies new information: "Did you know Sabine scratched a line on the wall for every day she was there? With her own fingernails!" True or not, it hardly matters. The girls are horrified. More gruesome details to pick apart.

In smaller groups, their imaginings grow even darker. How the monster must have undressed when he came into the cellar. What he must look like naked, how hideous he must be. How he dug pits in the middle of the night so he could bury the little girls. Did he put them in a bag first? Or just toss them into the hole, *alive*? How deep do you need to dig to smother a scream?

"I don't think there will be much left of them after a year," Sophie says.

At playtime she strolls around the schoolyard with Hannah. Arm in arm, a ritual Sophie relishes, moments when everything flows and feels just right. Garden-go-rounds they call them, their walks around the circular garden that only the nuns are allowed to enter, a commandment no pupil at St. Martin's would dare to disobey.

Hannah shakes her head. "No, it doesn't happen that fast.

First the worms eat away the fleshy part of your head. Your cheeks and bits of your nose, that kind of thing."

"Yikes!" Sophie pulls a sour face.

"It's true! I saw it in a film. Then insects lay eggs inside your body and in a few days larvae crawl out."

"Bleeuch! Hannah, don't be so gross!"

"And meanwhile the bacteria that help you digest your food when you're alive begin feeding on your insides. So in the end your body eats itself."

Sophie lets go of Hannah's arm. She doesn't want to hear any of this; she is terrified of death and everything that comes with it. It's been like that ever since she first found out that people die, ever since the meaning of the word hit home. She even tried to talk about it with Hannah once, in the depths of the night, as she lay on the thin mattress on the floor. Was Hannah afraid too? "No," Hannah had answered, "I have God."

As simple as that. As if God were a thing to have, to own, a tool to lighten the burden of mortality. But God works. Hannah is not troubled by dark thoughts that haunt her for hours and hours before she falls asleep. For her no never-ending stream of images about how it might end and how it would feel: a fall, a kick, a crash, a clot, a long and painful illness, alone in the hospital, knowing that the end is near and that you are about to disappear for good.

"Okay, Sophie. No more gory details, I promise." Hannah takes Sophie's arm, links it through hers again, and gently strokes her hand. But Sophie is beyond comfort. The dark circle is here again and she is trapped inside. At school the circle hardly ever finds her but the story of the kidnapped girls has changed everything.

Now there is no place to hide, not even inside the thick school walls. She wants to tell Hannah everything: about being afraid at night, in that awful house, about the many times she died and miraculously woke up again. About the pain, the unfathomable pain. But she walks on, another garden-go-round. It's safer not to tell.

KILLJOY

BACHTE-MARIA-LEERNE, 1996

THIS IS MY FRIEND SOPHIE." SOPHIE NODS AND FLASHES A SHEEP-
ish smile. She hates having to smile, especially when it turns
out sheepish, but what else are you supposed to do when you're
introduced to someone? A bunch of girls and boys glance ab-
sently in her direction and immediately resume the activity that
was demanding every ounce of their attention: rolling the perfect
cigarette.

On Friday afternoons, it's school uniforms wall-to-wall in
The Sloop: a swarm of gray, blue, and green, school ties and
knee-length socks. Like many a teen hangout, it's seen better
days: Oblivious to the peeling paint, sticky mirrors, and rusty
fittings, the underage clientele ignore the wooden benches and
wonky tables, preferring to lean at the long bar or lounge against
the walls.

Sophie wanders through the shabby room, thick with the

smell of rotting wood, cigarette smoke, and spilled beer. The music is so loud you can barely hear a word. Girls preen and boys whack each other chummily on the shoulder. Everything is moving, but without direction or purpose. Smoke, swill, joke, pester, hollow, shallow, sad.

Hannah is leaning against a wall, swaying to the rhythm of the slamming beat. She has ditched her green blouse in favor of a sleeveless top that promises FUN FOR YOU in bold letters. It's standard practice: almost all the girls have traded half of their uniforms for expensive little tops that leave as little as possible to the imagination.

To an average twelve-year-old, breasts are the ultimate status symbol. Sophie looks at the well-rounded cups of the radiant older girls around her and recalls her own humiliating visit to a lingerie store. A disaster, even the AA cup had room to spare. Anyway, she's convinced it's a sham, half the girls pad their bras with cotton wool. She looks at Hannah standing there between Andrea and Veerle. Are her breasts bigger than usual? No, she would never stoop to that. It's just a pity that Hannah's ignoring her after begging her—pretty, pretty please—to come along.

"It'll be fun, you'll see," she had insisted.

"But Hannah, I won't know anyone there."

"You know Veerle, don't you? And Mariëtte from sixth grade?"

"Yes, but I never talk to them."

"Sophie, we're only going for a drink. We'll stay for an hour and then we can cycle home together, okay?" And she gave Sophie her sweetest smile, the one that ensures she always gets her way.

Right now Hannah is regretting having asked her friend

along. Sophie isn't saying a word to anyone, just standing there gawping, like she's at the zoo, staring at a bunch of weird reptiles behind glass. But it's Sophie who's the weird one, Hannah thinks. Everyone gets a kick out of sneaking a cigarette and having a beer on the sly, everyone except Sophie. Her embarrassing silence is starting to make Hannah look bad. Can't she at least try to fit in for once?

Hannah chats to the other girls and turns her back on Sophie, who pretends not to notice. She feels completely lost. I *am* doing my best, Sophie thinks, but everyone's avoiding me. I'm way too small and the words stamped on my forehead are too big. No one here is interested in me. Why should they be? In a place like this, I'm *not* interesting.

Someone bumps into her and beer splashes over her skirt. She wants to swear but doesn't dare. A boy with a buzz cut shoots her a sullen look. The air is churning, prodding, tugging at her; she needs to get out of here. Now Hannah is talking to a tall boy with red hair and an adoring look in his eyes. Beanpole.

"I'm leaving, Hannah."

"Oh? Okay then." Feigned surprise and a fake Sloop smile.

"I'll cycle home on my own."

"Yeah, fine. Sure you don't want another drink?"

Beanpole and the girls exchange glances with Hannah and snigger. Sophie looks down at the beer glass she is clutching in one hand, still full to the brim. She had forgotten it was there. The sniggers become a roar.

"No, thanks," Sophie mumbles.

She hands her glass to Hannah, who accepts it in a reflex, then turns and walks away. Maybe Hannah will come after me, she thinks. Maybe she honestly didn't notice the glass. Maybe she'll say sorry and we'll both hop on our bikes, cycle home together and laugh it off tomorrow. She lingers on the stairs and dawdles down the street to where their bikes are parked. Slowly she slides her key into the lock, climbs on the saddle, and looks behind her one last time. Hannah is nowhere to be seen.

I WON'T BITE

NEW YORK, 2014

From the outside, Roberta's has all the charm of a bunker. Like much of Bushwick's nightlife, it keeps its appeal well hidden behind a bleak façade of grim concrete and bricked-up windows. Its narrow steel door, almost lost among the graffiti, is plastered with dog-eared stickers and deadbeat slogans—*I was not invited to your birthday, #fuckitandwhatever.*

Perversely, it's the most popular joint in Bushwick, packed to the gills on a nightly basis. Beyoncé once put in an appearance and even the Clintons figured it was worthwhile posing with a Roberta's pizza. The local hipsters will happily wait two hours for a table in its courtyard or one of two cavernous rooms.

Balancing a tray on one hand, Hannah navigates her way along the treacherous aisles between the tightly packed tables, an obstacle course of jackets, bags, jutting elbows, and stretched legs. But she does her best, checking the table numbers on the orders at the bar, ferrying pizzas to the customers and trying not to think too much. She enjoys the cacophony of voices that merge into a monotone buzz, bland as water, every sentence swallowed by another. A soothing, nothing sound.

"The Margarita was for?" A girl with cropped peroxide blond hair and blue-rimmed glasses nods. "And the calzones?" Two bearded young men raise their hands. What is it with hipsters and beards? Hannah thinks, and tries to block the image of crumbs and blobs of cheese clinging to face fuzz, the greasy smell of melted mozzarella. It's a means to an end, remember? This lousy job is paying for *The Plan*.

A month ago she had been sitting at one of these tables herself, after taking Irminia on a tour of the neighborhood. "What a fantastic place Bushwick is," Irminia had exclaimed as they tucked into two huge pizzas washed down with a good glass of wine. Irminia, always upbeat, supportive: a devoted mother figure, friend.

They had been sitting by one of the bricked-up windows where two men are currently engaged in an animated conversation. One of them is watching her. She can sense it, an instinct she has learned to trust. His good looks remind her of the Ken doll she used to play with, sterile and utterly sexless. She chewed his little plastic feet to pieces. *Poor Ken*. When she brings over their pizzas, his hand brushes hers.

"Sorry, I know this is going to sound creepy, but haven't I seen your face somewhere before? You're a columnist, right?"

Just what she needs, a spy from the right side of the river to witness how she has fallen from her pedestal. *No, not fallen. Jumped*. Shut up, I don't owe you an explanation, she wants to say. Instead she musters a sour smile and nods.

"Ha!" he says, pointing at his friend. "What did I tell you? I see her photo all the time in that magazine Vanessa reads." Triumphantly, he drapes his napkin over his lap and proceeds to make things worse. "Gotta be honest, I've no idea what your column's about but I just *love* those photos."

Across the table, Ken's dinner companion—a shabby guy with a ponytail—quietly picks at his pizza. He gets it, she thinks, he's been there: the embarrassment of the photographer working behind the bar, the singer clearing tables, the writer serving pizza. An ugly sort of embarrassment, so brimming with failure that she wants to fling her white apron at the wall and sprint for the door in her flip-flops. Either that or state loud and clear that this move was *her* choice and that nowadays she does far more *interesting* things than rub shoulders with celebrities. *Things like serving pizza*, she thinks, with a pang of realization.

"Well, thanks for dinner!" Ken says brightly and dives into his pizza. *Asshole.* A battalion of toy soldiers has lined up in her head: boom, boom, boom. She turns and walks away.

The rest of the night is murder. Everything seems to sap her energy: smiling for customers, joking with colleagues. Her arms are stiff from lifting and her feet are sore. Walking home at the end of her shift, she is ready to collapse into bed. What bed? All she has is a smelly mattress barely big enough to stretch out on. That and an empty fridge. No sofa, no table. Her stark apartment looms up before her and suddenly it's the last place on earth she wants to be.

She heads for a bar across the street: Hell's Forest, a name to live up to. The place is black, from floor to ceiling. At the bar sits a man with all the hallmarks of an alcoholic: a slave to the glass he's huddled over. A man smaller than his drink.

Hannah is in no shape to be choosy. With the sinking feeling that Hell's Forest is a fitting end to her evening, she orders a gin and tonic and slides onto a barstool at one of the tall tables. Pearls of wisdom are scratched into the black surface: *Johnny loves Maggie, Facebook is a fucking bore.*

She presses both hands to her face and rubs her eyes until she is lost in a black-and-white blizzard. She feels hollow. Her writing is at a standstill, the words that somehow made it onto the page are meaningless. She needs to get drunk.

"Hey."

Hannah looks up, sees no one.

"Hello-o."

She turns around, looks for the voice. Behind her at a corner table she spots a pair of expensive sneakers, then two skinny legs in black denim extending from a beaten-up Chesterfield. "Haven't I seen your face somewhere before?"

She peers into the black hole.

Cigarette smoke curls out of the shadows. "I thought I recognized you." He leans forward and a wide grin appears. Ken's bashful companion.

"Jess," he says. "Nice to meet you again."

The musty smell of tawny leather and nicotine reminds her of the Sloop. Jess takes a draw on his cigarette, head tipped back and a touch to the side, eyes half shut. James Dean in *East of Eden.* There are men who actually do that, quote shamelessly, and manage to pull it off too.

"Hannah," she says. "My name is Hannah."

He runs a hand through his hair, still tied in a ponytail, and stray blond locks fall gently around his face. Next to Ken he just looked shabby, but here in hell Bashful is more in his element. He comes here often, she thinks. That Chesterfield has roots.

"Sorry but it's been a long night. I'm not in the mood for conversation." She turns back to her G&T. The last thing she needs tonight is a flirtatious bad boy with a James Dean complex. Been there done that, Hannah. Let this train pass you by.

She peers into her glass and feigns an intimacy with her gin that no barfly can put asunder. Catching sight of the drunk at the bar, she's struck by the painful resemblance. Here she sits, a bundle of woe wrapped around a glass. And right on cue, here comes her bashful poser for a second pass.

"It must be hard work. The pizza place."

"Keeps me busy," she mumbles.

"You must have walked miles by the end of a shift."

"I don't keep track."

"You should. Get one of those step counters. Quantified Self is the new God, haven't you heard?"

"I'm not interested."

But not so long ago she was. In her Manhattan days she wore a watch that registered every detail, a device that knew her through and through: distance travelled, heart rate, sleep patterns, mood swings. "Self-hacking" was the term the guys at Boy's ad agency bandied about and she remembers how she used to tease him about his pitiful step score at the end of the day. Until he bought a treadmill for the office, a gleaming slice of the future that, within a week, was dubbed the "think-tank." Creative brainstorming turned out to be highly efficient when your legs were moving. From that moment on, Boy broke every record on the pedometer. He was number one again. Back on top. Suave Boy with his smooth face and silky skin, a walking soap commercial.

Bashful's face is weathered and tough. A texture you can actually feel when you run your fingers over it. Rugged, lined, veined. *So real.*

"So what *is* churning away in that pretty little head of yours?" He chuckles like a schoolboy. "Why the frown?"

With his right thumb, he smoothes the crease between her brows. "Stop thinking. It's vastly overrated, Anna."

"Hannah. My name is Hannah."

"Sorry. Hannah."

He gives her a playful little pout as his fingers trace a gentle line along her jaw. Slow, tingling, pleasurable. The train is ready to depart. Should she stay or climb aboard?

"What's wrong? Are you angry?" He takes another drag on his cigarette and a slug of his whisky, holding his head back as he swallows.

"No, I just need some time to myself. Time to think. Go talk to someone else. All right?"

No, not all right. There *is* no one else and she knows it. Apart from the drunk at the bar the place is deserted. A film set with too few extras. Hopper.

"My pal back at the restaurant upset you." She shrugs.

"Are you ashamed of your job?" She says nothing.

"What is it you really do?"

Really? I serve up pizzas in a Bushwick bunker and drink G&T's in deserted bars because I can't face going back to my empty apartment and my lack of a life. But *really* . . .

"I write."

"A novel?"

"I'm not sure. A book about women writers who disappeared."

"Ah."

Yeah, right. As if he gets it. No one gets it, so don't pretend you do, she wants to snap. But she sees him nod quietly, feels him letting her be. No opinion at the ready, no words of advice. No warnings or colorful anecdotes from his past that make her predicament so very relatable. They drink in silence and somehow she feels safe.

"It's an ode to women writers who were smart and strong, who dared to make risky decisions in their lives. I admire them. I want to be close to them."

"How can you be close to them?"

"By knowing what they knew."

A pause. A puff of smoke.

"But you'll always know more than they ever knew. You have the benefit of hindsight."

The man has brains. She smiles. Bashful is right. She reads articles and biographies to get to know these women. But how can she ever know them? Shamelessly she transplants them from their day and age to her own, from their own lives to hers. Is that knowing or instant appropriation? *Click, drag, drop.*

She takes a greedy gulp of gin. Bashful tells her about serving his time as a reluctant waiter until his career took off. Not to the Shakespearian heights he had dreamed of but a bit part in a popular daytime drama. His easy charm hit the spot and now he is one of a handful of characters at the heart of the soap, his charismatic face accompanying the opening credits. He is Harvey James in *As Time Goes By*, a male model fallen on hard times and manipulating wealthy women in a quest for revenge. "A Hamlet of sorts," he says dryly. She laughs.

Hannah has seen snatches of the show: cheap sets, hammy actors, preposterous cliff-hangers, millions of viewers. With groupies lining up to share his bed, he sometimes hides out here in hell. His lips brush her neck. Failure comes in many guises, Hannah muses, just like success. Like her columns and the enthusiastic reader responses that came pouring in month after month. Columns that filled her with shame. That was why she had to quit, make her getaway. And here she is, in Bushwick, and a familiar train is ready to depart. Bashful's story lifts her up, his calm words comfort her. She puts a hand on his arm, he runs his fingers through her hair.

"Shall we?"

She smiles. He nods to the barman to put the drinks on his tab and gets up to leave. *Bus or plane, car or train, we will have a trip today.* She shoulders her backpack, grabs her jacket, and walks out leaning against him . . . *Off we go, don't be slow, say goodbye and whisk me away.*

SH

You first."

A broad and tranquil stretch of water encircles the castle at Ooidonk, a fairy-tale collection of turrets and stepped gables. The castle and its rose garden are the pride of Bachte. It's where everyone comes for their Sunday stroll, topped off with fresh pancakes and whipped cream in what used to be the coach house.

Today is Monday, a warm and windless autumn afternoon. School finished early and Sophie and Hannah left as fast as they could. Sophie has come up with a plan—another crazy Sophie plan. They are giggling in anticipation when they cycle past the castle gate.

They throw their bicycles in the grass and run under a small tunnel that brings them to their secret passage to the garden. Loose stones beside the arch give them just enough of a toehold to clamber up. For years it has been their free ticket to the rose garden everyone else has to pay to see.

On one side, the castle moat flows to a drawbridge that's always down, on the other side it widens to form a modest, round lake. Sophie and Hannah are standing at the water's edge, silently looking across. In the middle of the lake there's a small island, barely twelve feet across. A no-man's-land. Until today.

Carefully Sophie takes off her shirt, her green skirt, and her sandals and lays them on a tree stump. Hannah pulls down her skirt and wriggles out of her patent shoes and sweaty knee-high stockings. There they stand, two girls in chalk-white underwear, so much smaller without clothes.

They giggle at each other and take a furtive look around. No one. Solemnly they gaze at the island with its thistles and in the middle its solitary beech tree. Sophie feels a tingle of excitement run through her body.

"Now?"

Hannah nods.

Hollering in unison, they sprint hand in hand toward the edge and take the plunge. Two naked girls land in a lake. Hannah splutters, Sophie sends spatters flying high in the air. The water is cold and exhilarating. With the deadpan resolve of explorers, they swim out to the island and clamber ashore. They scamper through the tall weeds to the big tree; thistles prick their ankles but they don't feel a thing.

They stand side by side under the majestic beech. Hannah opens her fist to reveal the penknife with the antelope. Their secret weapon. She hands it to Sophie, who flicks open the blade and carves a jagged *S* into the bark. Hannah follows suit, carving three straight lines to form an *H*.

From now on this will be their island. They sit and watch the world from across the water, distant and free. Sophie looks at the bark of the tree. Two letters joined for all eternity. Best friends. She looks into Hannah's eyes and smiles with endless pride.

THE SPEED OF LIGHT

BACHTE-MARIA-LEERNE, 1996

SOPHIE LOVES TO RUN. WHILE MOST OF THE GIRLS ONLY ENDURE the annual cross-country race for the hot dogs and the boys, she has winning on her mind. Even on these little legs of hers, she is convinced she can beat the rest of her year.

A steady drizzle has set in and the ground is boggy. Hundreds of sports shoes squelch through the wet grass. Sophie feels the sweat on her skin, the air glide over her body, releasing her, pushing her forward, a strange, exquisite pain.

Hannah is dragging herself around the course with a trio of exhausted friends, princesses whose main concern is keeping their hairdos intact and their long legs free of mud.

"I've arranged to meet Philip at the finish line," Veerle pants. "He's bringing his friends along." Sophie sees Hannah light up.

The course has been cordoned off with red and white plastic tape. The true athletes have already crossed the finish line and are strolling along the sidelines, grinning and flashing their medals at the lesser mortals who will have nothing but a stamp on the back of the hand to show for their efforts.

"Round the next bend is a spot where no one's watching," says Veerle. "We can slip under the tape and sneak off, okay?" Three girls nod in unison.

"But then we won't get our stamp," Sophie puffs.

Veerle rolls her eyes. "Like anyone cares. Look, this is the place."

The three of them prepare to make their getaway, much to Sophie's consternation. What a sad bunch of giver-uppers. She runs on as fast as she can.

"Ladies and gentlemen, there goes Sophie," Hannah yells from the other side of the tape. "Faster than the speed of light!" And the four of them disappear into the crowd in search of Philip and the boys.

SOPHIE IS RUNNING LIKE A CHAMPION. HER CHEST IS HEAVING AND her head is light. Her breath pricks like needles in her lungs. She's almost there: cheering faces and roaring voices line the home stretch. She doesn't know any of them but she pretends they have all come to see her, to cheer her on. She crosses the line in a triumphant burst and joins the queue to get her stamp: 175th place, better than last year!

Beyond the finish line, the festivities are already under way, complete with streamers, music, and ecstatic youngsters high on endorphins. Hannah and her friends have spread a plastic sheet over the muddy grass and are busy unpacking a hamper filled with plastic cups, fizzy drinks, and family packs of potato chips.

"What happened to you?" Hannah asks when she catches sight of Sophie. Her white T-shirt is splattered with mud, her face flushed, sweaty, and streaked with brown. Sophie proudly shows off the stamp on the back of her hand but it doesn't feel cool. Cool has been hijacked by a quartet of girls on a plastic sheet who had the nerve to sneak off under the tape when no one was looking.

"Who wants a hot dog?" Hannah asks, as if struck by divine inspiration. Eager nods all round. "Can you help me fetch them, Veerle?" In their sweatpants and muddy sports shoes they stroll over and join the hungry masses at the hot-dog stand, jostling for a royal helping of sausage, bread, and mustard. Manna from heaven to a bunch of kids in the throes of a teenage growth spurt who have just run for miles.

"That Sophie is weird," Veerle says suddenly. Hannah doesn't reply.

"I honestly don't know why you hang around with her."

Hannah shrugs. "We go back a long way."

"She trails along behind you like a lapdog. I mean, it's pathetic."

"Sophie is not pathetic."

"Well, what would you call it?"

"She has it tough at home. I don't know all the details."

Veerle waves her hands dismissively. "We *all* have it tough at home. The least you can do is make an effort to wash your hair and wear clean clothes. She *stinks* sometimes. Don't tell me you haven't noticed!"

Hannah doesn't want to hear. This hurts, cuts deep. "Sophie is just different, that's all," she snaps.

"All right, calm down. I was only saying . . ."

"It's okay. I get it."

The conversation trails off as a burst of laughter erupts from a bunch of bare-chested boys ahead of them in the queue. They look older than Hannah and Veerle, fifteen maybe. Out of nowhere, the tallest and cutest, with blue eyes and thick curly hair, gives Hannah a tender glance and smiles. She looks away shyly, but Veerle has noticed and tugs at Hannah's T-shirt.

"He's hot!" she whispers. Hannah can only blush. "Go on, talk to him."

"Are you nuts?"

She tucks her T-shirt tighter into her pants and eases her shoulders back. Hannah knows why the boys can't take their eyes off her. They can sense that she's a woman, a *real* woman now.

"Ladies first?" One of the boys extends an inviting hand to a muddy spot ahead of them in the queue. He has tied his white T-shirt around his head and Hannah can just make out the words *HERE WE ARE NOW, ENTERTAIN US*. For all his macho posturing, he looks like a Smurf.

"This way please, my lovelies." He smiles. The girls look at each other and giggle.

"Thanks, that's sweet of you," Hannah purrs and promptly steps in a deep puddle. Muddy water splashes in all directions, most of it up Curly's trouser legs.

"Take that, Damiaan!" the Smurf yells. "There's gratitude for you!" They crease up as Damiaan tries in vain to wipe away the stains.

"Sorry," Hannah says hesitantly. He looks at her a second time, a hint of mystery in his blue eyes. A warm wave rolls through her and she stands there in her puddle, frozen in the moment. Veerle nudges her.

"Sorry!" She speaks again. "I didn't mean it. Honest!"

He replies with the sweetest smile. "No need to say sorry. It's all part of the fun."

"Yeah, getting dirty's part of the fun," Smurf says with a chuckle.

"Down and dirty," their pal chips in and they roar with laughter again.

They reach the front of the queue at last and return to the girls' picnic spot with a stack of hot dogs. Sophie is lying on the plastic sheet, still recovering from her exertions. She looks up, sees the boys, and her gaze clouds over. Hannah knows what's coming: Sophie will sit there with a long face for the rest of the afternoon and treat the boys with contempt like she always does, while Hannah tries in vain to make her feel part of things.

Well, not this time. She's had enough. Sophie can fend for herself. Hannah settles down next to the boys. In stony silence, Sophie grabs a hot dog, fishes a book out of her backpack, and pretends to read.

With the book raised in front of her face, Sophie is as good as gone, but peering over the top there's no avoiding Hannah's sullen, accusing stare. Yet again Sophie is refusing to do what's expected of her: to make stupid, pointless jokes with a bunch of nitwits. "You need to laugh more, Sophie," Hannah had sighed the other day.

Sophie turns a page, watching the boys and girls inching closer together. The curly-haired boy rests his hand on Hannah's leg. It's the same old routine. They babble, huddle together, and

giggle about any old thing. But then Curly tilts Hannah's chin
and kisses her full on the mouth. A soft, seamless kiss, the kind
you see in movies. They look into each other's eyes and Sophie
holds her breath.

Where does he get the nerve? His hand stays on Hannah's
leg and without missing a beat, he goes right on talking. Sophie
tries to get back to her book but the kiss is whirring around her
brain. Such a carefree kiss. Such an easy prey.

Suddenly Veerle leaps to her feet. "My favorite song! Let's
dance! Come on!" Everyone gets up and Curly's hand goes from
Hannah's leg back into his trouser pocket. The whole group
walks away. Sophie stares holes in her book: As long as you're invisible no one can forget you or leave you behind. Hannah turns
back and heads straight for her. Here it comes, thinks Sophie: the
anger, the spite, the recriminations. *Why won't you join in? Why
can't you enjoy yourself? Why are you so boring?*

Hannah kneels in front of Sophie, takes hold of the book, and
snaps it shut. She smiles her sweetest *pretty please*. "Join us?"
Suddenly Sophie feels the warmth of Hannah's hand on her knee.

"Come on, Sophie. You like dancing, don't you? You don't
need to say a word. No one's expecting anything of you. I'll dance
with you, okay?"

Sophie looks down at the tender hand on her knee, happy and
sad at the same time. It's a feeling she doesn't understand, so she
opts for happy and nods.

100% LOVE, 0% CALORIES

NEW YORK, 2014

HANNAH WAKES UP IN BASHFUL'S PALACE. THERE ARE NO CUR-
tains and the afternoon light of Bushwick falls in perfect
crescent moons on the wooden floor. Bashful occupies an entire
story of a magnificently renovated warehouse. There are no di-
viding walls and ridiculously large objects punctuate the vast
space: a snooker table, showroom dummies, a motorcycle complete with sidecar, and a huge bed flanked by beeswax church
candles, which burned themselves out last night. He is still sound
asleep. She pulls on his gray T-shirt and pads across the creaking
floor to the toilet, tucked away behind an opaque glass screen. A
whiff of something in the air reminds her of school. Since when
did a New York loft smell of Belgian classrooms? *What is that
smell?*

She pees and walks back through the room, taking in the paintings along the way: moody canvases, all spatters and smudges, a

pathetic attempt at Pollock. She touches the thick layers of paint—solid, almost elastic—then moves on to a giant wooden wheel leaning against the wall.

"They used it to hoist up the cargo from the ships," he calls from the bed as he gropes for his watch on the floor. He sits up and holds the face comically close to his own. *Mr. Magoo*, he muttered last night after his third attempt to slide the key into the lock. He stumbles out of bed and drags his tousled hair and naked soap-star physique over to the kitchen.

"Coffee?"

"Please."

She looks on as he rustles up a couple of soy-milk cappuccinos with an old-school percolator and a dinky jug of milk. He heats the cups with hot water from the faucet. The light falls on his perfect ass, even better than Vermeer. This unfamiliar place feels oddly sheltered, safe.

Perched on two high stools at the breakfast bar, they eat yogurt with thick chunks of organic muesli from the deli down the block and talk Bushwick. He tells her Madonna recently bought a warehouse around the corner, where Brad Pitt plans to set up a drop-in center for intercultural parents. No doubt about it: Bushwick is booming.

She thinks of her tiny apartment five streets away where nothing is booming or blossoming or even taking root. Still filled with a fervent desire never to go back there again, she chats away assiduously and spoons her yogurt as slowly as is plausible.

"So what brought you here?"

"You tell me," he says and laughs. "There's something special about Bushwick, it's still a little rough around the edges.

Manhattan's had the life polished out of it and the only afford-able living space is no bigger than a rabbit hutch. Here you're within striking distance of the city without the tourists and the fat-cat Russians to bring you down. There's room to breathe." He throws his arms wide. A splotch of yogurt lands on the floor but if he notices, he doesn't mind.

"What about you?"

I needed distance, she wants to say. A river at least between then and now. There was no other way. Bushwick is an escape, not a destination.

"Likewise."

She pulls her bare legs up in front of her, chin resting on her knees. It feels good here. Another heaped spoonful of yo-gurt disappears into his open mouth. Greedy, she thinks, just like the sex. Flashes of her body on the floor, pinned to the mattress. Pure sex. Not the cuddle-me, tickle-me lovemaking Boy was so fond of, but classic fuck-me, fill-me sex. His face expressionless. Two naked bodies consuming each other.

His spoon clatters in the bowl. "Hey, I've got to go. I have a shoot in a while." She nods. He stands and looks at her for a moment, and she knows he knows. That she doesn't want to leave, to head out into a world where everything feels awry, where houses and cars are floating in a hollow pipe, where streets are rocking, tipping beneath her feet, where she will be lost again.

"Stay if you like, Hannah," he says. "I won't be back till later this evening."

Staying sounds wonderful.

"Maybe. I'll see how I feel."

He smiles, grabs a pile of well-thumbed pages from the table, and stuffs them in his bag. "Still got lines to learn but hey, it's not like it's Hamlet. I'm outta here. Catch you later, maybe." He takes her head in his hands, kisses the crown of her head, and strides off. The heavy door falls shut behind him.

The house is hers. She feels a sudden urge to rifle through drawers, cupboards, his toilet bag, to peer under the bed, behind the books, to expose, to unmask. That's how it was with Boy at the end, searching in vain for a love letter or a furtive email, for a sign that he was not a saint, for a valid reason to let him go.

Bashful's game is different. He flaunts his secrets, they are the tools of his trade. How can you catch someone out when they revel in the truth? Bashful didn't even pretend last night was special. He's lost count of the girls and boys who have writhed between his sheets. His bed is as big as his home. His heart is bottomless. Just like mine, Hannah thinks.

There it is again, that smell. Something in the air bringing back her schooldays at St. Martin's. The vast schoolyard, deserted. A little girl, all alone, walking across the gray flagstones. A girl with a pleated skirt, long white socks, two pigtails. Sophie. *And then . . . a cheek raw with pain, a bloody tooth. No, stop thinking! Not here, not now.*

Hannah reaches for her backpack and slides out her laptop. She flips it open, an action that always takes a mental effort. A young girl appears on the screen: Agatha, in a white dress, her hair in two long braids, lace collar buttoned tight and around her neck a crucifix on a chain. She is posing at a spinning wheel, her right hand loosely holding a wooden spool, her left resting on an open book. Her eyes are heavy-lidded, always a hint of ennui in her gaze. But ennui is the essence of her disguise.

Hannah clicks open a new document. A pristine page shoots up out of nowhere and blocks Agatha's image. Through the window she sees blue sky, pigeons dawdling over the roofs of Bushwick. No, it's time to focus. Agatha.

FREEDOM

LONDON, LIBERATION DAY 1918

THE WOMEN HAVE ALL GONE MAD. WAILING LIKE BANSHEES, THEY pour onto the streets of London, screaming, singing, delirious with joy. Hankies, towels, tablecloths are being waved, confetti, streamers, and toilet paper tossed high in the air. The Union Jack is flying everywhere. The streets are filled with noise: everything from groaning to hysterical laughter, animal, untamed. Many are drunk, all of them sound like they are. Release a German into this crowd of women and in seconds he would be torn limb from limb.

The end of the war has brought chaos the like of which Agatha has never seen and it weighs heavily on her. Order and calm fire up her imagination but this furor of colors, smells, and sounds is deadening. Skirting the crowds, sticking close to the buildings, she tries to reach her apartment as quickly as possible. At the front door, she drops her keys not once but twice, and swears loudly before finally stepping inside and closing the door behind her.

She dashes through the hall straight into the living room and slings her cloak on the sofa. Where does she think she is running to? There is nowhere to escape from the screams, they force their way in through the windows. She walks over to the mantelpiece, leans wearily against the cool marble, and vigorously rubs both hands over her face and eyelids, as if to wake herself up.

From the mirror above the fireplace, a woman of almost thirty eyes her impassively. Behind the reflected face is a room, wedged in among so many other rooms, houses, streets, and neighborhoods. A parlor furnished with strange sofas, elaborate patterns on the walls. The fashionably floral wallpaper she has never liked.

Agatha is not fond of this house. As much as she loves dear Archie, her handsome, doting husband, she is cold and indifferent to the place they now call home. Once he had returned from the war and the Air Force had stationed him in England, Archie had insisted they find an apartment of their own and London had seemed like an ideal place to settle. The bustle of big city life had appealed to her imagination, but in the end her imagination outshone reality. However many flowers she arranges, pictures she hangs, pieces of furniture she buys, their house refuses to become home.

Home is Ashfield, the rambling house in Torquay where she lived with her mother, where she learned to write and never stopped. Home is that place with its colorful tapestries and rich satin walls, the garden full of beech trees, where she could lie in the grass for hours and feel the long blades growing against her cheek as she dreamed of other worlds and far-flung travels.

No one understands Agatha as well as her mother. No one else can make her feel safer, more protected. For evenings on end, Clara would read her daughter Sir Walter Scott and Dickens, skipping the boring passages, for Clara had no patience with lengthy descriptions. Hanging on every word, Agatha would listen to the rise and fall of the voice that guided her warmly through the written world. Not only that, but Clara encouraged her daughter to put pen to paper and reveled in the stories, in the unbridled imagination of her *peculiar little girl*.

Agatha lingers by the mantelpiece. There is no let-up in the hysteria outside. She closes her eyes. As a writer, she has failed. Her debut was rejected by no less than six publishers. A seventh, The Bodley Head, has not even bothered to respond. It is steadily dawning that an existence as an amateur is the best she can hope for. A consolation prize.

In London she devotes herself to womanly duties. She has thrown herself into the role of "wife of"; no, she has flung herself at it. She attends cookery classes and a course in bookkeeping and has turned out to be an exemplary pupil, exceptional even. She does her best, not out of fascination or any natural aptitude for figures or for cooking. Truth be told, they barely interest her at all. What does interest her is playing the perfect wife to her handsome husband. If it is not something she can *be*, it is a part that she can *play*. Her very own doll's house. That is worth something at least.

She heads for the kitchen and peers into the cupboards to see if there is enough to make supper for Archie. Grocery shopping does not come easily to her and she often finds herself returning from the shops with the most unlikely ingredients. The essentials only occur to her after the fact. But she's not about to venture out today, not for all the tea in China. She will make something from the leftovers, a tasty dish for Archie. She will astound him with her powers of improvisation and be rewarded with a proud look of approbation. Archie, the man every woman falls for, has fallen for her. *For her!* It still fills her with a sense of triumph. Life's greatest victory is already hers. Charming, handsome Archie.

When he returns home that evening, she tells him everything. About the frenzied women and the deafening racket. He smiles. "Agatha, people want to celebrate the end of the war. You can understand that, can't you?" They are sitting side by side on the sofa. Agatha shrugs like a sulky little girl. He cups her face in his hands, searches her eyes, and asks, "Shall we drive to Ashfield tomorrow and celebrate this momentous occasion in style?" She brightens up, nods, and knows she looks like a drooling dog. But she doesn't care. All is right with the world. They are going to Ashfield. Going home. Where Clara will be waiting at the elegant front door, her arms open wide.

GHOST

BACHTE-MARIA-LEERNE, 1996

IS THERE ANYTHING TO EAT?"

Mom wanders into the kitchen, her pink bathrobe hanging half open. Sophie is in the living room doing her homework for the day after tomorrow. "I think there's a slice of pizza left," she calls, without looking up. "Next to the microwave."

She hears the clack of cupboards opening and closing. Mom always forgets where the dishes and the glasses go. *Where are those goddamn plates?* They once had a huge fight because she was convinced Sophie moved things around just to annoy her. It wasn't true, but ever since Sophie regularly rearranges the crockery and listens with a smile to the spiteful slamming of cupboard doors.

Mom shuffles into the room, chewing on a pizza slice. "Everything okay at school?"

"Yeah, fine."

"Did you get your bike fixed?" She had had a puncture the week before.

"Yeah, they replaced the tire."

"How's things with that friend of yours?"

"Okay."

Mom collapses onto the couch, bathrobe billowing around her like a pink cloud. A tall, dark-haired woman with a hooked nose, her thin lips always pulled tight. Now those lips seem to be smiling, so Sophie smiles back. This is how they have spent the past year, *acting* as if everything's all right, and in a way it is. As long as no one's watching. As long as there are no concerned onlookers to see that things cannot go on like this. And there are no onlookers, Sophie sees to that.

Mom switches on the TV and Sophie looks up.

"Am I disturbing you?"

Sophie shakes her head. "I was almost finished anyway."

A blond continuity announcer smiles at the camera and tells the viewers what the evening has in store: the tribulations of a bunch of Beverly Hills teens, a musical extravaganza starring ten unmissable Belgian singers, the shock doc to end all shock docs. *Sit back and enjoy the ride.*

Sophie clicks her pen and closes her textbook and notebook.

"Finished?"

"Yeah, I'm off to my room."

Mom nods.

As she passes the couch, Sophie catches a whiff of King Bourbon on her breath. She leaves him be, knowing now that he will always be there. Once she poured him down the sink and saw how nasty Mom could get. An almighty slap. She came down hard on the broken bottle and ended up with a scratch in her eye that would be there for good. A tiny scratch between me and you, just like the TV announcer talking into the lens. *I act as if I'm close to you, but I'm not. When push comes to shove: I am here and you are there.*

She pulls on a comfy nightdress and crawls into bed with a book. She loves to read; every page is a blanket. It's fall now and the dark comes early. At nine she clicks the light off and settles down to sleep. She feels a little ashamed, giving up on the day this early. Often she's not even tired. She thinks of the pictures of endless oceans on her bedroom wall, photos of far-away worlds she knows nothing about. Coastlines that curl around clear azure waters, small beaches where no one has ever been. She will go there one day and make her own sanctuary. She will build walls from branches and a roof of leaves, drink water from coconut shells, spark fire with stones. These are the things that help her fall asleep. A house of trees, a garden sea.

A FEW HOURS LATER SHE WAKES WITH A JOLT. DULL THUDS COMING from the other side of the door. The hall light snaps on. She slips quietly out of bed and opens the door a crack. Staring back at her with deep-set eyes is a ghost in a long pink bathrobe.

"Where is he?" asks the ghost.

She wants nothing more than to slam the door in her face. Work it out for yourself, Mrs. Korsakoff, with your boozy amnesia that lets you forget the cruelest things, time and time again.

"He's not here, Mom."

"Don't lie to me, I saw him just a minute ago."

"Dad isn't here, Mom. He's in Gdansk."

"Gdansk?" She looks shocked. "Gdansk?"

"Yes, Mom. He's selling lawnmowers to Polish people. That's where he is now."

"And he's never coming back?"

"He always comes back, Mom." With his tail between his legs. When his latest affair turns sour, when his latest deal flounders. Last year it was water beds, this year it's lawnmowers. Whatever it is, the customers are always far, far away.

"Go to bed, Mom. It's time to go to bed."

"But doesn't he know I'm here?" she shouts, unbelieving. "Doesn't your father know that I miss him?"

Sophie nods. Everyone misses Dad. Last time he was home she found a letter among his things, from a girl called Olga, an endless eulogy in broken English about how thrilling he was, how creative, how intelligent, how incredibly charming. She read it, scrunched it up as small as she could, and threw the wad of sweet-talk into his case. She didn't even try to cover her tracks. Nor did he.

Once she found a stray jacket hanging on the coat stand. He'd had the nerve to bring a woman back with him, to make love to her here in the house. Their so-called home. Where had Mom been at that hour? And what did that woman think of this desolate place? Filled with objects that are never touched, fossils barely worth dusting? A house of empty vases and faded pictures?

"Come on, I'll help you to bed."

Sophie takes her mother gently by the arm and leads her to the double bed where King Bourbon is waiting to cradle her to sleep. She pulls the quilt over her mother's weary bones and watches her sink into the depths of her mattress, the warm, soothing depths that ease all the pain.

NOW YOU SEE ME

NOANK, 2014

THE BEST THING FOR A CHILD IS A HEALTHY DOSE OF NEGLECT. AN honest mother, Agatha believes, treats her children like a cat treats her young: She is content to give birth and nurture her infant for a time, before returning to the business of her own life. Hannah stares out of the window at the trees rolling past in a blur of green, like a film reel that's running too fast—or too slow.

No one in America travels by train. The compartment is as good as empty, nearly always the case when she makes the journey from New York to Mystic in the middle of the day. Between the seat backs she can see a man in a suit tapping away at his laptop. Across the aisle a young woman is leaning against the window, the sleeping baby in her arms wrapped in a cotton sling.

An honest mother. But who *is* mother, Hannah wonders: a woman far away in Belgium or a dear friend close by, in New

England? She has known Irminia for years, feels cherished by her. No one can calm her or comfort her more readily.

It's roughly a three-hour trip from Penn Station to Mystic Depot, a modest two-track affair, one of the few stops on the Amtrak between New York and Boston. Hardly anyone gets off at Mystic. When the long train pulls into the station, three doors swing open and Hannah is the only passenger to get off.

She walks over the yellow paving stones and past the charming little station building, straight out of a nursery rhyme. A toy manufacturer once reproduced it in miniature and that's exactly what life feels like here in the town of Mystic: a trip back in time to an innocent, orderly children's world.

On Roosevelt Avenue she sees Irminia in her orange anorak, waving. A woman of almost sixty with silver-gray hair and the friendliest smile in the world. When Irminia smiles, the world smiles back.

"Mina!" Hannah runs up to her and hugs her tight.

"Oh sweetheart, it's so good to see you."

"How are things? How have you been feeling?"

Irminia dismisses the question with a wave of her hand. "That's for later. Let's drive home first."

In a red Mini they chase through the streets of Mystic, once a sleepy fishing village, now a draw for tourists eager to sample a slice of the Mystic Pizza served up by Julia Roberts in the Hollywood hit. Then they wind along the road to neighboring Noank. Hannah is looking forward to taking refuge in the comfort of the blue house, light-years away from the empty husk of her Bushwick apartment.

The driveway is still spilling over with weeds and wildflowers, the garden a sanctuary for moldering chairs, rusty watering cans, and weather-beaten gnomes. The front door still needs mending, but who would want to do you harm in the miniature world of Noank?

Hannah opens the door and wanders into the chaos she knows so well. The smell of the bread Irminia bakes whenever she comes: a sourdough loaf with seeds, to be devoured in thick slices with lashings of soft, salty butter.

Since Irminia is incapable of throwing anything away, the entire house is a shrine crammed with memories: knickknacks, teddy bears, battered books, unlabeled cassette tapes. A host of objects that no longer work or have long since ceased to function. Stray buttons, long-vacated cat baskets, dented umbrellas. Thick strands of dust hug the corners of every room. Nothing is neat or tidy, everything feels snug and warm.

THAT EVENING, AS CUSTOM DICTATES, IT'S DINNER AT LOBSTER IN the Rough, an upscale fast-food joint with the best lobster in town and a glorious view over Beebe Cove. Irminia brings Hannah up to speed on Noank's residents, who never change and occasionally find themselves locked in a furious battle to defend their beloved status quo.

Once the lobsters have been taken away and their greasy bibs are lying spent on the table, Irminia brings up the subject of her new life in Bushwick.

"I'm still finding my feet."

"That's only natural. You're trying to do a lot at once."

Irminia turns the Styrofoam cup of white wine in her hands. "Do you miss Boy?"

"No."

"Can you still remember why you wanted things this way, Hannah?"

"I think so."

They fall silent and look at one another. Hannah senses that Irminia is on the point of saying something maternal in that soothing, deliberate tone she so clearly relishes—a tone Hannah will only tolerate from Irminia.

"I didn't try to stop you, Hannah, because I believe in making your own decisions and I trust you to do right by yourself. In all the years I've known you, I've never tried to hold you back. But you're not making it easy on yourself. And lately I got to wondering . . ." She hesitates. "Sometimes I wonder whether this has anything to do with me. With my situation."

Hannah shivers. Please, let's not talk about the *situation*. It's something she can't handle. Period. She wants to, she is trying to, but ever since that afternoon in the consulting room at Mount Sinai, she hasn't been able to think about it, never mind talk.

"I am going to give you our honest assessment," the doctor had said to Irminia with a deadpan expression. "The breast cancer has spread to the lymph nodes and the lungs and although we cannot provide you with an exact prognosis, our estimates suggest that you have between two and six months to live."

That was the second opinion. They had come in search of hope, a brighter prospect, only to be handed down a new verdict more damning than the first. The cancer had long since smothered every glimmer of hope.

Hannah could not bring herself to look at Irminia. Instead, she stared at the back of a photo on the doctor's desk: a triangular standard sheathed in leather propping up a gilded frame. The portrait on the other side probably showed two happy children and a radiant wife, the very picture of health. She wanted to slam the frame against the wall. No tears, Hannah, not now. She felt Irminia take her hand and squeeze gently. *No*, Hannah thought, *that should be my hand squeezing, I should be the shoulder to cry on. Everything's different now.*

"I don't know, Mina. I still find it hard."

"We *can* talk about it, you know, darling. Things aren't so bad. Those pills they gave me make the pain more than bearable. I'm doing much better now."

Better? Sure, thanks to the morphine or whatever other poison is eating away at your insides, destroying you bit by bit while making the pain oh so very bearable. Hannah looks away. She cannot talk about it, forces a few words from her throat. "That's good, Mina. I'm glad."

It's a lie but it seems to work. Irminia takes a deep breath and smiles. "Until things take a turn for the worse, we can just continue where we left off, you and I. Okay?"

Hannah nods. Of course we can't.

BABY OF MINE

TORQUAY, 1924

M UMMY, WILL YOU HELP ME?"
Rosalind is sitting at the table with a sheet of paper, a box of colored pencils, and a pair of scissors. She is trying to cut out a shape, a mask. She is only five years old, too young to complete the task unaided. Agatha does the decent thing: She smiles at the child and nods.

Rosalind was born at Ashfield, a bouncing baby girl, the final act of a troubled pregnancy. The birth of her daughter hit Agatha like a landslide, an almost incomprehensible event. How can this be, she wonders. In a fraction of a minute—the time it takes for a small, slippery body to make that astounding journey, to slither into the world—how can a woman go from daughter to mother?

Her eyes settle on the mask Rosalind has drawn. It is green and uninspired. A mask, nothing more.

"Why, it's beautiful," she says.

Rosalind smiles. *Does the girl actually believe her?* She sits down beside her daughter and looks at the drawing: a green oval with two dull circles where the eyes should be.

Every day she comes up short. She sees herself doing everything as it ought to be done: Here we have Agatha making a tasty treat for Rosalind, Agatha smiling as she dotes on her toddler, gaily throwing a ball to the little girl who looks back at her in wide-eyed surprise.

Slowly but surely, Agatha feels herself giving up. Why be a perfect mother when she would much rather be a perfect daughter instead? The all-embracing love she saw in her own mother's eyes is nowhere to be found. She cannot be a Clara to her Rosalind. She is the lesser mother.

"This is where the holes go." Rosalind points proudly. Agatha picks up the scissors and pierces the paper. Turning it patiently, she cuts two neat holes for the eyes. She takes a spool from the drawer, snips off a length, and knots the thread on either side of the paper. Rosalind looks on breathlessly. Agatha hands her the mask but she shakes her little head firmly. "No Mummy, you put it on. It's for you!"

Agatha hesitates, then raises her hands and slides the mask into place. Her sight dimmed by the paper, she peers at her cheerful child.

"Oh Mummy, it's so pretty!"

She tilts her head from side to side to heighten the hilarity. That's how Archie does it: larking about, playful and free. Going through these motions, she feels anything but free. She is making a spectacle of herself—a mummy in a mask.

Through the small holes she studies Rosalind, whose long

hair hangs in two neat braids, like her own used to. A girl whose cold eyes she cannot read. A dear child, but not truly hers. Her real child would have an unbridled imagination, devour book after book, lie daydreaming in the long grass at the bottom of the garden. Her child would have Clara's tender gaze, not the blue-eyed Archie stare. Rosalind is *Archie's child*.

"My turn, Mummy!"

The girl seizes the mask with her chubby fingers and presses it to her face. The eyeholes are too far apart, but she doesn't care. Her little hands turn into claws, she growls.

"Who am I, Mummy? Who am I?"

Archie's child. Out of nowhere, an idea comes to Agatha: Perhaps they should have another child, one that is truly hers. A second chance to become a proper mother. Perhaps the next child will bring the maternal devotion she is missing, the instinctive joy on which happy mothers thrive. Mothers who live for their children, who surrender unconditionally, something she seems incapable of doing. Mothers who fill up existential emptiness with new life, plug craters with kiddies; children as a means to an end.

Perhaps that is where the trouble lies: Agatha's landscape knows no craters. Her writing fulfills her, every single day. Now that her talent has been recognized and her stories are being read, she has become unstoppable. After ten months, when all seemed lost, The Bodley Head came to her rescue. She rewrote the denouement as requested and signed a contract for her debut novel: *The Mysterious Affair at Styles*.

More capitulation than contract, she now knows, worth all of twenty-five pounds. A piddling sum, but enough to silence her skeptical sister Madge. Agatha has what it takes, not least an undeniable mastery of plot. One reviewer even dubbed her the "Queen of Mystery." She prefers to see herself as an illusionist, mesmerizing the audience with her dexterous left hand while all along the key is hidden in her right.

Still wearing the mask, Rosalind slides off her chair and starts running around.

"Woo! Woo-ooo!"

She tears through the room, a sudden outburst of energy that leaves Agatha at a loss. So she smiles and her eyes follow the girl, under the table, over the sofa, until her bare feet catch the edge of a rug and she hits the floor with a smack. Rosalind wails. Agatha leaps up and dashes over. She kneels, takes her daughter in her arms, and pulls off the mask.

"Are you all right, sweetheart? Does it hurt?"

Rosalind sobs, a lip-trembling show of dismay. Agatha strokes her hair, plants a kiss on her forehead. At times she catches herself thinking the unthinkable: What if Rosalind were not here? What if she were to vanish as abruptly as she came? Would that make everything easier? Would that make her feel freer, happier?

"No, Mummy, pain's all gone now."

"That's good, darling. I'm glad."

Rosalind clings tightly. Agatha holds her and tries to cherish the warmth of this small, strange creature in her arms.

ONE MORE THING

BACHTE-MARIA-LEERNE, 1996

CYCLING'S NOT EASY WITH THREE BAGS OF MICROWAVE MEALS and defrosting pizzas hanging from your handlebars. Sophie wobbles her way along the cinder track, taking a shortcut behind the castle so that no one will see her. It feels all wrong for her to be buying the groceries; most people have a mother for that sort of thing. So she does it on the sly, early on a Saturday morning while the supermarket is still deserted.

She does her best to keep the bike in motion but it's like cycling over sand strewn with pebbles. Before she can gain enough momentum it's too late. Her front wheel jams and she comes crashing down. *Damn!* A searing pain shoots through her shoulder. There is blood on her knee but worse still, a puddle of pink and white sauce is spreading from the handlebars to the saddle. She stares motionless at the thick gloop. Sometimes she just wants to give up. Really. When something goes wrong, something stupid like this, she would give anything just to let go.

She sets her bike upright and finds some dry leaves to wipe down the saddle. It helps a little, and a little is good enough for now. As long as she can be on her way before anyone sees her.

One of the bags is full of slops: boiled potatoes and steamed salmon in a creamy béchamel sauce. She divides the clean groceries between two bags, collects the mess in the third bag, and dumps it in a trash can. In the puddle on the ground, she spots the penknife with the antelope grip, covered in thick white sauce. She picks it up, wipes it off, and puts it back in her pocket.

Just as she is about to gather the fallen pizzas and climb back on the saddle, there is a crunch of cinders behind her. She jumps and prays it's no one she knows or that half-blind neighbor who never says hello anyway. She holds her breath and wishes the ground would swallow her up.

"Sophie? Are you okay?"

She looks up and finds herself face-to-face with the one and only male teacher at St. Martin's, her English teacher, Mr. Verhoeven.

"Are you hurt?"

"Not really."

"But you're bleeding, Sophie."

Tell me something I don't know. "It's just a scratch."

"Come here, let me give you a hand."

Mr. Verhoeven picks up the pizzas, still scattered across the path like giant autumn leaves. He smiles. "I'm guessing you folks really like pizza!"

Us folks. If only it were that simple. "Yeah, we do."

When he smiles, his eyes smile too. A man in a freshly pressed shirt and fashionable jeans, almost a boy. He is carrying a sports bag and smells of deodorant. At school, in his suit, he looks much older. Here he seems so ordinary, a real person you can reach out and touch. She watches as he picks up the broken bottle with the little man with the walking stick and the top hat. King Bourbon. He says nothing. It follows the dirty bag into the trash can.

"There now. That's better, isn't it?"

"Thank you, Mr. Verhoeven," Sophie murmurs.

"The least I could do. And call me Sven. I have a first name too, you know." Again she feels that strange sensation. This is not how a teacher talks to a pupil. He is crossing a line, although Sophie cannot say what line exactly, or why it makes her feel uneasy.

"Sorry. Thank you, Sven."

"Look, I live just around the corner. Come with me and I'll get you cleaned up. It'll save you having to answer too many questions when you get home."

Sophie looks down and sees white sauce clinging to her blouse like long trails of snot.

"Come on."

His hand on her shoulder. So this is how it feels when a strange man asks you to come home with him. Only Mr. Verhoeven is not a stranger. He is her teacher. He hangs one of the bags on his handlebars and puts a foot on his pedals. "Ready?"

MINUTES LATER, SVEN IS GIVING HIS JAMMED KITCHEN DOOR A GOOD shove to get it open. It wasn't even locked. Sophie thinks this strange. She always makes sure every door and window is bolted before turning in at night. No one ever told her to, she just always assumed it was necessary. Now she wonders why.

"All right then, put your bags down over there." Sven points to the corner and lays his sports bag on the kitchen table. He walks over to the sink and comes back with a tube of detergent and a brush. From a cupboard, he pulls out a clean tea towel.

"Okay, sit down here. It'll be easier."

The room looks kind of pretty, with red-and-white checked curtains, a big wooden table, and six mismatched chairs. Sophie has always wondered what it would be like to live right next to the woods, just a stone's throw from the castle.

She gazes up at the wall, plastered with photos of pop groups, a flyer for *West Side Story*, postcards of New York, and reproductions of wild, weird paintings she has never seen before, as if someone's chucked paint at the canvas. Her eyes settle on a photo of Robert Redford grinning from under a baseball cap.

Sven smiles. "Good-looking guy, eh?" He winks and she blushes.

"Now, let's see." Sven knees in front of the chair and touches her blouse. He rubs the stain with the brush and a dollop of detergent, his face very close to hers. Long white lines streak the fabric. Her blouse feels damp and sticky, and seems to be even more of a mess. Sven shuffles back for a clearer look and sees it too.

"Perhaps you should take it off."

An electric charge shoots through Sophie's body. An eel that slithers up through her chest and scorches the back of her throat. She looks up in alarm. It happens in a flash, less than a second, but Sven registers it. He puts a hurried hand on her shoulder and looks her straight in the eye. "I didn't mean here. It's okay, Sophie. Never mind."

Still life of man and girl. A brush dripping suds.

"How about a cup of tea?" he asks at last. He stands up, walks to the sink, and fills the kettle. "I'll give you a bowl of water in a minute, so you can wash out the soap. Once it dries, the worst will be gone." He opens another cupboard, takes two teabags from a box, and puts two mugs on the table. All Sophie wants to do is get out of here.

"I hope you don't mind me asking, but do you like school?"

Such a plain, innocent question, but Sophie knows what he is trying to do. He wants to rekindle trust. It's too late for that. The cozy charm of the red-and-white checked curtains has been betrayed, and nothing will bring it back. This house is not different, only more of the same. Her only aim now is to make it out of here in one piece. Wait for a polite opportunity to grab her bags and head for home.

"Sugar?"

"No, thanks."

"Does it feel different now?"

She hesitates. What does he mean? School? No, not that different, except for that one thing you seem so keen to change. A teacher is not a friend.

"No, not really."

"Have you thought about what you want to do? Later, when you leave school?"

That's none of your business. I don't think about what I'll do when I leave because I still have to make it that far. And if I make it, I'll be free and then everything will be better.

"No, not really."

"What are you afraid of, Sophie?"

How dare he ask such a question? Sophie gets up. "I'm

sorry but I have to go. My mom will be wondering what's keeping me."

"Are you sure?"

But Sophie is already in the corner making a grab for her plastic bags. She has almost made it through the door when Sven lays his hand on her arm.

"One more thing, Sophie. I want you to know that you are always welcome here. Will you remember that? I want you to remember that."

He squeezes her arm gently. "I know what it's like, Sophie. We have more in common than you think."

TAKE ON ME

NEW YORK, 2014

A TRAIL OF DROPLETS WEAVES ITS WAY ACROSS THE LOFT. FRESH from the shower, Hannah's hair is still wet as she stands before a mound of clean clothes beside his bed. She fishes out a pair of panties and pulls them on. They fit loosely around her hips.

She thinks of her bashful lover and how sweetly he urges, "Come on, eat something, babe." Two tubs of yogurt and a drawerful of vegetables greet her when she opens the fridge, along with a big jar of kombucha that forces her to look away. Yellowish pus floating on murky liquid. A living organism bobbing in a glass reservoir, seething, pulsing, growing. Hannah gags, bites down hard on her lip, and slams the fridge door shut.

At St. Martin's the girls used to jot down everything they ate in neat notebooks full of dubious lists. *Such a little slice of bread only counts as half, surely?* Everything that went uneaten was a shining victory, a mark of character. Obsessing about food gave structure to the days at school, where time dragged by at such an agonizing pace.

Now her life has no structure and Hannah forgets to eat. Her stomach feels hollow and has done for months. Emptiness aches where once a fragile life had taken root. One little spot, bruised and raw. Can you learn to live your life around an empty space?

Perhaps she needs to head out into the open air, like Agatha who traipsed over the moors for hours on end. Perhaps then the words will come.

Agatha, who first began to write out of sheer boredom; the empty days at Ashfield had to be filled somehow and so she made up an endless string of stories, poems, and songs. Boredom is an excellent reason to start writing, Hannah agrees, but these long days in Bashful's loft have brought her book no closer. All she has are fragments of a writer, stray scenes typed in a daze.

What she wants is to tap into the essence of Agatha, bring her to life in the here and now. By describing her not as the famous writer she was, but as a person, as a mother, as a lover. So that everyone can understand why such a successful woman drove off into the dark one night and vanished into thin air. Agatha held the secret of what it means to disappear; she knew the seductive qualities of being able to break away. Without being lost, like Sophie, vanishing into the woods, forever. No, don't think about Sophie. *Never think about Sophie again.*

A pair of oversized raincoats are hanging by the front door, partially obscuring stacks of DVDs, box sets of *As Time Goes By*. Hannah slides a disc from its sleeve and sees the sultry stare of Bashful, perfectly coiffed and wearing a white coat, a publicity still from the season when Harvey James abandoned modeling and found his true calling as a cardiologist.

Harvey James, a handsome man of many talents. Just like Archibald Christie, the suave military officer who could wrap the ladies of Torquay around his little finger. Archie, handsome Archie. Agatha had danced with him one night at a party. Ten days later he turned up at Ashfield. Her mother called in a panic. "One of your young men is here. What on earth am I supposed to do with him? Come home at once, will you, Agatha?"

He had driven over on his motorcycle to see her. To see *her*! "I had an awful time getting your address and finding you," he said. They talked and ate the cold leftovers of the Christmas turkey. From that day forth he turned up at Ashfield on a regular basis, until one evening he insisted in no uncertain terms that she had to marry him. There was nothing else for it, even if she was engaged to someone else. She smiled and said, "I am twenty-four years old, Archie. I can decide for myself what is best for me."

Hannah tosses the disc aside. Harvey, Archie. *Charlatans both*. Next to the DVDs are piles of old scripts and fan mail from women Bashful has never met. Good for a one-night stand at most. "That's fame for you," he said. "When it's all handed to you on a silver platter, you're hardly going to refuse."

He gently caressed the contours of her breasts, her hips, her thighs as they lay in bed. She kept on asking and he kept on telling. About the affairs with his costars, often juggling several at the same time. Sticky sessions in the backseats of taxis, the best blow job ever in the elevator up to the Peak Bar in Tokyo. Things she definitely does not want to know, rendered in intimate detail. Fans who stripped for him and satisfied his every desire without a single word. Women he declared his love for without meaning it for a second. Just because he could. Just to see what would happen. How easy it is to fill a heart and pump it dry, how ludicrously easy.

Bashful does not want to know anything about her. He doesn't even ask. "It would only make me jealous," he whispers. She doesn't believe him. It's lack of interest, nothing more. In this they are alike. Her own interest is purely strategic. She feeds off his confessions, thinking this knowledge might set her apart from all the rest, from the other women he has ridden to climax in this bed.

"I don't mind," she says. "I don't need to own you."

"Well, how cute are you?" He laughs, and her stomach turns.

"Come on, eat something, babe."

THE TENDER TRAP

NOANK, 2014

HANNAH IS SITTING ON A FOLDING CHAIR IN NOANK'S VERY OWN theater, a simple structure sandwiched between the town library and the cove. Two slender columns flanking the entrance do their best to lend the place a certain cultural cachet. But it remains a clubhouse by the water, the sound of sloshing waves, bumping boats, and shrieking gulls clearly audible through its flimsy walls.

Shakespeare's 450th birthday has not gone unnoticed here, and a special tribute will be performed by the scant acting talent that has washed up in Noank over the years. The hall is empty but for a few chairs and Hannah feels privileged to have been invited to one of Irminia's rehearsals. She's the first to get a sneak preview of the one-of-a-kind Shakespeare medley the Noank Theatre Company has created.

So far the tribute has been a bumpy ride: The company's octogenarian director bowed out six months ago and a replacement is nowhere in sight. By then, the three performances of the play had completely sold out, so it was decided unanimously: on with the show.

Hannah tries to make sense of the many characters that enter and leave the stage at a hurried pace. The Immortal Bard must be spinning in his grave, she thinks. The tribute is a kooky medley that has Ophelia rubbing shoulders with Cleopatra, King Richard with King Lear, a completely beatnik mash-up of midsummer night's revelry and bloodcurdling regicide.

In the hall where only this morning Noank's sprightlier senior citizens creaked their way through their weekly yoga class, elves are now jumping, kings raging, maidens wooing. The improvised decor is woeful, the acting even more so, but Hannah decides to lean back and revel in the spectacle.

"What, jealous Oberon?" Irminia is Titania, queen of the fairies, skirt over her jeans and two cotton wings dangling from her shoulders. "Fairies, skip hence!" With a grand sweep of her arm she takes to the stage. Here, among the cheap seats and velvet curtains, Irminia is in her element, outshining the rest of the cast with ease. She is the undisputed star of the company, brimming over with unfulfilled promise.

Little do they know that nearly twenty years ago she was giving her all in the latest Broadway production of *A Chorus Line*, on the verge of fulfilling her dreams. Until one momentous decision changed her life for good, blew her off course, and took her from the Great White Way to stamping books at Noank public library. This chapter in her life occasionally surfaces in conversations with Hannah, but her accounts are always fleeting and sketchy. Not at all in keeping with her flair for drama.

From her front-row seat, Hannah can feel Irminia's energy, practically feed off it. These days it's a fire that comes and goes from one moment to the next: a look across the cove, a shiver in the wind and Hannah knows Irminia is back in the consulting room, trying once again to understand what has happened, what was said, and what it really means. The color drains from her face, as if her veins have stopped and her blood is holding its breath. But then she sees Hannah looking at her and recovers her composure, a faltering effort.

Ben is Oberon, the king of the fairies. Good old reliable Ben, the town handyman, jack of all trades. A nut and a bolt for every household calamity but not a thespian bone in his body.

"Ill met by moonlight, proud Titania," he mumbles.

"What sayest thou?" Irminia exclaims, cupping a hand to her ear.

"Uh . . . that's not your line. It says here—"

"I know what it says, Benjamin, but I can barely hear you. And if I can't hear you, the audience has no chance."

"Ill met by moonlight, proud Titania," Ben mumbles a little louder.

"What, jealous Oberon? Fairies, skip hence!"

THAT EVENING, HANNAH AND IRMINIA TALK FOR HOURS ON THE porch of the blue house as they so often do. Two basket chairs and a stool just big enough to hold two glasses of wine and a bowl of nuts. Irminia has wound a cotton scarf around her head and draped a blanket around her shoulders.

"So how's the book coming along?" she asks. Hannah sighs. *Not the book, please . . .*

Less than six months ago, she had shared the idea for the first time on this very porch. For weeks she had been grieving the little girl she lost; not eating, not getting up, staying in bed for days on end until Boy had literally dragged her out and put her on the next Noank train.

"What do you want?" Irminia had asked and to her surprise, she had answered.

"Something meaningful. I want to write a book."

"What about?"

"A kind of biography about three female writers who inspire me, three strong and complex women who dared to fight the demands and the limitations of their time. Famous authors that I want to describe as the ambiguous women they were."

Irminia had seemed intrigued, something that sparked Hannah to continue: "I need to understand what they can teach me, what they wanted to say. They were talented, wise women who raised their voices and then suddenly became silent. Why? They all disappeared, you know."

Irminia had taken a big gulp of wine, looking uncharacteristically tense, and then, almost reluctantly, as if going against some invisible current, she had simply said: "Hannah, do it."

And here they are: six months later. Same porch, same book, no words. An awkward question and a wretched deadline breathing on her neck. She's never going to meet the stipulations of her fancy contract. Her publisher will be displeased; she will officially be a failure.

Irminia is staring at her from under her colorful cotton scarf, concerned. Hannah looks away, spots a broken garden gnome between the leaves, crushed for as long as she can remember. A hole in his side, a crack between his eyes.

"Well? Hannah?"

"It's an unmitigated disaster. I have a deadline in two weeks and I've hardly written anything at all."

"Do you still want to write the book?"

"More than ever."

"Then just do it." She leans forward as if she wants to reach into Hannah's mind and brush the dark cobwebs away. "These women are yours, Hannah. Let them take you where they will. They are your private league of writers."

Yeah, right. Guided by dead writers: *some league*. Out of nowhere, she thinks of Damiaan. His blue eyes, his whispered words. "We're in the same league, you and I." And everything in her tingled, because it was true.

"Only you can write this book, Hannah. It's all there, in your head, and if you let the words out, it will be a book. Simple as that."

Agatha once said: *Writing a book is like driving a car at night.* That's how she feels: cruising aimlessly through a moonless night. *You can only see as far as the headlights, but you can make the whole trip that way.* Wise, wise Agatha. Just do it. Nobody ever says *just think it.* Hannah steps back from the edge and raises her glass: "To my writers!"

Irminia grins from ear to ear. "That's my girl."

They toast and the good old times are back: drinks, jokes, the ebb and flow of intimate conversation. Tonight nothing will remind them of the scene at the hospital. It will be as if it never happened. They dance barefoot on the fluffy carpet and Sinatra croons their favorite tune. *Those trees, that breeze, they're part of the tender trap.*

Later that night, still tipsy from the wine, Hannah is lying in her room. She stares out through the small window that grants her a distant glimpse of Beebe Cove. The water is the same as ever. The town is the same as ever. Irminia is the same as ever. She can refuse every change. Yes, it is possible. Nothing will change unless she allows it to. *Do you accept the changes in this document?* No.

Irminia comes in, sets her glass on the bedside table. Lying down on the bed, she puts her arms around Hannah and holds her tight.

"My little girl," she whispers.

Hannah smiles. The blue house seems more beautiful than ever: the chairs warmer, the carpet thicker, the bed stronger, the sheets cleaner. She curls her whole body against Irminia's. If only she could disappear among the soft folds of her warm flesh . . . Her hand feels for Irminia's hand. No one is going to take this away from me, she thinks. No one.

"Don't ever leave, Mina."

"Of course not, sweetheart. I'll always be here with you."

IT'S OH SO QUIET

TORQUAY, 1926

REALITY IS REFUSING TO BECOME REAL. CLARA IS ILL, DESPER-ately ill. Agatha hardly leaves her mother's side, dabs the sweat from her brow with a damp cloth, brings her fresh pillows, clean sheets, and hot water bottles. Her long skirt rustles in the overwhelming stillness of the room. Clara speaks less and less, does not so much as touch her books. In this big house, she seems so small and insignificant.

"What time is it?" she asks. "Are the children indoors?"

"There's no need to worry, Mama," Agatha reassures her. "Sleep a little longer."

She closes the door to the room and sits down at the typewriter in the parlor at Ashfield. Every sentence is a struggle. The insatiable public appetite for her books has changed the writing. The romance has gone. She is no longer a creative force, but a tradeswoman delivering her wares to her clientele at designated intervals.

She hears Clara moaning through the wall, the plaintive sound of a stricken animal. In a reflex Agatha jumps up, hesitates, then sits back down. She thinks of Rosalind as a baby, how every whimper had her dashing over to the cradle. Mothers and daughters. Perhaps that is the nature of things: A daughter becomes a mother when she has a child of her own and a mother who needs looking after becomes a daughter once again. Calm down, Agatha, make a little time for yourself.

On their travels, time had been her own. Far away everything was better. Ten months touring around the world with Archie, leaving Rosalind behind with Clara. They trekked along the South African coast, conquered the hills of New Zealand and the waves of Hawaii. She wrote to Clara, long, colorful accounts of their experiences: coming face-to-face with a hippo in the Zambezi, eating the juiciest peaches in Cape Town, being one of the first Europeans to surf the waves of the Pacific. She can still feel the fitful buoyancy of the water beneath her, feet anchored to the wooden plank, the surrender demanded by the waves and the pleasure, the sheer pleasure they gave!

Clara, surfing is one of the most perfect *physical pleasures that I have known, truly!* And she underlined the word "perfect" as she underlined every important word in her letters, to give the language a little lift.

And now the globe-trotter is home again, back to being a mother and a housewife. She can't help but see it that way: back in your corner now, pipe down. The only sound we need to hear is the rattle of your typewriter. It's stories we want from you. Come along, chop-chop!

She runs a hand through her blond hair, unwashed for days,

and stares at the typewriter as if for the first time, as if a hippo has surfaced in front of her.

She presses a random key and watches the metal arm swing at white paper, eager to stamp a black letter into the grain: W. It could have been any letter. Typed on a whim, much like the stories she writes. Everything she invents exists. The colonel's moustache could just as easily have been a beard, the secretary's winsome smile a killer's disguise. The thinnest of lines between what is real and what is not. And as for her—the formidable writer, the failed housewife—how much of her is real? Even Archie seems not to notice her these days, every spare minute spent with his chums at the golf club. Agatha doesn't care for golf.

That evening, when enough letters have been stamped on paper, she climbs quietly into bed beside her mother and for the littlest while she becomes herself again. Lying next to Clara, she remembers who she is, the child who lay still as could be on her pillow so as not to let Clara's bedtime hugs slip away between the sheets. Lying motionless for hours in the warm nest of Ashfield, clinging to the resonance of that last touch, straining not to let go.

Now a girl again, she lays her head on Clara's shoulder. "Don't ever leave me, Mama."

Clara opens her eyes, raises a heavy arm to Agatha's face, and smiles.

"Of course not, darling. *I'll always be here with you.*"

BLUE MONDAY

BACHTE-MARIA-LEERNE, 1996

NOBODY TALKS ABOUT IT BECAUSE IT IS PLAIN AS DAY. THE world of St. Martin's is divided into pairs: Vicky and Conny, Lisa and Anneleen, An and Karlijn. A tomboy and a girly girl: Big and tough paired with small and tender. No deal was ever struck, no rules prescribed; that's just the way it works. The laws of gender insinuate themselves, even into the sexless Catholic straitjacket of St. Martin's. These couplings are not easily broken, another unwritten law. They are bound by a loyalty and intimacy to rival any love match. Veerle and Evelien. Hannah and Sophie.

On the playground that isn't a playground they stroll arm-in-arm during breaks. Their white socks pulled up over the knee, identical stiff pleated skirts, identical green blouses—intimate as twins. Now Hannah is holding Sophie's hand; they talk and gently nod whenever they cross another couple. Sophie glows. I belong to someone, she thinks. And what a joy it is to belong to Hannah, even if it's only within St. Martin's slightly tilted walls.

When the clock strikes four and the school day is over, they cycle home together. Sophie cherishes their trips along the Steenweg, picking over every detail of the day's news: who got the best grades, who had the coolest shoes, the bugbear Sister Gregoria chose to harp on about at morning assembly.

"Did you know Veerle managed to sneak into Backstage at the weekend?" Hannah asks wide-eyed. "Said she was sixteen and that chump on the door believed her."

"You're kidding!"

"Honest. She said it was amazing in there. All her drinks were paid for and she didn't get home till four in the morning."

"Wow."

"God, I'd give anything to get in there. What about you?"

Sophie nods. The Sloop is dumb and childish, but Backstage is something else entirely: a proper nightclub where people dance and drink the night away, *real* people who have left school, for whom real life has begun. She would love to know what it's like on the other side of that door but she knows she doesn't stand a chance of passing for an adult, not with her scrawny physique.

"I look way older with lipstick on," Hannah muses. "Hey, d'you know what we could do?" Her face lights up. "Dad's working late and Mom will be at her computer class. We can raid her wardrobe and try everything on."

Why has she never thought of it before? Her mother's drawers full of makeup, racks bursting with clothes. She has never dared venture into her mother's sacred walk-in closet before, but with Sophie at her side anything is possible.

"You're on!" Sophie nods eagerly. "See you later!"

They wave goodbye and Sophie cycles home, one street away. Home is a designer bungalow from the 1970s, a building sightseers happily take a detour to marvel at, though there's nothing to see but a white box obscured by a cluster of beech trees. *Who wouldn't want to live here? It's so adorable.*

She opens the back door. No sign of Mom. Then she spots the note on the kitchen table. *Gone to the hairdressers.* It makes her smile. A note means that Mom is having a good day, and the hairdressers means things are really looking up. She turns on the oven and grabs a pizza from the freezer.

It's almost dark by the time Sophie taps on the kitchen window. Hannah flings open the door with a wide grin. Tonight they are sixteen! They rush up to her parents' bedroom and plunder the drawers for mascara, eyeliner, nail varnish, and lipstick. There seems to be no end to them. When it's all spread out on Hannah's dressing table, they go back and dive into Mom's closet: a wonderland of dresses, skirts, blouses, and bikinis. They drag the full-length mirror across the landing to Hannah's room. Just as they are about to start dressing up, Hannah leaps to her feet.

"D'you know what we need?"

Sophie shakes her head but she knows it's bound to be something cool.

"G&T's! Mom always drinks gin and tonic at parties and I know where she keeps it."

Sophie starts to say something, but seeing the elation on Hannah's face, all she can do is nod.

Hannah charges downstairs and returns with a squarish

bottle under one arm, two cans of fizz under the other, a tub of ice cubes, and two glasses. "This is what you serve it in," she says knowingly, holding up a cut-glass tumbler and pouring in a glug of gin followed by a slosh of tonic. She has no idea how much of each to pour, but fifty-fifty seems like a safe enough bet. She tosses in two ice cubes and they clink the way they do in the movies, a thrilling, grown-up sound. *Shaken, not stirred.*

Just holding the glasses makes them feel all grown-up. Sophie sniffs at the bitter mix. She has never drunk alcohol before, though her house is full of the stuff.

She takes a mighty swallow that glows at the back of her throat. Not bad. Hannah takes two swigs in quick succession and looks around at the boudoir they have brought to life in a young girl's bedroom. The desk is a riot of color and a glorious array of clothes is spread out under the watchful eye of Jesus, hanging from his wooden cross above Hannah's bed. They close the door.

"Okay, let's get started."

Sophie nods and they plunge into a whirl of fashion and fantasy. They start with the dresses and shiny blouses, apply wet clots of mascara and lashings of lipstick. Their world becomes a beauty pageant on a Caribbean island and they are the only two candidates remaining. The excitement builds. Only one of them will be crowned *Miss Tropical Paradise*. A jury of experts is on hand to judge every category as they strut through the room like Spice Girls, cheeks flushed, lips shining, strong and sassy.

Glowing with happiness, Sophie sips from her fuchsia-rimmed glass. She slips into a silver swimsuit with laces she can pull tight at the sides, so it fits snugly enough even though it's too big for her. Balancing on a pair of outsized white mules, she totters across the room feeling fabulous. Hannah is wearing gold sandals and a leopardskin-print bikini fastened with two thin straps around her shoulders. Hips swaying, they parade up and down, feeling sixteen and sensational.

It's Sophie's turn to scrutinize. As head judge, she frowns and examines Hannah from head to toe. Hannah wiggles her behind and pouts her full lips. She does it well, licking her glistening lips, feeling blissful and warm inside. She takes a step toward Sophie, and thrusts her breasts forward.

Sophie's eyes drop to the thin cord pulled tight around Hannah's waist. She reaches out and strokes the soft skin below her navel, a sea of warm, soft flesh. Hannah closes her eyes and feels Sophie's other hand glide over her thighs and the curve of her buttocks. A kiss, tentative at first, then firm. Lipstick thick on a moist tongue. Hannah tastes the sweetness of saliva, the bitterness of the lipstick.

They both knew it would happen again tonight. It's something they always look forward to, but never talk about. That way it stays unimportant, unnamed and uncondemned. Just something that happens between them.

Sophie slides the straps from Hannah's shoulders and the top falls open to reveal her breasts, full and round, with perfect pink buds. She presses her face to them and leaves a trail of fuchsia across her hard nipples. Holding her breath, she hears Hannah's heart racing.

Slowly they fall onto the bed, blouses and dresses gliding under their naked bodies. The bottle topples and a splash of gin anoints their moist skin. Touching every spot, caressing every curve. It goes unspoken and so it is allowed. Two young girls disappearing wide-eyed into one another.

Outside in the darkness, an engine purrs. A car eases into

the driveway and stops in front of the house. The girls don't hear. How a door opens and closes, a briefcase hits the floor and a glass is filled with water. How someone climbs the stairs, alarmed by too much silence, and slowly walks toward the bedroom door, sensing something is wrong.

He opens the door and freezes, sickened by what he sees, an image he cannot understand. Two naked girls pawing at each other's bodies with an eagerness, a hunger he has never known. It chokes him and excites him. It hurts.

Hannah looks up, sees her father standing there. A statue in a smart suit, one hand still resting on the door handle. She looks into his unblinking eyes and screams. Sophie jumps up in a reflex, dives for cover behind the dressing table. She clutches her hands to her breasts and clamps her legs together, tries to make herself invisible.

A moment suspended in time. No one moves, no one speaks. One word, any word, would only make this more real, carve it into the here and now, never to be erased, make it part of a world in which it has no place. A car zooms past. The Barbie clock ticks in the closet.

Could it still be a game? A silly mistake we can laugh about later? Sophie's mind is racing. It *was* only a game, wasn't it? But she looks at Hannah's father and the panic in his eyes blocks every escape route. Slowly, mechanically, he turns and walks back downstairs, without a sound. Hannah begins to sob. Sophie buries her face in her hands. This isn't right, this can't be right. This never really happened.

THERE SHE GOES

BACHTE-MARIA-LEERNE, 1996

THE STREET IS DARK AND EMPTY, NOTHING FOR THE LAMPPOSTS to light but bare patches of front garden. It feels like such a long way home. Her T-shirt is on backward and the label scratches at her throat. They dressed in a hurry, Hannah sobbing all the while. Sophie tried to say something but Hannah wouldn't even look at her, so she left. Tiptoeing through the hall, she saw Hannah's father sitting bolt upright in front of the television, as if he had been turned to stone. She crept through the front door, which slammed loudly behind her.

Sophie's head is pounding as she tries to grasp what has happened. She wants to hurry on but her feet refuse to move, two open-laced sneakers glued to the tarmac. It's like walking on bubblegum, a sticky thread stretching and pulling her back with every step. Trapped between two houses. If only there were somewhere else to go, a choice between walking on and turning back. If only there were other streets to take.

She looks back and sees Hannah's rustic villa, the house that once felt safe. Inside, a shadow is dashing around, picking up dresses and putting them on clothes hangers, back in Mommy's closet. Pretty little Hannah, making it all better. As if what just happened could ever be tidied up and put away.

T<small>HE HOUSE IS QUIET.</small> S<small>OPHIE LEAVES THE LIGHT OFF;</small> <small>DARKNESS IS</small> better. Everything looks less real in the dark. She sees the contours of a living room—a lounge suite, a television, a cabinet—the decor of a life that is not hers.

The windowsill ornaments cast freakish shadows on the carpet. From every business trip, he brought back a souvenir. Not the pretty gifts from the local craft shops but cut-price clichés snapped up at the airport kiosk minutes before boarding: a plastic Eiffel Tower with twinkly lights, a ceramic pizza, canary-yellow clogs, and a wooden flamenco dancer. Her mother never wanted any of these things, but every time he left a little present for her on the kitchen table.

Mom never opened them. It was Sophie who unwrapped the presents after a day or two and gave them their place at the window. Eventually he noticed this and stopped bothering. No more gifts, just a windowsill of failed attempts.

She walks slowly past the ornaments, touching each one lightly. Her fingertips brush the Polish doll's long braids. Big Ben gets a pat on the head. Her skin picks up dust, a powdering of gray on her index finger, and she resolves to clean them more carefully. She lowers the shutters. Broad slats tumble down, the slits between them zip tight and swallow the last of the light.

Sophie only feels safe once the shutters are down, when the

house becomes a fortress that cannot be captured by anyone. Not even by him, if he wanted to. That way she sleeps soundest.

She walks to her mother's room and eases the door ajar. Her shutters are already down and her bedside lamp is on. Mom is lying on her side, arms stretched out in front of her as if they are reaching for something, or have just let go. Sophie watches for a while. Her mother looks so calm when she is sleeping, so peaceful, curiously content.

After a while she closes the door and tiptoes to her empty room. She takes off her clothes and throws them on a chair. Something cold and hard is digging into her wrist: an armband belonging to Hannah's mother, unnoticed in her rush to escape. She switches on the light and sees an elegant snake of copper and gold winding around her arm. She tries to pry it off but it won't let go. Her skin is clamped tight between the reptile's head and the curl of its tail. She pulls harder and thick red lines score her wrist, then harder still until the metal cuts her skin.

The snake relinquishes its hold, flies through the air, and glances off the bed. Her wrist is free but Sophie feels a scream rising up inside her. *Hannah, why wouldn't you say anything? Why didn't you help me?* We could have cleaned up the mess together. We could have comforted each other. She slams her fist into the mattress.

You wouldn't even look at me and now you've left me alone in this empty house. Fist after fist pounds her pillow. *Hannah, you spoiled little bitch.* But punches you cannot feel do not help. She unclenches her hands and slaps her cheeks until they sting. It's a trick, nothing more. Pain to make the pain more bearable.

Her skin burns and smarts. She is calm again. It's over. On

the wall across from her bed are photos of white beaches and blue seas that really do exist. It doesn't matter where they are or what they are called.

"There's always an island somewhere, Sophie," he said. "A place you have yet to discover. Remember that, my little one, always remember."

ETERNAL FLAME

SUNNINGDALE, 1926 / NEW YORK, 2014

H E LEANS AGAINST THE DOORPOST, WATCHING HER UNNOTICED from the darkness, her cramped hands pounding away, the typewriter lost in shadow. From this angle she looks like a thing possessed, her movements compulsive and spasmodic.

Why can't Agatha do what is expected of her? Be there waiting with a cup of tea when he comes home, take his coat, engage in pleasant conversation about the weather? Why can't she come to bed at a reasonable hour and receive his affections willingly, without aversion, without restlessness or, as she puts it, a head that is buzzing with stories.

Every evening he returns to a dark house, one dim lamp burning on her table. It tells him all he needs to know: She has been sitting at her typewriter for hours and twilight came and went without her so much as noticing. He sees her hunched over that mechanical monstrosity that spits and snaps, driving him to distraction with its infuriating rat-tat-tat.

He speaks her name and she jumps, turns around, and gives him that familiar distracted look, scrunching her eyes as if he keeps swimming out of focus and she can barely make him out. It's dark, he thinks. To her I am always standing in the dark and she cannot see me. But now there is someone who can, and that makes all the difference.

Since achieving an unprecedented success as an author, Agatha has devoted herself to her writing as she has devoted herself to nothing in her life before. Not to their daughter. Not to him.

"You are incorrigible," he says. "Come to bed, Agatha."

"I'm not finished yet," she replies.

"No, but *I* am." He steps into the lamplight and tries to look at her sternly, knowing it will make no difference. She will go on writing, he knows, deep into the night, with a diligence that will cut him adrift.

"I'll just finish this chapter and then slip between the covers with you, all right?"

No, it's not all right. Their bedroom at Sunningdale is roomy but their bed is small and Agatha's *slipping between the covers*, as she likes to put it, only serves to wake him. And so they have placed an extra bed beside the double bed, so that she can *slip between the covers* to her heart's content without disturbing him. A writer's bed for Agatha with a *writer's* pillow, a *writer's* blanket, a *writer's* sheet. "Incorrigible," he mutters as he leaves her to it.

And I have a *writer's* mattress, Hannah thinks. And a *writer's* actor. She glances over to where Bashful is lying, on his side. He is naked and the moonlight on his skin reminds her of an ad for yogurt that earned Boy an award once, in a different life.

She is sitting with her back to the wall, laptop bobbing up and

down on a cushion stuffed between her outspread legs. She saves
the words she has just written under the title "Eternal Flame,"
and the document is automatically slurped up by a file named
Agatha, joining documents with titles such as "Freedom" and
"Baby of Mine."

Isolated moments from Agatha's existence—disjointed, un-
connected. The scenes appear to her in fits and starts, plucked
haphazardly from the flow of time. How can these fragments of
Agatha ever pass for a whole?

She drinks from the bottle beside her on the floor, a nip of
vodka to help the words flow. As a writer, she is aware of her
power to make Archie do anything she wants with her Agatha.
He could storm over to his wife, shake her violently, and growl an
ultimatum. "If you don't come to bed this very minute, Agatha,
it's over! Do you hear me? Over!" Would their history have been
different if he had?

He could seize her by the hair and drag her to bed, maul her
like an animal, give his pent-up urges free rein at last.

Again, Hannah gazes at Bashful and the bed where she is
writing their history. She could storm over to him, shake him
violently, and demand that he choose her and only her. Other
women will have to stake their claim to eternal happiness elsewhere.

She could smash the vodka bottle against the wall, pick out
a particularly nasty shard, and force him to swear that he will
never, ever leave her. Anything Archie can do, she can do better.
But deep inside she knows, the facts are very different. Archie no
longer loves Agatha. Bashful never loved her at all.

She refuses to think about which is worse and returns to the screen. So there you are, Agatha, you've just lost the woman you trusted and loved more than anyone. And Clara's death was just the beginning. I wonder, if she would have been alive at the time, could she have protected you? Would she have made the shock, the pain more bearable? Your guess, Agatha, is as good as mine. What we both know with certainty is what happened next in that sacred, mourning house.

HANDICAP

TORQUAY, 1926

"THAT WILL BE ALL, LILY. THANK YOU. NO NEED TO SHUT THE door on your way out."

The maid nods, gives a swift curtsey, and heads for the door with a modest tread. Through the open crack, Agatha watches as the young girl shakes out her apron and disappears down the long, dark hallway with a chipper gait. Soon she will jump on her bike and cycle to a happier place, away from the mourning that has seeped into every fiber of this house.

Clara is dead. Ashfield slumps and leaks. The roof is on the brink of collapse, water drips from the ceilings, and a lifetime of possessions needs clearing up. In her final months here, Clara's life was played out in two rooms, an immaculate island at the heart of a musty labyrinth. Agatha looks around at the sea of things spread about her in purposeless piles and clusters. Ashfield is no longer a home, but a warehouse stacked with furniture, suit-cases, books, and assorted junk.

Every day she wanders through their lives together: what to keep, what to throw away? Should she cherish and keep what is valuable or do things only become valuable because they are cherished and kept? Are Clara's things steeped in memory or are they hollow shells that pretend to know who Clara was? A dress without her body. A pen without her hand. "Burn everything," Archie tells her. "Torch the lot! End it now and make a fresh start."

That's the last thing she is about to do. Like a creature possessed she works her way through each room in turn. Yes, that is how she feels, possessed. To stay here is torture, to leave is simply impossible.

With Clara gone, there is no denying that *home* is now the fortress in Sunningdale, the somber mansion that, in a fit of madness, they christened "Styles." Named for the red-brick pile whose uncomfortable rooms and contrived garden provided the setting for her debut novel. A house cut out for murder and skullduggery. Admittedly the neighbors are nice and stop to chat now and then, but mostly she feels like an outsider among the gin-swilling, suffocating Sunningdale community.

The fortress had been Archie's choice, not too far from London, convenient for work. Agatha would rather have lived out in the country or, even better, on an island, in a big house with ultramarine shutters and a sea view.

Lily has gone. Agatha has packed away her typewriter and is resolved that this evening she will welcome her husband just the way he likes it. From the kitchen she fetches a silver tray with a teapot and two cups, and places it on a round table by the hearth. An image of Clara floats past, resting by the fire, nodding off with Dickens in her hand, reading glasses perched on her noble nose.

The images come day and night, a restless stream. But in a while Archie will be here and she will share her sorrow at last. He knows better than anyone how deep her love for Clara ran. He will gaze at her fondly and hold her tight. She will bask in his care awhile, an indulgence she has earned. She drops two sugar cubes into a cup. Yes, that much she has earned.

The wait is long. She tidies the room and wraps a few presents for Rosalind, whose birthday is tomorrow: shiny paper covered in stars and tied with a cheerful bow. What could be keeping Archie? It's after ten, he should have been here by now. She reads a little by the fire, makes a fresh pot of tea. Then she hears the crunch of tires on gravel and the dying of the engine. *Archie!* She jumps up and runs to meet him, happy as a child.

He appears in the hall, dripping from the downpour despite sprinting from the car to the front door. He is wearing a long Burberry, a well-tailored suit, a pained smile.

"Archie! Archie dear!" She flings her arms around him. "Here, let me help you."

She slides the wet raincoat from his shoulders and hangs it on a chair. He walks briskly to the fireplace and rests his left hand on the hot mantelpiece. A grand, almost regal pose.

"Agatha, there is something we need to discuss."

"Discuss?" Suddenly she sees: Something is wrong, terribly wrong. His skin is gray, his gaze is dull, as if someone else has crawled into his body and is looking out through his eyes. Someone who ought not to be there. This is not Archie, her husband. He might look like Archie but he is acting like one of the murderers from her books. She quickly suppresses the thought. What on earth is wrong with him? Please no, don't let him be ill. Not cancer, dear God! Or is money the problem? Yes, that might explain the scoundrel in his eyes.

"Agatha, I have made no arrangements for our trip to Italy." They were due to leave for Rome the following week. A little getaway, like in the old days, just the two of them. Ah, so that's it. She shrugs and smiles.

"Oh Archie, that hardly matters, now does it? We'll stay in England. I'm sure that will be just as nice." She walks over to him, arms outstretched, but he fends her off with one hand. *Who is this man?* He clears his throat and speaks.

"Do you remember the dark-haired girl who used to be Belcher's secretary? We had them down for a weekend once, a year ago. And we've seen her in London once or twice."

Agatha knows the girl he means.

"Her name is Nancy Neele. I've been seeing her in London this summer."

A dalliance. He has been flirting with another woman. It comes as a shock, but her first instinct is relief. At least it's not some horrific disease. Nancy Neele. The girl liked to play golf, she recalls, a passion of her husband's that she has never taken to. Should she have been aware?

"Oh, what of it?" Once again she shrugs.

Archie stands there motionless with his scoundrel stare. "I've been seeing her *very regularly* . . ."

No, no, no. A flirtation is hardly going to threaten their future together. She had not expected this of him, her loyal, earnest Archie, but these things are not uncommon. She is far from naïve.

"It can happen in the best of families."

What a ridiculous thing to say. Worthy of a spineless ninny from one of her novels. Of course it was improper of him to flirt with another woman while she was here at Ashfield, mourning her mother, going through hell. But then Archie has never responded well to illness and misery. It is something he cannot help, a deeply ingrained aversion. No, her mind is made up. This time she will forgive his foolishness. *Silly Archie.*

"I understand, Archie."

"Agatha, you do not understand."

She looks inquiringly at his cool gaze, Rosalind's eyes. She sees impatience and something else besides, something close to disgust. And now she knows what is coming. She knows for certain. The one thing she does not know is how they sound, the words that break a world; how blunt, how vicious, how loud? Here it is again, the emptiness she felt at Clara's bedside as she waited for her to slip away.

Hush, Archie. Please. Keep them to yourself. Just a little longer.

"I've fallen in love with her, and I'd like you to give me a divorce as soon as it can be arranged."

THE LADY VANISHES

SUNNINGDALE, 1926

FOR SO MANY REASONS.

Because Clara is dead, because Archie is gone, because her daughter does not feel like her daughter. Because no matter how hard she works, she seems incapable of satisfying her readers' and publisher's endless demands, because the dream is over and her doll's house has come crashing down.

Agatha's plan is a masterstroke, steeped in mystery, dripping with venom. It will be her glorious revenge. A score settled by absence, an attack sprung by running away—such a gratifying irony.

The search for the celebrated author who vanished without a trace will soon be on, and as in the best detective stories, they will steadily unpick the truth, one clue at a time. An extensive investigation will narrow its focus to the one prime suspect she has in mind: handsome, treacherous Archie.

It is not the truth but what of it? The truth does not matter when she is writing, so why should it matter now? She will go on living, elsewhere, and no one will know. You can look for me, but you will find me gone.

Agatha closes the front door behind her, starts the car and disappears.

II

BARBARA

DON'T LOOK BACK

BACHTE-MARIA-LEERNE, 1996

No, SHE MUSTN'T LOOK BACK, THERE IS ONLY HERE, ONLY NOW. These limp arms, aching muscles, cinders stinging the soles of her bare feet. She runs along the path, the pretty garden, the little bench with its friendly carved heart.

At the door she stops, presses her forehead to the cold wood, briefly closes her eyes. She can still turn back. *Back where?* There is nowhere else, there is no other house. Only this path at the edge of the woods, the red-and-white checked curtains, a door that jams but is never locked.

She steps into the kitchen, waits in front of the water heater, catches her breath. Her stained white dress flickers blue in the pilot light. She calls out his name. His school name, though she doesn't know why. School suddenly seems so far away.

Mr. Verhoeven?

Stumbling, creaking floorboards, thudding on the stairs. A

figure appears in the dark hallway, naked but for his boxer shorts. He stares at her, bewildered, shocked by the image of a girl in a bloodstained dress crying on his kitchen floor. She begs him to help her. *Please.* Her whole body is trembling.

His hands reach in an open drawer, all the way to the back. He takes something out. She hears it fall. He picks it up quick, walks past her to the door, locks it. He doesn't ask a thing.

He opens a chest, takes out a blanket, walks up to her, and kneels. Gently he wraps the blanket around her shoulders, takes her in his arms. Her head in the hollow of his neck, his skin oddly familiar, warm.

Up the stairs they go. To a bed with a crochet bedspread, downy pillows, crisp white sheets. An old alarm clock ticks on a rickety table. A room from long ago.

His hands, kind and gentle. He pulls back the covers. It's all right now. Someone to save her. At last there is someone to save her.

She sinks into the pillows and slowly drifts away.

THE WHITE MARCH

BRUSSELS, 1996

A RIVER, WHITE WITH RAGE, WINDS ITS WAY THROUGH THE streets of Brussels. The people have come in their hundreds of thousands to join the White March, the biggest demonstration in Belgium's postwar history. White balloons, white flowers, white ribbons, white faces. Symbols of innocence betrayed.

It has gone beyond the horror of Marc Dutroux. The six young girls he abducted, the four he murdered. The public outcry has spilled over into incredulous disgust with the authorities: the police, the courts, the politicians—no one can be trusted. ASHAMED TO BE BELGIAN! END THE COVER-UP! Little people clutching giant banners. PROTÉGEZ NOS ENFANTS! FOR THE SAKE OF OUR CHILDREN! Protesters joined in scathing indignation, a sentiment that unites a country like no other.

The girls from St. Martin's High are there. So too are the

boys from St. Barbara's, among them Damiaan and his pals from the cross-country race. Once again, the boys and girls are thrown together in a crowd. The boys have painted their faces white and are carrying a banner: ENOUGH IS ENOUGH! Hannah is walking hand in hand with Damiaan. Sophie trudges along behind them, caught between a big cross bearing a photograph of the murdered girls and a paper heart trimmed with white roses. WE DEMAND THE TRUTH!

The truth is that Hannah has no idea what this afternoon is about. She is not thinking of the dead girls or of Marc Dutroux, the monster with the filthy hands and the sweaty moustache— she is thinking about Damiaan. How four streets ago he took her hand and now they are marching as a couple. It has made Sophie miserable. She maintains a serious expression and does her best to concentrate on why she is here. She tries hard to feel it, the fear of the girls, the horror, the injustice of it all.

"The streets of Brussels will turn white with fury," the man on the radio said that morning. And even though Sophie is stuck in the middle, she can feel the immensity of it, how exciting it is to be inside history, to embody the movement, to be the event. This is what momentum looks like, what it smells like, how it sounds.

A stocky man with a megaphone thrusts his fist in the air, and the crowd cries out, echoing his words at the top of their voices. We must never forget. *We must never forget!* Leave no stone unturned. *Leave no stone unturned!* Unmask the pedophile networks, end this nightmare. *End this nightmare!*

The people march on, furious yet meek as lambs. Sandwiches in their backpacks, parking permits tucked safely in their coat pockets. A mother wipes her tears while her newborn baby turns in its sling. An elderly couple shuffle past looking desolate. A collective shudder. *End the cover-up!*

Sophie feels sad too but it's a strange, indiscriminate sadness, a sorrow that has lost its way and is clinging to the image of two little girls trapped in a cellar. And then it hits her. This is not about the girls. What she feels, marching with this mass of grieving people, is her own despair. Not the girls' sadness. *This girl's sadness.* The White March is not a battle against injustice but an avalanche of personal suffering, violent woes wrapped in white and dumped out in the streets.

The march turns a corner and enters a narrower street, a bottleneck that squeezes the crowd together. A handful of police officers urge everyone to remain calm. Sophie feels wedged in. Moving among so many people is like wading through molasses. She lets herself drift to the side of the street and ends up in the doorway of an apartment building. On the stone steps, she sits down beneath a large panel studded with doorbells, plastered with names. She is in her own little bubble, a spectator watching grief ripple past.

Dredging up your own sorrow is one thing, but radiating happiness like Hannah is doing? Just because the high school hunk has grabbed her by the hand? Damiaan is the catch of the century for girls their age, even Sophie can see that. Mouthing off at The Sloop about all the stuff his artist father lets him get up to, reciting bad poetry, pretending to be bowled over by the mathematical grandeur of pi. He flaunts an intelligence he barely possesses. It's all show, but he has the girls eating out of his hand. With his steel-blue eyes and dark curls, his full lips and his tight body. She sees it, of course she does, but it leaves her cold.

"Do you know where Hannah is?"

Suddenly he is standing there. White face, dark curls, steel-blue eyes.

"I . . . I only just got here, it was so crowded I mean . . ." She breathes and recovers her senses. "No, I have no idea where Hannah is."

You were the one holding on to her, she wants to say, and now you've lost her? How the hell did you manage that?

"Shit. I went over to say hi to someone . . . I told her I'd be right back."

He sinks to his knees and flops down beside her on the stairs. A boy who, at any other moment, would never give her the time of day. He pops her bubble, it bursts. She sighs.

"It's getting to you, is that it? Today?"

His concern confuses her. All she can do is nod.

"It's a lot to take in. All this emotion. I saw a woman in a wheelchair crying so hysterically that she slid right off her chair." His eyes twinkle, waiting for a laugh to reward his cool irreverence, but Sophie doesn't react. They sit in silence. The beautiful boy and the girl he doesn't know what to do with.

"Are you always so serious?"

She shrugs.

"You were the same at the cross-country race. You just sat there on your own, reading. Why do you do that?"

She doesn't answer. She doesn't know why. She certainly hadn't been *reading*.

He wants to say something else but can't find the right words. They stare at the bottom step for a while. Then he slaps his knee.

"I think that's kind of special, you know. Classy. What's the point in always tagging along, copying everyone else? The great minds of our civilization were lone wolves, not sheep. Einstein had no friends, Mozart only ever did what *he* wanted." He nudges her arm. "That makes you one to watch out for."

He laughs sweetly. She laughs back, and her laugh startles her. No, not her laugh but the way their laughter meets halfway. A kind of *ting* in midair, a bright sound like a spoon against glass. A beautiful sound. She blushes.

"What do you say we go looking for the others?" He gets to his feet. "I come to Brussels all the time with Dad. There's a shortcut to the Grand Place. We can wait for them there, okay?"

They walk through streets strewn with empty cans and discarded plastic. The march may be white but it's far from spotless. Between the houses they happen upon a children's playground, deserted but for a mess of leftovers in the sandpit and a half- empty bottle of beer on a picnic table. Damiaan shakes it and puts it back down. He sprints toward the swings, swivels around the rusty pole, and lands with both feet on the round seat.

"What are you waiting for, Sophie?" he asks and extends a playful hand. Of course she would be a fool to trust this invitation, but what else can she do? What does she have to lose? Cautiously she clambers onto the rocking surface. He pushes off with his foot and they swing to and fro, hinges groaning under the weight of two oversized children. In the distance the impotence of a furious nation drones on, but Sophie feels lighter than ever.

The swing flies high, recklessly high, but fear doesn't stand a chance. They could come crashing down this instant and she would accept her fate. She looks him straight in the eye and he looks back. He sees her as no one has ever seen her. She breathes the fresh scent of the trees, feels the strong chain threading through her fists, sees the boy and his loving look. *This* is how momentum feels. And it lasts and lasts.

When he drops onto the seat, his warm body glides against hers. Her head rolls onto his shoulder, and everything falls into place. "You're special, you know that?" And he strokes her glowing cheek. Now, Sophie thinks. She leans forward and kisses the softest lips, savors the taste of his mouth. He smiles. A smug little smile but she doesn't care. Her hands want to touch him, to grab, to own him, here and now—claws clutching at what will disappear all too soon.

Damiaan gets to his feet and slings his bag over his shoulder. He pats the top of her head and lifts her from the swing like a child of six. She feels sick. "I think it's time we found the others." He winks. "What about you?"

She nods. Anything else would be utterly naïve.

BRIEF ENCOUNTER

NEW YORK, 2014

THE BOOKS ARE BRUISED AND FADED IN A MILLION SHADES OF gray. They lean wearily on the shelves or lie in crooked towers against doorposts, under chairs, cramming every inch of Michael's apartment.

Hannah finds a damaged edition of Borges's *The Book of Sand*. Some pages have been torn from the book with brute force, leaving ragged edges, severed words. *Who would do such a thing?* According to its own myth, *The Book of Sand* should be able to heal itself, sprout new pages like leaves on a tree, spinning out the story until the wound of the past is healed and only the finest of scars remains. She fingers the rough paper seam. No healing for this beautiful edition—no healing for this Hannah. In her new world next to nothing sprouts or grows so far.

Irminia called yesterday: "You need to go see Michael. He has something for you."

Michael, the friend Irminia keeps referring to as *the hand-some player with the golden hands* who, three decades later, Hannah dubs *the old misfit with the shortsighted dog*, owner of a secret second-hand bookstore located in a dark prewar apartment just off Central Park.

"And how's the book coming along?" Irminia asked. "Did you make the deadline?"

Hannah sniveled. Sure, she made the deadline and she didn't. She has written a few chapters on Agatha that she'll never allow anyone to read. Her little scenes, ephemeral observations of Agatha's life, seem pointless. "Motive," Agatha would have muttered. "Hannah, where on earth is your *motive*?"

She can't answer Agatha, nor Irminia, and her publisher already left five messages on her voicemail urging her to deliver the manuscript. *We have a schedule, Hannah, where's that tremendous text of yours?* Great expectations mocking her, but she needs to push on. She's not a quitter, she needs to succeed, even if it's only for Irminia.

So here she is, wandering between *Baffling Stories* and *Biography*, words scrawled on yellow Post-it notes stuck at the end of two aisles. Brazenhead Books is what Michael calls the improvised bookstore where the labeled sections are wildly flexible; *Anna Karenina* rubs shoulders with a French edition of *Planet of the Apes*; a stack of wartime memoirs is topped off by a book on grooming dogs. She returns Borges to his designated place.

This is where she wants her book to be washed up one day, right here in Michael's lap. His house of books feels like an island, sheltered and familiar. She's been here so many times that she knows the exact sleight of hand required to find the light switches behind the shelves, she knows which chairs are comfiest and where Michael stashes his cheap wine.

With his shirt buttoned open semi-Italian style, his long gray beard and lively eyes, Michael looks every bit as singular as the books in his apartment store. Many times Hannah has pictured him as a younger man: broad shouldered, with that firm jawline and the same charming, cheeky smile that promises: *I'll take you anywhere, I'm up for anything*. Much like Bashful's smile, she thinks. Nothing like Boy's at all.

In a previous life, Michael had been one of Irminia's flings. As a puppeteer, he had toured Upstate New York and New England accompanied by his self-made marionettes. Performing in Mystic one night, he noticed a bright-eyed woman sitting front row with whom he spent a wild night talking, drinking, and somehow ending up making love to among the lobster traps in a fishing boat.

Soon after Michael quit the puppets—or the puppets quit him—he began selling secondhand books. Hannah remembers kneeling among the empty shelves of his first bookstore, helping to unpack boxes by the hundred.

When business hit hard times, Michael hit the booze. Bankrupt, he may have given up hope but he never gave up his books. He moved all the books that were left in his store to his tiny apartment on the Upper East Side, where literature took over every closet, niche, doorway, and crevice. Words voracious as longhorn beetles ate up his entire living space. Eventually, he moved, the books took over, and a clandestine secondhand bookstore was born. By appointment only. A secretive success.

"I've got something for you." He smiles at her with the glow of anticipation.

She nods. "I know."

He turns and ambles on ahead, leaning on his walking stick, Poe the white bull terrier scuttling along behind him. Reaching his desk, he slides open a drawer and removes a flat, narrow box.

"Three guesses?"

"Michael, you know I hate guessing games."

He shakes the box enticingly from side to side and she snatches it from his hand. Carefully she tears the cardboard lid and pulls the book from its snug little nest. She takes in the looping letters and a running dog, the emblem of Knopf books. *The House Without Windows*, a novel from 1929, the year when the stock markets imploded and doomsday seemed just around the corner. The golden years of Barbara Newhall Follett.

"You were planning to write about her, weren't you?"

She nods and beams. Only Alfred A. Knopf Inc. was willing to take a chance on a debut by a complete unknown, a twelve-year-old girl at that. A girl whose writing was beautiful enough to win over even the most caustic of critics.

One of the century's most remarkable books, proclaims the blurb on the back flap. The paper smells dark and sweet, like a musty Belgian attic. *Everyone has dreamed of fleeing from their daily existence, and this is the story of a little girl who did just that.*

"Oh Michael, it's wonderful," Hannah whispers. She wants to ask him how much it costs but she knows all too well that an edition like this doesn't sell for under five hundred dollars. Barbara would have cracked up to hear that.

"Write a wonderful book," Michael replies. "Like Barbara did. Then we'll see."

She nods and wants to hug him. But a hug is the last thing you give a loveable curmudgeon like Michael.

"Thank you, you sweet old man." She looks at him and he chuckles.

"*Dirty old man*, more like," he says with a wink.

She opens the cover and sees a photograph of Barbara as a girl. A face in grainy monochrome, two long braids and a white dress. A girl looking unflinchingly into the lens, hands folded. Smiling, unaware of how soon her flame will flicker and fade, of how easily a literary promise can be broken.

VISITING BARBARA

NEW HAVEN, 1922

W HAT IS *THAT*? "
    Father jumps and turns his head to see a little girl with two long braids staring wide-eyed at the typewriter and pointing. He clears his throat the way courtiers do in fairy tales before announcing the guest of honor.

"That, Barbara, is a machine for writing with." He gives a demonstration, the desk trembles beneath his leaping fingers.

"But what kind of things does it write?"

"Why, anything you want it to. Any thought that comes into your head."

She eyes him suspiciously: *any* thought?

"How do you mean?"

"Come here and I'll show you."

He lifts her onto his lap, close to the thing that she always hears rattling. She sees the letters on the keys: B for Barbara and

W for Wilson, her father's name. She is only six but she can already write and she likes letters. Especially the W, the way its two sweeping curves join together.

She practices every day, but with a pencil in her hand the letters come out different every time. No curve is ever the same, however hard she tries. The letters on her father's page are perfect as can be. She runs her hand over the big shiny box. This machine knows how it's done. It lines up perfect letters, like soldiers all in a row.

He takes hold of her index finger and places it on a key, steadies her little fingertip on the letter and pushes down until a crooked arm shoots up. *Whack*.

"I pressed a letter!" she shouts, and he laughs at her delight.

From that day on, Barbara never stops whining. She wants to press *real* letters and she wants to start now. She sneaks into her father's room to type stories in secret but that infernal rattling betrays her every time.

One month later, on her birthday, she walks into her bedroom to find it standing proudly on a little table at the window. It is secondhand and covered in white scratches but she doesn't care: she has her very own typewriter. The door to Barbara's room swings shut and an incessant rat-tat-tat begins.

Within weeks her first novella is finished: *The Life of the Spinning Wheel, the Rocking Horse and the Rabbit*. She cuts out a piece of card from the side of a box, takes her pencil, and draws a girl with two braids and a cuddly toy. Under the drawing she writes: *by Barbara Newhall Follett*. Her father beams with pride.

SINNERS ALL

BACHTE-MARIA-LEERNE, 1996

Mrs. Lange is standing at the blackboard declaiming sentences in Latin. Sophie gets the gist immediately, Hannah hasn't a hope. With no one to do her homework for her, Hannah's grades have taken a tumble. *Serves her right.*

These days Hannah chats to other girls in the morning. She no longer lines up beside Sophie and at break time she is nowhere to be found. When the day is over, she cycles home with Veerle. They still sit next to one another in class but the days of swapping secret messages are over. There's a distance between their desks that was never there before.

Orantem frustraque iterum transire volentem portitor arcuerat. Ovid. They are told to translate six verses, in pairs. Hannah and Sophie stare at the sentences.

It feels uncomfortable, exchanging words over a dead language. But then everything they say feels dead. Sophie wants to bring it back to life, reclaim what's been lost.

"Hannah?"

"Yes."

"Is something the matter?"

"No, why?"

"Because we don't cycle home together anymore." Sophie feels a pang deep inside, feels that she is about to suffer for what she has just said.

Hannah shakes her head wearily. "It's a free country, Sophie. Now can we get on with this?"

Hannah has never wanted to get on with anything. She always had a hundred excuses to get out of doing her schoolwork. But here she is, staring intently at a jumble of Latin words she cannot begin to understand. Sophie writes down the translation in silence. Her hand accidentally brushes against Hannah's woolen sweater, a soft, familiar feeling. Hannah is always cold. Sophie has lost count of the times she has taken off her own sweater and lent it to Hannah. *I'll keep you warm.* But now there is a chill over everything and nothing to talk about except the misadventures of Orpheus and Eurydice.

As soon as the lesson ends, Hannah disappears. She hurries across the schoolyard, heading straight for the gates where no doubt Damiaan is waiting for her. Hannah is only allowed to go to The Sloop on Fridays, but now she's sneaking over there on a daily basis. Sophie runs after her. Among a crowd of girls, she grabs Hannah by the sleeve and pulls her aside. The others press past them. Sophie is sweating, panting. Hannah stares at her, dumbfounded. *What do you think you're playing at?*

"Hannah . . . Hannah . . ." The words won't come. "Is something the matter?" A feeble echo of everything she's said before. She knows there will be no answer. Hannah rolls her eyes.

"There's nothing the matter, okay?"

She frees her sleeve from Sophie's grasp and smoothes it out.

"I have to go, Damiaan is waiting. Everything's okay, Sophie. Come down to The Sloop with us if you like."

With the most beautiful boy at her side, Hannah strolls up to the bar. All thoughts of Sophie banished, she is intent on having fun in The Sloop. "How on earth did you pull it off?" her friends ask. "What made him choose you?" She simply smiles and that heavenly feeling washes over her. He has chosen her. The handsomest boy has chosen the prettiest girl. They order their drinks from one of the two men behind the bar. The place is packed as usual and everyone is pressed tightly together. The music is loud and she leans back contentedly while Damiaan recounts his latest exploits to anyone within earshot.

Damiaan has opened up a whole new world to her. Last weekend they went to an art installation in Deurne. Hannah had never seen anything like it: they entered a cave and waded through water in their wellies, peering into dimly lit chambers with floating candles and mysterious statues.

In a narrow passageway behind one of the chambers he had pulled her to him and kissed her, tongues and everything. It was one of the most exciting moments of her entire life. She lays her head on his warm shoulder and wallows in the memory.

A sudden bang sends a shockwave through the room. A glass smashes, someone screams. Girls look around in panic and dive for cover. Hannah turns around, follows their frightened stares. There in the doorway stands the stooped, sturdy figure of Sister Gregoria, flanked by two scowling nuns who elbow their way in and pluck every green, pleated skirt from the crowded bar.

Sister Gregoria has done this before: *cleaning up The Sloop,* she calls it. Picking out her pupils, jotting their names on a black-list, and calling their parents. "Were you aware that your daughter has been frequenting a *bar* after school? Where tobacco and alcohol are served to minors? Where *drugs* circulate?" The parents react with surprise, feigned or genuine, and scurry down to collect their daughters from a classroom where they have been corralled together, watched over by a nun with a pained expression. *In all likelihood your child is beyond salvation.*

Hannah abandons her beer glass and sees that the door to the toilets is tantalizingly close. She can still do it, make her getaway if she's quick and clever enough. She forces her way through, shoving people aside. Unwittingly, she elbows her way past a blue habit. The nun spins around and fixes her with a withering stare through thick spectacles, before grabbing her by the arm and marching her to the door.

Caught red-handed, Hannah feels the shame rising—what will everyone think, what will *he* think? She can already feel her father's anger, his disappointment. He has barely even looked at her since that night. *Why hast thou forsaken me?* Head bowed, she trudges back to school with the rest, sinners all.

WALK THE LINE

NOANK, 2014

Bᴜᴛ ɪs ɪᴛ ꜰᴜʟꜰɪʟʟɪɴɢ?" Iʀᴍɪɴɪᴀ ᴀsᴋs, ᴀɴ ᴇᴀʀɴᴇsᴛ ɪɴQᴜɪʀʏ ꜰʀᴏᴍ beneath the brim of the straw hat they have just bought at Tom's News & General Store. Irminia in a straw hat: It's all Hannah can do to keep a straight face. In all the years she's known her, stylish Irminia never once succumbed to cheap beach paraphernalia. Then came chemotherapy. Now her balding head needs protecting, even from the wan November light.

"Yes and no," says Hannah. "It's a kind of temporary fulfillment, the same way instant soup stills your hunger for a while." Irminia raises her penciled eyebrows, shakes her head and laughs. Hannah has been living with Bashful for three weeks now. If you can call it living; taking refuge is nearer the mark. She spends her days indoors, dozing or staring at her laptop. She is there waiting when he gets home in the evening and rustles up a meal from whatever's in the fridge. At night they fuck like wild animals. Dawn comes and she waves him off, watching until the heavy front door swings shut.

She feels happy in a precarious kind of way. As if her happiness is a shell that is hiding something else. The clingy attachment between a baby and its mother. A handcuffed, almost helpless kind of happiness.

She can feel herself becoming more timid, more careful about what she says, how she behaves, who she is. Withdrawing, like she did with Boy, into a safe world that is not her own. She always believed it was the immensity of her love for Boy that made the relationship impossible for her to bear. But her lust for Bashful is nothing like her love for Boy. For him she yearns in some absurd, probably neurotic way. Yet here she is: experiencing the same distance, withdrawing to the same dark place. She curses herself.

"Instant soup doesn't still your hunger, Hannah. All it does is make you thirsty." Motherly one-liners; Irminia does them so very well. She renders them in a soothing, heartfelt Yoda-like tone of voice, with a nine-hundred-year-old certainty Hannah relishes in. She nods and smiles.

They stroll down Water Street to DuBois Beach with its old stone lighthouse. Fall is losing its grip and the trees are almost bare. Could that be what's making me sad? Hannah thinks. Irminia is undergoing her therapy, managing the pain, laughing the way she used to and yet something is teetering on the brink, about to fall away, something she can't let go. But she has no say in the matter. There is no point in protest.

"Penny for your thoughts?" Irminia asks.

"I wasn't thinking anything much. Just that it's beautiful here."

Irminia nods. "Enchanting."

A hum of activity out on the water. A gleaming white sailboat glides past a clapped-out old sloop. The tourists are winning out over the fishermen.

"These days there's nowhere on earth I'd rather be. But there was a time when I felt stifled. You know, the small-town mindset, the people here. I was a big city girl: I wanted New York, action, life lived to the fullest."

At least there had been options for Irminia, a luxury *she'd* never had.

"So why did you leave, Mina? If everything there was so great?"

Irminia sighs and lets the silence speak, exudes a quiet dignity. She points at the pier, where a fisherman is locked in a tussle with his floundering catch.

"Well?"

"You make choices in life, Hannah, and I made mine." Pregnant pause. "And I have never regretted it. Not a single day."

Irminia, a talented actress on her way to the top. Sensational in *A Chorus Line* and married to one of New York's most celebrated directors. A turbulent marriage characterized by everything that characterized a seventies showbiz marriage: other men, other women, drugs, gurus, ideology.

"I can't explain why I left, sweetheart. Not yet."

Hannah looks at her. *Not yet?*

"What's that supposed to mean?"

"It means that I have my story too, Hannah. Just like you have yours."

"Didn't he love you?"

"Heart and soul."

"So you didn't love him?"

"Every bit as much."

"So what was it, Mina. *What?*"

A wave of the hand. Not now.

"I don't get it. Why the big secret? What happened? I thought we told each other everything. I know everything about you. Why can't you tell me this?"

She hears her own voice growing louder. It's the last thing she wants but still she won't let up. "If you don't tell me soon, it'll be too late." *Stupid, petulant child.*

Irminia falters. Her knees buckle and she throws out an arm. In a reflex, Hannah catches her, shores up her wilting body. They stagger over to a bench under a bare tree.

Did she falter because she can't help it, or because it lets her off the hook? With Irminia you can never quite tell, but the answer hardly matters. The fact of Irminia's weight, the leaning, the lending of support, these are the things that matter. I can never be small again, Hannah thinks. No longer play the daughter. Worrying about, caring for. From now on, the world will be bent out of shape.

"I'm sorry, Mina. I'm so sorry."

They sit on the bench, looking out across the harbor from where the lobster boats sail, red cranes jutting high above the water. Shining sloops in search of the gold that inhabits this coastline. The local fishermen love their boats, call them "she," paint proud names upon their bows. Hannah reads the bright red letters on a passing sloop: *FURIOUS.*

The water is calm, the horizon clear. The last fisherman leaves his catch, takes up his nets and baskets, and heads for home. The sun is sinking slowly. And suddenly she is standing there. At the end of the wooden pier, motionless and upright. A vague outline, short and slim. It looks like a little girl. What could a child be doing out there at this hour? Hannah blinks and the girl comes into focus.

"We'll talk about it, I promise. Just not now. Okay?" Irminia closes her eyes.

The calm water turns red. Hannah recognizes the child and holds her breath. On the pier stands a girl in a spotless white dress. A girl with two braids and a face in grainy monochrome. Her feet planted neatly together, arms hanging at her sides. She smiles and moves her hand. Faster than slow motion, slower than real life. What is she saying? Hannah wonders. But she isn't saying anything. She is beckoning.

DAMNED PUBLISHERS

NEW YORK, 2014

Tick-tick-tick goes the pen on the desk, a sure sign that he is *not* amused. His Tom Selleck moustache seems bushier than ever, poised to give the books and manuscripts piled in front of him a thorough dusting at any moment.

"*One* chapter, you say?" He repeats the words slowly just because they sound so grim: five months, one chapter. "In all this time you have managed to bring a single chapter into the world. What can I say, Hannah? Congratulations. I'm assuming I will be allowed to read the fruit of your labors?"

She shakes her head, determined to keep what she has written to herself. He wouldn't understand anyway. He's only thinking of his spring catalog and the fact that she needs to be in there with a fetching photo while her face and her name are still ringing bells with magazine readers. Hijacking momentum, she knows the tricks of the trade.

"So I'm not even being allowed to lay eyes on it?"

She stares hard at the toes of her sneakers. The grubby rubber edging is peeling off.

"Don't take this the wrong way, Hannah, but are you okay?"

She squirms in her seat. Five months ago she was still capable of wafting in here, radiant in a lilac dress. She practically perched on Max's lap as he all too willingly signed for her debut. This was it, her chance to actually write, and she was grateful. The fact that everyone was telling her she had lost her mind didn't matter at all. She could do it, would do it, prove them all wrong.

Whether she *can* actually do it is what Max is now wondering. She sees the doubt in his eyes. No, she will not make the spring catalog. And is that lilac dress in Bushwick or still at Boy's place? Somewhere, a clock is ticking.

"We gave you that advance for a reason, Hannah. An advance means trust." Tick, tick, tick, something is happening, but what?

"If there's something wrong, Hannah, you need to tell me." It sounds like a command. He wants to get the business end in order, warn the legal guys, fill the hole in the catalog with another *dream debut*.

Hannah's eyes wander, taking in the posters for Max's past publishing successes, books that actually got written. She sees a photo of a lake and suddenly she is back in the woods. Then come the raised voices, clawing branches, feet covered in blood.

"Let's meet a month from now, but I expect to see words on paper."

He tries to look forbidding but with that ludicrous moustache upstaging his eyebrows, he hasn't got a hope.

"Any more obstacles and we'll need to take action. And the

last thing I want to do is reach for the contract, Hannah." She knows exactly what he means.

"Come to André's launch Saturday, will you? There's a bunch of people you should meet. And for God's sake wear something less . . . angsty."

She looks down at her black top, black skinny jeans, and her disintegrating sneakers. *You're my publisher, Max, not my fucking stylist.* From the corner of her eye she sees him nod pityingly, a bobble-headed dashboard doll, jittery but unimportant. He has no say in this. She's the one in the driver's seat.

Barbara has beckoned and she will listen. She will write about the gifted little author and the man. The one who, like impatient Max, craved for her written words. The one who taught her how to type. The one who gave her what he wanted. The one who left. The one.

RAFT

NEW HAVEN, 1927

Dear Daddy,

The water in the lake is still high. I am starting to think that we shall never win from the rain. It pours incessantly. I sit here looking out of the downstairs window and it makes me sad.

Of course, the wet weather brings good things too. To begin with there are all kinds of mushrooms in the wood: brightly colored toadstools and penny buns. The odd trumpet-shaped ones are so incredibly beautiful. I have remembered where they grow so that, when you come to visit, I can show them to you as soon as you arrive.

A little squirrel pays frequent visits to the garden. I think his little home must be close by. I tried to make friends with him by scattering cookies and bread under the oak tree, and saw him creep over, sit up and nibble the crumbs from his claws in the most charming manner. What an adorable creature! I think I shall write about him in my next book. Winnifred strikes me as an elegant name for him.

I have also started collecting red salamanders again. Thanks to the wet weather they are everywhere. I now have nine in a box. They are delightful, especially the funny way they walk, their back foot trying to catch up with their front foot on either side. When you put them on the palm of your hand they wiggle over to the edge, and when you bring your other hand alongside, they hesitate for a moment as if they don't understand why they should be expected to do the same thing all over again. Doing things over is not always different or better, as you know.

Last week I discovered a garden in the wood that reminded me of the glade where we saw that vast array of flowers: anemones, violets, yellow adder's tongue. How long ago that was. I have always remembered that walk and although I no longer recall why we found ourselves in the woods or where we were living at the time, I can still see the yellow anemones carpeting the hillside and remember how we longed to pluck them, each and every one. Now I would like to bring each and every one of them to you, to the big city where I am sure no flowers grow.

I miss you terribly. I have not been back to our raft since you left for New York. Back here we think of the big city as a kind of gaudy palace full of temptations, traps, and trickery. A place that seduces its visitors and turns them into helpless victims.

Do you miss us, Daddy? We hope that you will let us know where you are staying. Once I know where you are, I will be able to picture it when I think of you. Now I imagine how you spend your evenings sitting in a deep armchair, reading books with your red pencil to hand. You read until sleep makes your eyes droop and then you climb into a four-poster bed and lie there under a thick quilt all alone.

You are the one I lean on, Daddy. You have the strongest shoulders of all of us. I am counting on you and I am looking forward incredibly to seeing you again.

Much much much much love,

From

Barbara

To

Dear Daddy-Dog

SIGN YOUR NAME

NEW YORK, 1928

N O ONE CAN SEE HER SHOES. SHE SPENT A LONG TIME THINKING about which pair to wear, but the black tablecloth reaches all the way down to the floor. "You only have one opportunity to make a first impression," he had warned. "Contact with your readers is of vital importance. They are the ones who will have to take the trouble to go down to the store and buy your next book, Babs. So smile, scribble your name, and wear a pretty dress."

With all this in mind, she ran down Fourth Avenue through the rain in her patent leather shoes. Soaking wet they arrived at Strand, the literary bookstore where they were expected. *Three Miles of Books*, six beaming faces, and a table bearing a carafe of water, a pen, and stacks of novels. Her novel with the ivory cover, the looping black letters, and Knopf's running dog. Beside the table a large sign on a painter's easel:

BARBARA NEWHALL FOLLETT (12), THE LITERARY SENSATION,
SIGNING TODAY AT STRAND.

A photograph that shows her smiling at the camera, wearing her white dress with its embroidered collar. Her hands are folded, something she never does, but the photographer thought it looked especially intelligent. Bows tied around her braids. A childish smile, a picture of a girl she no longer is. Will people recognize her? Won't they be disappointed to see that she has grown?

Her father fills his glass, presses a warm hand on her shoulder, chin up, beaming with pride. *Yes, we are ready.* The people form a line, shuffle closer. He watches her open the cover and scribble attentively. *Could you add a dedication?* To my grandson Edward. To my wife, Emily. To my daughter Laura, my father, Steven. Mark, Mary-Lou, Jonas, Ellen, Archibald, Rosalie.

Ever since the first glowing reviews, her star has risen rapidly. *The New York Times*: truly remarkable. *The Saturday Review of Literature*: unbearably beautiful. In no time, a legend had been born: so very young and already such a talent. As if talent grows by the inch; often it's quite the opposite.

Her father had judged it perfectly. He knew exactly when her book was ready. How he had scratched away with his red pencil and how she had cursed his endless comments, but each draft was a step on the way to the book that now stands on the shelves. *The one true tale of Eepersip, the girl who ran away from home to live in the woods and be one with nature.*

More and more faces appear among the bookcases. *Why Eepersip? However did you come up with such a name?* The same questions, time and again. The bookstore is stuffy. Her stockings make her legs itch and scratching simply will not do. Barbara looks around.

Her father is holding court, the center of attention, gesturing expansively as he addresses his audience. He looks dazzling in his new suit and a young woman with blond curls is gazing up at him adoringly. Barbara pretends she can't hear but she is tuned into every word. *When did you first discover that your daughter could write so beautifully? Doesn't it frighten you, a child with such an exceptional talent?*

Next in line is a lady with a kitschy flower brooch, who leans over the table. "I see myself in Eepersip," she says with half-closed eyes. "That little girl comforts me." Her breath stinks from too little food, the same restless smell she knows from her mother. You and Eepersip? she thinks. I see no resemblance. Eepersip is wild and free, she would never squeeze herself into such prim and stuck-up clothes. She ran away to the wild woods where she found happiness. There she runs with the deer, dances with the butterflies, sleeps under the trees in the long grass. Not you, Miss Kitschy Flower Brooch. You sleep surrounded by the cold stone of New York. Your feet are glued to your expensive heels. You understand nothing.

"Barbara, come here a moment."

She dashes off another signature and leaps from the chair. Her father is standing beside a smartly dressed young man, grinning from ear to ear. "This is Benjamin Bass, the owner of Strand. The man who has so kindly organized this book signing." Hands are shaken, nods exchanged. Barbara taps her father's arm. He excuses himself and takes her aside, happy as a clam. It's an expression that keeps bugging her this evening: *happy as a clam*. There is a flush in his cheeks that she has never seen before.

"Daddy, I want to get out of here."

He shakes his head. "Darling, you can't simply leave. Look," and he points at an aisle full of damp raincoats. "All these people have come specially to see you."

"But I don't want anything to do with those people."

"Barbara, it's only this once. We agreed. Remember what I said about establishing a good rapport with your audience? That is not to be underestimated, Babs. It is the very least you can do." And he gives her a kiss on the cheek, a fine kiss that makes her glow. She goes back to the table, sits down, and works her way through the raincoats.

How different home is to this bunker in New York. A city without windows. She longs to go back to New Hampshire, to the tree hut where she sleeps soundest of all, to the river, and the raft she built with her father.

Eepersip had never before been so happy. Every day she felt as though she loved the animals, birds, and butterflies—everything of Nature—more than the day before.

And here she sits, scribbling away next to a sign, an animal put on display, to be leered at by the paying public. Surrounded by people who will never understand what really drives Eepersip. They do not really see her, have no idea what it's like to dance in the fields *lart ain caireen ien tu cresteen der tuee, darnceen craik peen bun.* In human language: like a little fairy in a golden dress, waving in the wind. For Eepersip takes her own words into the woods, her own language. A girl like her can never be pinned down. Though sometimes she is captured, she always breaks free.

The sound of breaking glass reached their ears all too late; for

Eepersip, on the little fawn's back, had vanished toward the field.
Though they heard trampling hoofs, they knew that it would be of no
use to follow.

That evening they dine at a long table in the restaurant of a
swish hotel. Plush red seats, crystal chandeliers, mirrors everywhere. *Distinguished company, Babs.* There are publishers, agents,
and writers at the table; she has no idea who they are. They eat
lobster. Everyone wants to talk to her.

Barbara imagines how Eepersip would behave if she were
sitting at the table. She would hate it, despise the guests, collect
each and every lobster and throw it back into the pool.

"Do you already have an idea for your next novel?" one old
biddy asks.

She nods. "Yes, I plan to go on a long sea voyage and write
a logbook."

The woman looks at her father with raised eyebrows and then
turns back to Barbara. "All by yourself?"

She nods. Her father gives a nervous laugh: "Yes, well, we'll
have to see about that."

"You said I could, Daddy. You promised."

"Barbara, this is not the time."

He flashes a forbidding stare. *Do not ruin this, Barbara.* She
keeps quiet. He can say whatever he likes, she is going. Over the
sea and far away, to places that really matter. Places worth dis-
covering.

He nudges her with his elbow: "Why don't you tell them
about our raft, Barbara?"

She ignores his request, breaks off a lobster claw, and bites
down hard till the juices run out.

BOOM BOOM ROOM

NEW YORK, 2014

Everyone loves the Boom Boom Room with its golden ceilings, endless windows, and killer views of nighttime New York. Not to mention the private hot tubs, to which you can retire with as many people as you want for as long as you want. Boom boom till your body turns flaccid and your fingertips scrunch into numb water wrinkles. The bubbles in those tubs have borne witness to the most unlikely trysts: Bon Jovi and Lil' Kim, Lindsay Lohan and Corpus J.

This is where Leonardo DiCaprio swung from a vine at a jungle party and Jennifer Lopez cartwheeled across the gilded bar. An amusement park for the rich and famous with rides the plebs down below can only dream of. Hannah dished half the dirt and maintained a discreet silence about the rest. After ten years she could gauge the sleaze threshold of her gossip-grazing readers to perfection. No running mascara, punctured arms, or celebrity slapstick. No slithering across toilet floors slick with vomit or slipping on pills discarded next to the shagged-out jacuzzi. They want Timberlake as he struts through the door in his crisp suit and his dicky bow. They want the It girls flaunting their designer dresses in mint condition, before they are mauled by hands too important to refuse.

The club is *invitation only* but Bashful can bring anyone he wants, including Hannah, under duress. They are sitting in an alcove on mocha leather sofas and he is following the showbiz party code to perfection: drinks ordered by the table and extravagance designed to boost the credibility of your star rating at all times.

God, he looks delectable in his immaculate white shirt, and jeans that are molded to his slender hips. Hard to believe he's the same shabby soul she met slumped on a beaten-up Chesterfield in a Bushwick bar. Tonight the grimy beer glasses have been exchanged for champagne flutes. The more he drinks, the less bashful he gets. He is playing Harvey James, as seen on TV. And she is not playing along.

Harvey is attracting an audience: A bevy of shiny young things beat a path to his wide-open door. "Say, aren't you . . . ?" You bet your sweet ass I am and what are you drinking? She had hoped to lean on him this evening, snuggle up to him and watch the world go by. She wanted to let the empty chatter ripple past her like water, to emerge into the night unsullied. But now there are three adolescent girls, a faux-lesbian couple and an off-duty waitress between her and him. "Did you know my girlfriend once dated George Clooney?" Hannah orders something strong, sweet, and fast. Wait, make that a double.

He insisted that she come out with him, that arriving home to find her waiting every evening was getting him down. The domestic sex slave routine was wearing thin. His words broke the spell. Some relationships only exist as long as they are undefined. Label them and they are no longer viable. There is no way back.

So she nodded, fetched a slinky little dress from her cursed apartment, and for his sake squeezed into a mold that no longer fits. She let him make his entrance with Hannah the Society Scribe in a world still eager to suck her in. There were perfunctory looks of recognition, familiar people smiling at her: *"Welcome back, Hannah. And look who you're with!"*

She's trying to avoid their gazes, hiding in a corner of a crowded sofa. *I'm here but I'm really not.* Bashful is talking to a teenager in a pink halter top who flashes her clear green eyes and fondles his bicep. "So strong!" Pretty girls like ticks, digging their mouths into the shiny coat of celebrity. *Is that what she herself was like?* He takes a drag on his cigarette and flashes a fake smile. She didn't even know he had one. It must be Harvey's. Mr. James is turning out to be one hell of a disappointment.

He invited her to this friggin' party and now he's forgotten she is here. She feels a sting, a pain, sharp and old. Why is she even here? And who the fuck is she tonight in this fake Wonderland? If not Hannah-the-celebrity-columnist, *then who?*

She slams her glass down on the table and sweeps past him, sashays over to the dance floor. He doesn't even notice. She begins to move, twisting, swaying, shaking, sweating, a drunken whirlwind in the pounding light. Of course he was only in it for the sex, but she was *the best sex he'd ever had*. That much she needed to believe.

Yet here he is, with some underage trio who will soon be draped across his bed. And he will do them the way he did her, pin them to the same mattress, three for the price of one. The image sickens her. She stamps and shakes it off, surrenders to a furious dance.

A body is moving closer to hers. Hands grab her by the hips, push and pull, to and fro. She rides the wave, it doesn't matter who he is. Bashful will see. He will see and think, *Fuck, what am I doing surrounded by children while the best I've ever had is being snatched from under my nose.* She thinks this and knows it's not true. She thinks this and forgets it's not true.

Her nose brushes his collar, inhales a bland mixture of sweat and deodorant. She presses closer, hungry for that scent, the forbidden scent, that sweet fucking forbidden scent, and she whispers. *Sophie. Sophie.* Her skin is his skin now, his cheek wet with her tears. He feels her, scoops a hand through wet hair and holds her tight, as if he understands.

When she looks up, she sees dark eyes, a friendly face, baby-smooth skin. Her knees buckle, he catches her. To get back at Bashful, she kisses him. *Boom, boom, boom.* She sees them through his eyes, greedy tongues on the dance floor, sensual and unashamed. But the soldier sits in his alcove like a fox in his lair, his cold blue eyes fixed on new horizons. She kicks and kicks at the indifferent little soldier who will not fall down.

UNINVITED

BACHTE-MARIA-LEERNE, 1996

T IS DARK AND THE LIGHTS IN HANNAH'S HOUSE ARE SHINING warmer than ever. Sophie watches as Hannah puts down the phone and wanders into the kitchen. Through the window, she sees her open the fridge and pour herself a glass of juice. She waits a few seconds to make sure there is no one else around, then taps on the windowpane.

No response. Did Hannah see her? Or was she mistaken? Why won't she look her way? Instead, Hannah turns and disappears into the hall. The red glass is still on the kitchen counter. Where has she gone? It's already past ten, too late to ring the doorbell. Hannah always used to let her in through the back door so they could sneak up to her bedroom and talk in whispers deep into the night.

Sophie turns to go, then hesitates. Maybe she should wait. Hannah has forgotten her drink, she's bound to come back for it.

If she taps louder, Hannah is sure to hear. Suddenly the back door swings open. Hannah's father is standing there in a pillar of light, glowering at her.

"What are you doing here, Sophie? It's late."

Sophie tugs at her blue track jacket.

"What do you want?"

"I wanted to speak to Hannah."

He nods. It's the answer he was expecting. "But Hannah doesn't want to speak to you, Sophie. She's upstairs doing her homework."

Hannah and homework, yeah right.

"But I have to talk to her. It's urgent."

"I'm sure it can wait until tomorrow, Sophie."

He says her name in every sentence, heavy with emphasis and revulsion. This is not the man she knew. The man who drove them to school in the rain and the cold. The dad who treated everyone to ice cream on a hot summer's day. Who spoke the kindest words when he sat at the head of the table and said grace, words like *gratitude* and *harmony*. The father who made her envy Hannah all these years.

"I don't understand."

"Sophie, you come here and hang around my back door late at night because you want to see Hannah. And when I say she doesn't want to talk to you, you won't take no for an answer. That is inappropriate behavior, I'm almost inclined to say rude. Now go home."

But Sophie doesn't want to go home, to the dark rooms where shadows linger even when all the lights are on. She wants to stay here, in the warm glow of the twilight lamps, a house where there is fresh juice in the fridge. She wants Hannah.

"Please, let me talk to Hannah."

He takes a step toward her, leans in close to her face. "Do you honestly think nothing has changed, Sophie?" he hisses. "No one here wants to talk to you. Least of all Hannah."

His face turns red and his eyes glare. The same panic she saw that night.

"I don't understand," she repeats and feels the tears come.

"Go home, Sophie. Don't make things worse than they already are."

A noise from the kitchen.

"Daddy, let me . . ."

Hannah comes and stands next to him. She sees Sophie crying and although she's had no second thoughts about the story she told her father, her version of that awful night, she can't help but feel pity.

"It's okay, Daddy, honest."

Her father takes a few steps back but hovers close to the kitchen door.

"Sophie, things have changed. I'm with Damiaan now. You'll find a new friend. It's best if you don't come to the house anymore. We'll still see each other at school."

"But even at school I never get to see you. You don't want anything to do with me." Her words sound hoarse and ugly, the squawk of a wounded crow.

Hannah hesitates, wavers, but the stakes are too high. She shakes her head. "I'm sorry if it's hard for you to understand, Sophie. But I'm with Damiaan now, okay?"

She turns and disappears into the house.

Hannah's father waits, too polite to shut the door in the face of a crying child. Sophie wanders off through the garden. She feels sadness and something else besides. At a spot where the light can no longer reach her, she sits down in the wet grass. The damp seeps through the thin fabric of her pants, turns them clammy and cold. *Dirty.* She feels dirty. That's the worst thing of all.

The back door closes. Everyone in Hannah's house retreats into a room. The red glass is still standing on the counter as a callous afterthought.

IN THE NAME OF THE FATHER

NEW YORK, 1932

H^{*E.*} Barbara sits at her desk and types his name. For there is only one *he*. The *he* who encouraged her, who gave her the confidence to write. The *he* who made notes with his red pencil so that Eepersip became better than she already was. The *he* who celebrated her first book with her and oh how ecstatic *he* was when the glowing reviews hit the newsstands. *He* told anyone who would listen about his daughter's genius, her literary success. And as *he* basked in the reflected glow, his child became a means to an end.

Five years have passed since her triumph, her debut. She is eighteen now, living in New York. Streetcars clatter past. From her window she looks down on Fifty-Third Street, where people in hats and thick coats bustle down the sidewalk. A man at a stall is selling apples for five cents apiece, fumbling for frozen coins with woolen mittens. It's bitterly cold for November.

The door flies open and Jacky struts over in her tube skirt, slaps a stack of paper down on the desk, and peers like a schoolmistress over her black-framed spectacles.

"Don't forget now, Barbara. These have to be sent off by four."

She nods and waits until Jacky has left the room before looking back at the black letters she has pressed. Her father is not a man.

He never came back, but found happiness in the big city with a secretary by the hideous name of Margaret Whipple. The divorce papers arrived in the mail on her fourteenth birthday. She persuaded her mother to go on a voyage. Carrying a suitcase and two typewriters, they set sail across the ocean.

The water was calm and eased their troubles. They made friends on the islands and the wind took them in a new direction day after day. Tahiti, Fiji, Samoa: destinations every bit as exotic as their names. By the time they went ashore in Honolulu their money was spent and their journey was over. She types:

Far away everything was better.

When a man divorces his wife, Barbara decided, he also divorces his daughter. Now she lives with her mother in a cramped apartment and they both work to pay the ridiculously high rent: she as a secretary for Fox Film, where she types up one synopsis after another. America's next great novelist is an unqualified drudge trapped in an office not much bigger than the average New Haven closet, with an iron desk and a sad little conifer for company. At first she had planned to brighten the place up with potted plants, but after two days of typing in silence she understood that slavish surrender would be the least painful path to take.

The black Underwood in front of her is faded and scratched, a monument to unfulfilled potential: a typewriter that only spits out numbers, lists, and the tamest of scripts. She types:

I am a machine.

This is what she does: type, eat, clean, and sleep. She misses the waves. Her dreams are ebbing away. And then comes the unbearable thought:

I cannot do it without him.

Her last two novels have been returned by every publisher under the sun. They lie complete and rejected in a drawer of her desk. Did she need his annotations, his connections, his talent in order to be published? In her memories he is everywhere: at the book launch, at every reading, every interview. At every glorious moment he stood beside her, beaming. The more she thinks about it, the less the success of five years ago appears to be hers.

Stepping-stone.

But he used her as a stepping-stone too. She gave him a shortcut to success he would never have found on his own. He used her to access another life, one in which she had no further part to play: a new wife, a grander home, a better job. All this she gave him willingly, for fathers and mothers always expect a return on their investment. They want to be reimbursed by the people they put on this earth. A desire that seethes like tiny ants beneath their children's skin.

When she gets home from work that evening, she walks through the apartment with its narrow hallways and dim windows, over the dusty carpet, straight to the bathroom. In the mirror she sees an eighteen-year-old girl with two brown braids and a pale face. A beautiful, unhappy girl. It is time.

She slides open a drawer in the medicine cabinet and removes a big pair of scissors. With two short, sharp snips she slices through the braids. The scissors chirp and grind, and the braids fall like bloodless limbs to the floor. Satisfied, she looks at her new face. There, now. Daddy's girl is gone.

THE HURT LOCKER

BACHTE-MARIA-LEERNE, 1996

THREE BIG SUITCASES LIE GAPING IN THE LIVING ROOM. HIS THINGS are scattered everywhere. Gone in a flash, back in a flash. Unannounced and overbearing as ever, he has taken over the house. Music is blaring, a cassette tape churning out wailing fiddles and a twitchy tambourine. She tosses her school satchel among the shirts and papers on the couch, just as he pops his head around the kitchen door.

"My little Sophie!"

He charges toward her with long, bounding strides and two flat boxes clamped under one arm. His big bald head leads the way, while his lumbering frame and flabby belly do their best to catch up. He is wearing nothing but a pair of baggy jeans.

"There's my girl!" He pinches her cheek and plants a wet kiss on her forehead. She rubs it off as inconspicuously as she can.

"I've got pizza. Fancy a bite to eat?"

She nods and takes hold of the boxes.

"You're a sight for sore eyes, little lady."

"Is it just you?" she asks.

He shrugs off the question. "Of course it's just me! Fresh off the plane. Hightailed it here from Brussels Airport." His beefy fingers bulldoze assorted items to one end of the couch. Fallen from the sky, he hasn't changed a bit: an angel with a flabby gut and restless wings.

A pile of brochures on the coffee table show a range of busty beauties perched on lawnmowers that look like mobility scooters.

"How was it?" she asks, because it's what you're supposed to ask. "How was Poland?"

"Great, great," he says with a grin. "Business is booming. Lots of grass over there, *a hell of a lot of grass*." His thundering laugh bounces off the walls. "Polish farmers like their fields neat and tidy, but there aren't enough hours in the day."

"And that's where you come in."

He smiles and winks. "Indeed it is, little lady. Indeed it is." He says it with knowing pride, as if he has played the Polish market to perfection. The man with the plan.

"How are things here?"

"You've got sauce on your cheek." She points to the corner of his mouth.

He wipes the splotch away. "So . . . how *are* things here?"

"Okay."

"Okay *no-kay*, Sophie. How's high school treating you?"

"It's not that different, really." She takes another bite of pizza and suddenly it begins again, skin flaking from his bald head, a swarm of skin flakes drifting her way.

"Did Hannah go to St. Martin's too?"

"Yeah, we're in the same class."

"Good, that's good. And sports? Are you still outrunning the lot of them?"

She nods; no point in telling him she gave up athletics ages ago. The yellowish flakes drift closer. She holds her breath. He munches greedily on his pizza and tells her a story about one of his lawnmowers landing in the water during a test drive, farmer and all. And how he sold two lawnmowers that day: one for the grass and one for the frogs in the ditch. His laughter echoes through the house. She pretends to laugh along and all the time her brain is thinking feverishly: *Where is Mom? Does she know he's here? Has he been kind to her?*

"Those Poles make fantastic fireworks, did you know that? I saw a demonstration when I was out there, amazing! Nearly loaded up ten trucks and sent them straight here." His top lip is shiny with grease. He winks and waves a pizza slice in the air. "Now there's a business worth getting into."

His bald head continues to shed its sickening swarm, tiny flakes of skin seething through the air toward her, growing. Once it starts, it never stops. She wants to leave, run to her room, can't keep this up much longer. *Act normal, Sophie. Keep things normal for as long as you can.*

"Will you be going back?" she asks, forcing out the words.

"Yeah, but I've got a few things to sort out here first. No idea how long I'll be staying."

The pizza boxes are empty but for a few crusts. "Will you clear everything up?" she asks, nodding at the exploded suitcases.

"Yeah, yeah. Little Miss Fusspot. And what are you going to do? Watch TV?"

"No, I've got homework to do." Good, now she can go.

"Hang on there, missy, I've got something for you." He gets to his feet and gropes around in one of the cases for a plastic bag. Inside is a big box. She opens it to find a strapless dress with a lace bodice and a wide, white skirt. He never remembers that she always wears pants.

"It's a dress," she says.

"Well spotted. And . . . do you like it?"

She sighs. "For a dress it's very pretty."

"What's that supposed to mean?" The cloud is coming faster now, flakes shooting forward like a shoal of tiny fish. She has no choice but to breathe them in, tries not to think about those filthy fish swimming down inside her body.

"I don't wear dresses. I've told you that before."

He shrugs.

"Even so, I know it will look fantastic on you. Every girl in Poland would kill for a dress like that. Cost me a fortune." The chastened look of a beaten dog. He wears it well. Tail between his legs, a monster pleading for pity.

"Thanks. Now, I really need to get that homework done."

She picks up her satchel and goes to her room. She does not ask him if he has seen Mom. The less she says, the less can go wrong. In the clean air of her bedroom she takes a deep breath. And another. And another. She tries to read but her mind keeps wandering. Around ten, she hears him leave. The front door slams and she climbs into bed with all her clothes on.

IT'S ALMOST HALF PAST THREE WHEN SHE WAKES UP TO A LOUD THUD in the hall. A body has fallen and staggers back to its feet. A chink of light at the bedroom door, a voice that groans. "You still love me, don't you, Sophie? *Say you love me, my darling girl.*" She pretends to be asleep—like she always does. He pretends to believe her, creeps in and closes the door behind him. Her heart pounds in her chest, so hard she can hardly bear it. He approaches quietly, sits down on the edge of her bed. The scent of way too close. She pretends to be asleep and lets her body go.

THE SEAS ARE RIGHT THERE ON THE WALL, WAVES ROLLING GENTLY over white sand. And beneath the waves the fish, so many different colors—orange, pink, blue—darting and gliding in all directions, fickle, flighty. She can hear the waves now, rushing in. No, not the waves, another sound. Something at the bedroom door. Nails scratching on wood. The slow, mechanical scraping of someone slumped against the doorpost like a paralytic cat. Crippled, humiliated. A voice that can only cry, drawn out whimpers of impotence and longing. Was that the sound she heard when she was born? When she was a toothless baby born to look after her own mother?

HER BODY IS A SHELL NOW, SHE FLUTTERS HIGH ABOVE IT. A BUTTERfly on colored wings that beat quickly, brightly through the gloom. Light as a feather, she is, full of grace, paper thin. Bright yet almost invisible. Here, there. And everywhere, as long. As her wings keep beating she. Does not feel the pain she. Feels nothing at all. Poor, beautiful butterfly.

NO, SOBBING IS NO GOOD. SHE HAS TO BREATHE. THOUGH SHE FEELS the weight crushing her. Lungs though there is no life in the.

Air she is breathing she. Must go on now she. Survived five times survived. She counted just like Sabine. In the monster's dungeon Sabine. Survived it too she knows. It can be done to die. Five times and then. Simply.

Wake up again.

MAD RIVER

BROOKLINE, 1939 / NEW YORK, 2014

THREE-FOOT DRIFTS IN BROOKLINE. SNOW WAIST-DEEP ON THE path to their house. Barbara wades to the shed to fetch a shovel and starts clearing the path so Nick will be able to get through when he comes home. Back inside, she gets changed, swaps her thick winter pants for a long black dress with lace sleeves. A dress she never wears, a dress he loves. She has cooked for her husband, waits for him. Hours tick past. The potatoes turn cold in the dish, the prime cut of beef dries out in the oven.

The best advice for a happy marriage is never to marry, Nick had read aloud from the Sunday paper on their honeymoon. Oh how they had laughed, secure in the knowledge that in their marriage everything would be different. No cliché or cheesy one-liner would ever apply to their perfect, all-encompassing, purely devoted love. Let the unhappily married couples complain all they like. We are better, cleverer. Too clever by half, ha-ha.

With a fork, she scrapes the cold potatoes off a dish into the garbage can. When did all that change? When did their brave new world come to an end? The image will not leave her: her husband sitting with another woman, a stranger. She happened to pass Dolly's Tearoom when she caught a glimpse of a familiar face. She peered through the window to see him at a small round table opposite a dashing woman, sharing a perfect slice of red velvet cake that hadn't yet been touched. Instead, the woman touched his hand and gazed at him. His eyes were shining. Barbara saw their glowing faces and her face between them, peering in, reflected in the window glass. There she was: a ghost who had no business being there.

She walked on, churning with disbelief, she kept walking and walking, unable to stop. She walked the streets and then the parks and back again. As if she could outwalk what she now knew, somehow make it undone.

By the time she returned home that day, Nick was already sitting on the sofa reading a magazine about trees. He greeted her the way he always did, she greeted him back. He asked her about supper and she understood how things would be from now on: As long as she did not say a word, *the other woman* would not exist. Day by day the facts would fade to become mere figments of the imagination, a reflection in a window that had long since disappeared.

That's what women do, Barbara thought. Literature is littered with women who try to hold their tongue, know their place, meanwhile digging their own graves. Heroines of the tragic fall: Anna Karenina, Emma Bovary. *Doesn't it make the blood boil?* She scorned it, the passivity she suddenly understands. To keep quiet means to refuse. *To refuse all changes.* Refuse to allow another to steal what is yours by law. She won't say a word, nor will Nick because it would pain him so to hurt her. The saint.

The sack of shit. Hannah takes a greedy swig from her beer bottle. She wanders barefoot along the Hudson in a damp party dress, stilettos dangling from the strap of her bag. The night is over. Five a.m. has come and gone, and the sun is slowly rising. An early jogger plods his rounds. A street cleaner pulls a roll of gray plastic bags from his cart and wrestles with an enormous trash can.

Bashful left the club with three girls on his arm. Now they are probably slinking around his loft, impressed beyond belief. Sliding into the sidecar of his motorbike, snapping pouty selfies with the showroom dummies, nodding intelligently as he explains his giant wheel. Props with no need for a script, same routine every time. Once the mandatory oohs and aaahs are over, he can get on with playing World of Fuckcraft on the snooker table.

What if she went over there right now? She still has his keys. Blow their little shagfest sky-high. But she knows it's not within her power. When you mean nothing to someone, the party is not yours to blow. Her lips tremble. Her legs are heavy. She walks on and takes another swig. Nothing else for it.

IN THE SUMMER AFTER THE SCENE AT DOLLY'S, WHEN BARBARA WAS staying with a friend, Nick sent her a letter. He needed only a single page to tell her it was over. Just like that. A slip of paper, a chit, the death knell for their marriage.

In a state of panic, she travelled back to Brookline, trembling all the way. She waited at home for him to come. It took him three days. By then the trembling had stopped and she had decided to be reasonable, not the hysterical Barbara, but a rational woman talking facts, figures, and practicalities.

Even so, she cried when he confessed what she had known

for months. She begged him for another chance, one last chance. *Please, let's give it a try.* I promise you: no more typing through the night, keeping you awake with my endless string of words. No more screaming when I think you don't understand what I'm trying to say. No more running out into the rain in my nightdress when I feel sad. I will make coffee every morning and breakfast, and if you want them to, my hands will caress you every night until you fall asleep. *I can change, truly I can.*

Hesitation in his drawn face, his bloodshot eyes. Her impassioned plea left him no room for resistance. He nodded. A small movement, a sliver of hope.

After their conversation she wrote to her friend: "I think that, if I can really prove that I'm different, maybe things will work out. He still doesn't quite believe, as he says, that a leopard can change its spots. He thinks that in a month things will all be wrong again. So I say, at least let me have that month! I think I'll get it and I think I can win if I've got the strength . . . if I can make a pleasant sort of life for him, I think he'll stay."

On the surface all is calm, terribly calm, like water that barely ripples before the storm strikes. They both perform their tricks, their clumsy little tricks. Subdued Barbara and contented Nick. She keeps on believing, has to believe, because otherwise she cannot live.

Hannah leans on the railings by the Hudson, smells silt on the fresh breeze, or is that just her imagination? She looks at the mooring posts in the water, splintered, useless things.

A toothless woman shuffles past, pushing a shopping cart.

She sees Hannah and extends two wrinkled hands toward her, weathered palms with baby-pink lifelines. She too is barefoot but her soles are tougher, hardened by the city. They make a mockery of her little princess feet in their Louboutins. What does she know of life? She thinks of the Observer with his acclaimed photos of violence and starvation, a man who knows so much of life, and who is now back in Johannesburg, not thinking of her at all.

The old woman sits down on the bench. Taking off her fuzzy woolen hat, she wraps it around the bar of her shopping cart and lays her head to rest. Her dull eyes remain fixed on the water, the splintered posts, the calm before the storm. Hannah walks over, sits down on the bench, and takes the last beer from her bag. She offers it to the woman, who nods, takes it, and drinks. No gratitude, no contact, just two people who have nothing to say to each other, drinking beer and watching the water wake up. Hannah's eyes fall shut and flicker open, on the edge of sleep.

Nick braved the snowstorm and came home at last. The long wait, the black dress, the wasted potatoes, another broken promise. They must have quarreled, though no one knows what was said.

That December evening, a neighbor saw Barbara leave the house. She had a notebook with her and thirty dollars in the pocket of her coat. She walked into the night and was never seen again.

Nick waited two weeks before notifying the police of her disappearance. The search that followed proved fruitless. The only plausible explanation that remained was that Barbara Newhall Follett had erased herself.

If Barbara were alive today, she would be exactly a hundred years old. Hannah closes her eyes. The bag lady scrambles to her feet, murmurs what might be a farewell, and wanders off with her shopping cart full of junk. It's only when the sun becomes too bright and she gets up to go that Hannah notices her Louboutins are gone.

A CONVENIENT TRUTH

BACHTE-MARIA-LEERNE, 1996

DAMIAAN SHAKES HIS HEAD AND FROWNS EMPHATICALLY.
"You mean you left her standing there at the back door?"

They are sitting in the garage of his parents' house, a popular hangout crowded with beaten-up chairs and sofas, rickety wooden stools and a knobbly old rug. There is a pool table with too few balls and an old jukebox that plays when it feels like it. The wall bears the painted handprints of everyone who drops by regularly. Hannah's hand is next to Damiaan's, a fact that fills her with pride.

He is lounging in a leather armchair, dirty white stuffing bulging from the cracks in the upholstery. Hannah is sitting cross-legged on the floor at the other side of the Scrabble board. In search of distraction—Damiaan was winning, like always, and she didn't really want to play on—she had brought up the subject of Sophie. She can't remember why.

"What was she doing there?"

"She wanted to talk to me, I guess."

"What about?"

"How should I know?"

"Huh?"

"I didn't feel like talking to her."

"So you left her standing outside?"

Hannah sighs. "Yes, I did. Okay?" *And you are not the only one with a story to tell*.

"That's pretty damn mean if you ask me, Hannah. To leave her standing there without even listening to what she had to say. It might have been important." He raises his voice and rolls his eyes. "I mean, Jesus, what kind of friend are you?"

Hannah doesn't get it; something has shifted. The roles have been reversed but she doesn't understand how. Who's the guilty party here? Who was the one to abuse a friendship?

"I have my reasons, Damiaan."

"You do?"

"Yes, but I can't say. And where do you get off taking Sophie's side anyway? You barely even know her."

Okay, that *did* sound mean. She's going to have to watch herself. There's no bigger turnoff than a nagging bitch and she's sworn never to make that mistake.

"Sorry. But I had good reasons for not seeing her. You don't know what happened."

"So . . . what *did* happen?"

She swallows hard. This is all going wrong.

"What happened, Hannah? You know you can trust me to keep a secret."

Yeah, you and secrets, Hannah thinks. Every story blabbed

in your vicinity is common currency in The Sloop by sundown. Those tall tales of yours keep us enthralled, but they all come from somewhere. From someone who pleaded *please don't tell.* And who got the answer: *Trust me, I can keep a secret.*

"I can't say."

He shifts restlessly in his armchair. Hannah picks up the bag of Scrabble tiles and shakes it. A hard, piercing sound dampened by the bag. Sounds are good, sounds disrupt, make way for a new moment, a new topic of conversation.

"Hannah, Sophie is a sensitive girl and I need to understand why you left her out there in the cold."

Oh, so now it's *out in the cold.* "I don't want to talk about it."

"Well I do." And he leans forward till his face is right up next to hers.

This could be it, Hannah thinks. Breaking point. He'll go off me, decide he can't trust me and I'll have lost him. And all because of Sophie? Half the girls at St. Martin's are dying to take my place.

"Have you got something to hide, Hannah?"

She shakes her head.

"Well then, tell me."

Her tears come suddenly. They startle him. Tears that won't stop, prompted by something she cannot say. Damiaan sits down beside her on the rug and puts his arm around her shoulder.

"What is it, babe? What did she do to you?" He presses her to him, the warm chest where she loves to lay her head. Because he is a man, not just another boy, but a real man. With him she does things you only see in movies. Things most girls her age can only dream about.

"She . . . she wanted to do things."

He frowns. "What kind of things?"

She goes quiet again.

"What kind of things, Hannah? Come on, you have to tell me." His persistence wears her down.

"Things to do with sex."

Shock in his eyes. Sex. An ugly word, an open wound in the Belgium of Marc Dutroux. A country mired in shame.

"What? You mean she forced you to have sex with her?"

Hannah nods. Such a small, innocent movement. A chin that bobs up and down.

"Naked?"

She nods.

"Like actual sex?"

She nods.

"Oh, my sweet girl."

He holds her tight and rocks her gently. He does not ask how one child can force another child to do such things. The sorrow in his arms is enough for now. Poor Hannah. Her sobs become louder, she shudders, the wreckage of a sorrow that runs deep, deeper than the need to save her own skin. It will all be fine, it will. A little white lie never hurt anyone.

MOCKINGBIRD

NEW YORK, 2014

H E THROWS TWO APPLES, THREE CARROTS, AND A CHUNK OF ginger into the machine and hits the green button. A sound to set your teeth on edge, jerking fruit, splintered by metal blades in a plastic tub. The pain behind her eyes isn't helping either. He scatters in a few spoonfuls of some superfood or other and puts two glasses on the bar.

"Juice?"

She picks up a hint of something in the air, a hint of some-one different. The smell of his horny triplets lingers, a sweet scent that does not belong here. She takes in the empty space, scanning for souvenirs, traces of the night before. *Spot the differences*. She looks but finds nothing. She drinks but tastes nothing.

"Hannah, how can I put this?"

His tone is lighthearted, almost nonchalant. This is routine.

"I've had a great time with you."

Had.

"But it's time to move on."

"Where to?"

He gives her a weary look: *How hard are you going to make this?* As hard as it gets, jackass, harder than you can imagine. I am going to gnaw my way under your skin, hold you, treasure you, rip you to shreds. *I understand you*, she wants to say, *I know you through and through.*

"It's over."

"What's over? When did it start?" She takes a gulp of juice.

"Hannah, I was up-front from the beginning. You knew how things stood. I don't do relationships."

Yes, she recalls the words. And recalls thinking: *pure semantics.* But even the nothing they had is too much for him now. She shakes her head.

"In that case, there's nothing to break up."

"Hannah."

"Don't Hannah me. I don't need anything from you, you don't need anything from me. Let's just see where it takes us, or not. Why are we even having this conversation, this cliché? Is this really what you want?"

Silence. A sigh that says: *and this is exactly why I want out.* He is right. A surge of pain behind her eyes.

"You're one passionate girl."

She closes her eyes. "I still want to see you sometimes."

"Why?"

"'Cause I don't want to be dumped over a glass of carrot juice."

He laughs. That's more like it.

"I'm not dumping you, Hannah, but I can't go on like this. It doesn't excite me anymore."

"What doesn't excite you?"

He hesitates. "You don't excite me."

"I bore you, is that it? Predictable? Stale? Run out of props?"

"I don't want you anymore."

She shivers. He starts to say something else but she fends it off.

"Shhh! You've said enough."

Bashful withdraws into the coy silence he wears so well. All part of his repertoire.

If only it were part of hers. She unravels too quickly. Gives far too much, way too fast. Can she claw her way back to the start and become a mystery again? Scramble the code and revert to an enigma? She would do that for him. Close her petals, back into the soil. Shrink from butterfly to chrysalis.

With a sudden sweep of her arm she sends papers and keys flying, slides across the bar in her slinky dress and kneels in front of his face. Her chin nestling in his open palm, she whispers.

"One more time."

Even as she says the words, she senses his body harden, hermetically sealed, like a cell, a suit of armor.

"One more time, the last time. For me."

"Hannah."

"One more time."

Out of the corner of her eye, she spots a patch of black on the bed behind him. A dress. *What the hell are you doing, Hannah Karenina? You pathetic creature, you idiot.* A long, black, sleeveless dress with a thigh-length split. Not hers, but whose? Is she still here? *The woman who belongs to this dress? Is she here?*

Something stirs behind the milky glass screen by the toilet. For fuck's sake, one of his whores has been there behind the glass all this time, listening to every word. As soon as she's out the door they'll have a good laugh about it, Bashful and his brand-new slut, piss themselves laughing at her expense.

"What's the matter?" he asks.

"Where is she?" She skids off the bar and runs toward the toilet. "I know she's here somewhere!" But the toilet is empty, seat up, a copy of *Hustler* curling from the wall. Bashful stares at her as if she has lost her mind. Has she? The dress, the dress is really there. She walks over to the bed and picks it up. Soft, silky fabric glides through her fingertips. The dress is real, so who does it belong to? A beautiful, stylish woman, the dazzling success story she once was.

The penny drops. All this time he has not been sleeping with her, but with *Hannah the Society Scribe*. Two rising stars, a golden couple, always ready for their close-up. Perhaps he thought she could write about him, once she got her shit together. Chances are he never even believed her when she said she was writing a book. Hannah, you *idiot*.

"Take your dress with you," he says.

She looks at him, bewildered. "What do you mean, *my* dress?"

"Hannah, why are you acting so crazy?"

"You're the one acting crazy. This dress isn't mine. It must belong to one of your other whores. You're starting to get us mixed up."

"Believe me, Hannah, the dress is yours."

A chill runs down her spine, more confusion than sorrow. He sees it and walks over to where she is standing. His touch feels wrong.

"Hannah, honey, calm down."

"I am fucking calm. You're the crazy one. You're lying, you're confusing me. Why are you trying to confuse me?"

"Hey, come here."

Minutes ago, those words were all she wanted to hear. Not anymore. I am not your camera-ready Hannah. You don't know me, don't see me for who I am. You don't even fucking *see* me.

"Fuck off!" She pushes his arms away. "Stop playing games."

"Games? Hannah, listen . . ."

"No, I won't listen!"

She walks over to the bar and grabs her backpack. So it's back to that deadbeat apartment of hers. Pigeons coo in the gutter, stupid, dirty creatures. But they fly, pigeons fly too. She is about to turn and walk away when out of nowhere a shadow hits the corner of her eye. *The last thing she wants to see.*

She blinks but the little girl is standing there. The ghost girl who looks at her and laughs. She laughs! The child is laughing at her!

Her mind is playing tricks. No, this is real: The sky is blue, the walls are white, and there she is, the child with her cruel laugh. She looks over her shoulder at Bashful and knows he does not see the girl, no point in even asking. But she cannot block her out or make her go. *The ghost girl is laughing at her.*

"Get lost. Leave me alone. Go on, leave!" But the child does not leave.

In a rage, Hannah lunges for one of the glasses on the bar and hurls it straight at her face. Windowpanes smash, pigeons shoot away. Thick orange gunk drips from broken glass.

The little girl has gone. Good. She shoulders her backpack and walks away. Somewhere behind her, she hears a voice screaming. "Hannah, what the *fuck* has gotten into you?"

IT TAKES TWO

BACHTE-MARIA-LEERNE, 1996

*D*EAR *HANNAH, PLEASE COME BACK*. THESE ARE THE WORDS
Sophie wants to say but she is afraid she won't be able to find
them. She leans against the wall, clutching a ring binder to her
chest, and stares at the black-and-white tiles on the floor.

The corridor is deserted. Most of the girls are in the refec-
tory having lunch but Sophie saw Hannah go into the toilet and is
waiting for her to come out. She looks down the quiet hallway at
the mustard-yellow walls and oak panels stretching away on one
side, the tall windows with no curtains on the other. Through a
half-open door she peers into a classroom: neat rows of wooden
desks, a few words of Latin chalked on a blackboard, a plaster
bust of Socrates.

The time has come to win Hannah back. It takes two to make
a friendship. You can't drop somebody just like that. Not when
they really need you.

Her heart is beating faster. What could be taking so long? Has Hannah made her escape? Did she clamber out through a window, the way some girls do so they can sneak off to The Sloop in the afternoon?

The door swings open. Hannah sees Sophie and sighs. This is the last thing she needs right now: more yammering and whining. But she walks up to her. To walk away would be heartless.

"What do you want?"

Sophie hangs her head. It's a while before she can say "I miss you, Hannah."

There, she's said it. There are no other words.

Hannah looks at Sophie and sees a little girl. A child whose pleading eyes make her look so vulnerable, so desperately defenseless. Her blouse is grubby and creased, her shoes scuffed, everything about her is wrong. Can't she see that childhood is over? Hannah is a woman now. A *real* woman, with this child still clinging to her skirts.

"How many times do I have to tell you? I'm with Damiaan now, Sophie. Why can't you just accept that?"

"We never do anything together anymore. You're so different."

"I'm different? You're the one who's different, Sophie. Moping around all teary-eyed, always whining. Moldy bread in your lunchbox. Your clothes smell and you haven't even brushed your hair properly. You're a mess, Sophie."

"You've changed so much. I don't understand."

Hannah shrugs. "I just don't want to be around you anymore."

"Why?"

"Because I don't want to put up with this. Or that other thing. It's over, Sophie."

"But why?"

"That's all there is to it, Sophie. Okay?" Hannah shakes her head and walks away.

"Why?" The senseless word echoes down the corridor. Hannah turns around.

"I'm with Damiaan, Sophie. What part of that don't you understand?"

"I don't want this!" she screams and bites down hard on her tongue. The red flesh throbs in her mouth and again she screams, "You used to be with me!"

Hannah spins around and screams back: "Yes, and now I'm with Damiaan, *Damiaan*! Can I help it if you're a jealous little bitch?"

Suddenly the words dry up. Sophie runs at Hannah, clutching the ring binder in her hand, and slams it into her head, hard. Hannah staggers back in shock. *What are you doing, Sophie?*

Sophie lashes out again: the sharp plastic slices into Hannah's shoulder. This feels good, a door is flung open, something's moving at last. Hannah groans, twists away. Sophie strikes again, hits the other shoulder, again and again and again. As long as it takes for her to listen.

Hannah falls, scrambles to her feet, and slams her fist into Sophie's stomach. *Stupid fucking kid!* Searing pain, Sophie doubles up, finds her footing, and kicks Hannah hard between the legs. Nothing now is sacred. Smash it all to hell. Hannah hits back, a head thuds into a wall, a cheek that throbs, a bloody tooth. She kicks and scratches and screams. Girls come running down the corridor to witness something that never ever happens at St. Martin's.

Hannah pulls Sophie's long pigtails, drags her to the floor, and hurls her full weight on that small, flailing body. One hand on her throat, the other on the floor. *Jealous little cow!* Sophie snaps her head round and sinks her teeth into the arm that is pinning her down. Deep enough, long enough for a trickle of blood to show, a thin red line on Hannah's delicate skin. She bites again, and again. Thick red rings in her darling flesh. Hannah howls, crawls backward, and everyone stares in horror at the arm she is holding out in front of her. *Sir! Sir!*

Two hands grab her and pull her to one side. Mr. Verhoeven forces his way between the girls, clamps his hands on Hannah's shoulders, and asks her if she is all right. Hannah gives a bewildered nod. The onlookers are silent. He turns to face them. "Everyone back to your classes. Now." The huddle of girls reluctantly backs away. "I said now!"

Sophie is still lying on the floor. She sees the grooves between the tiles, tastes the blood in her mouth. The corridor spins around her, the walls crowd in, the floor tilts and slides away. *Where is she?* At school. *What has she done?* Something stupid, something unforgivable. She looks up at Hannah, deathly pale, talking to Mr. Verhoeven.

What are they saying? The words sound muffled and far away, like voices behind glass. Hannah stands up, hand pressed to her forearm. She nods, Mr. Verhoeven pats her gently on the shoulder, and she walks off down the corridor. He turns around to Sophie. *Hello, sir. Can you wipe away a stain? A little red stain on the arm of the one I love the most?*

He doesn't look angry; he looks sad. He glances around, falls to his knees, and holds her tight.

SQUARE ONE

NEW YORK, 2014

THE SWEET SMELL OF DECAY. HANNAH OPENS THE DOOR TO FIND a moldy loaf and a bag of mushy apples sitting on top of the fridge. It's as cold and drafty in the apartment as it was out in the hallway. A washing machine rumbles below, an upstairs neighbor is pounding away at a double bass.

Home sweet home. The apartment with the big Bushwick windows, love at first sight, still has no table, no chairs, no sofa. If anything it seems emptier, devoid of domesticity. If only there were no windows, Hannah thinks. At least then she could hide away. Then not even the New York night could see how she had squandered every opportunity, tossed away all her aces.

She throws the rotting gunk into a bag, knots it, and drops it outside the front door, before flopping onto the thin mattress with its unwashed sheets. The synthetic floral scent of fresh bed-clothes always used to bring a smile to her face. Thick towels, fluffy and straight from the wash, courtesy of the housekeeper who assisted her and Boy. That was the word, she *assisted* them in a life that needed no assistance. A TV ad of a life, sheer perfection. Until a little life began to grow, so fragile that when it slipped away everything else slipped away too.

She peers into the shoebox beside her makeshift bed, stuffed with clippings and pictures of Barbara in the snow, among the bushes. Barbara posing with her father and the publisher when the good news was announced. *We are going to conquer the world, Babs, the world! You and me together.*

Burn everything, Archie had said. Perhaps she should. One more purge, one more attempt to shake off the one thing that always catches up with her. That night in Bachte. The deep, dark woods.

Hannah opens the fridge and finds a half empty bottle of gin. She pours a decent splash into a mug: *KEEP CALM AND LOVE BEARS*. How can she keep calm in this room? Sophie is in here somewhere. Deep in those cardboard boxes that never stop whispering. *Come here*, they whisper. *Open us if you dare.*

She leans against the wall, stares and drinks and stares some more. *Fuck it.* Slamming the mug down on the fridge, she descends on the boxes. Down on her knees, she tears open a cardboard lid and starts pulling out clothes, records, assorted junk. No, it must be another box. Wildly she scrabbles among her old things until at last she sees it.

There, at the very bottom: a small backpack held shut by two buckles and a clasp. She digs it out of the box and it flops into her lap like an oversized hand puppet. Will-less. She twists the clasp, clicks the buckles, and slides her hand into the bag.

Carefully she pulls at the collar and takes hold of the narrow shoulders. A small blue jacket. She holds it up at arm's length, an invisible girl in a blue track jacket. They look at one another, Hannah and the girl, and it's quiet for a moment, as if neither of them knows what to say. Sophie is back. The felt letters across the shoulders, the broken zipper that got caught among the branches. When her little feet ran for help, for someone to undo what had been done. Can a mystery dissolve? Wash away like a stain?

The fabric of the track jacket feels stiff and heavy. Hannah knows why. It smells of darkness, smells of fear. Her hand fumbles in the right pocket and finds the knife. A bloody antelope in her palm. She pulls open the blade. Rusty steel, runny stains. *Oh Damiaan, dear God, Damiaan. What have we done?*

WONDERWALL

BACHTE-MARIA-LEERNE, 1996

THE PARTY TENT CASTS A LONG SHADOW ACROSS THE COBBLES. A
string of lights illuminates the square where the cycle race
ended that afternoon, where coffee and pancakes were sold at
sensible prices, where the winners of the pie-baking contest were
rewarded with a year's supply of free goodies, and where Mireille
Melodie and her accordion trio belted out sing-along favorites
with their usual gusto.

Three evening gowns sweep across the old pavements. A
trio of young girls giggle, gaudy swathes of fabric rustle, dresses
crackling with expectation. Every year the new pupils of the
nearby high schools are invited to what is announced as "The
Grand Bachte Ball." Many have been looking forward to this
night for months. For most of the students it's their first dance,
first time in a tuxedo, first chance to wear an evening dress.

Ooidonk Castle shimmers in the distance, like a mirage

conjured up by the hopes and dreams that fill the party tent. Midnight is only half an hour away and the full moon is shining clear as a torch. The three girls have made their entrance now and the square is all but deserted. Under that pounding white tarpaulin is the place to be.

Two tuxedoed boys are having a cigarette by the entrance. The shorter one slaps his lanky pal on the shoulder and laughs. Sophie cannot hear what they are saying. She is standing under a big oak tree at the edge of the square, invisible in the shade. Not long now until the party ends and Hannah and Damiaan emerge, crowned king and queen of the ball. The most adorable, exciting, in-love couple of the evening. But it is only Hannah Sophie wants to see.

Her suspension from school since the fight has felt like an eternity. The days spent at home are long and empty. She wanders around the house doing nothing, feeling almost as useless as Mom, who spends her days mostly in bed. One more ghost. Sophie waits at the crossroads for hours until Hannah finally cycles along, waves at the shadow of her friend who zips past without so much as a glance in her direction. She has never had a chance to tell her how sorry she is. Tonight is her chance.

She has dolled herself up and is wearing the strapless prom dress from Gdansk like a penance, her blue track jacket pulled over the white lace to keep out the cold. From the pocket she takes the antelope knife, holds it tightly in her fist. A soft rain begins to fall. The boys stub out their cigarettes and go back inside.

Two rows of candles lead up to the tent. Slowly Sophie walks the path between the flames; it is wide but feels thin as a tightrope. She pauses in front of the slippery, cold plastic sheeting.

Only two flaps of thick plastic between her and Hannah. She pushes them aside and enters.

The dance floor is teeming with bodies, writhing, whispering, fondling among the streamers and lanterns. Girls in huge dresses, with wet-look perms and glossy red lips. The sickly scent of young bodies doused in Mom's perfume. Boys in tuxedos, barely moving as they gaze breathlessly at the high-heeled dancing girls around them. Off in the distance, Sophie hears the music. It barely registers, as if she is screened off from the rest. In a tent within a tent.

Before long she spots Hannah at the edge of the dance floor, holding her glass of beer as if it were the finest champagne. She looks stunning in a pink dress, her wild summer-blond hair swept up into an elegant knot. Damiaan is at her side, black dicky bow dangling loose around his neck, chatting away to a group of gawpers hanging on his every word. He rattles on, his gestures grander and more animated than usual, telltale signs of drunkenness Sophie knows all too well. Hannah hasn't seen her, but Damiaan has. His words continue to flow while he clocks her every move. A cold, angry look, not a hint of the tenderness he showed her on the day of the march. Just as she thought: that too was an act. Leave here now, his gaze commands, you are poison. Scare her off by staring? Does he really think he has that power?

The music becomes even more muffled as Sophie walks on in a daze. She shuffles through the crowd, which obediently parts to let her through. Girls shrink back, sensing her power. She heads straight for Hannah. *Sorry* is what she will say, tell Hannah she understands why she wants to keep her distance after everything that has happened. It will be all right. If only she will come back and love her again. Hannah, the name she carved in her arm yesterday, all for love. It's still there to read. *Hannah*. Stay with me.

Damiaan's lips stop moving. The girls see Sophie and start whispering. *Look, there's the girl who sank her teeth into Hannah's arm. The girl who attacked her. The girl who raped her.* Sophie's eyes grow wider. What did they say? Hannah hears it too and their eyes meet.

Sophie's lips tighten. "What did they say, Hannah?"

Hannah's face is frozen. The glass is shaking in her hand. Damiaan comes and stands beside her.

"I'm warning you, Sophie. Don't come near her. Leave now before there's trouble. You don't belong here." He shoos her away with a drunken hand.

Sophie comes closer. She can smell Hannah now, smell the booze on her breath.

"What did they say, Hannah? What did you tell them?"

The girls whisper. *You can see it in her eyes, she's out of her mind. And what's that in her hand?* Damiaan points.

"What the fuck are you doing, Sophie? Look what you're doing!"

The edge of the blade is digging into her clenched fist. The antelope is bleeding. *It hurts, but only a little, eh, my little Sophie?* A scream cuts through the air, rising above the voices, above the music. The dancers stop moving, the girls are silent now. Who is that screaming in the middle of all the pretty streamers and shiny lanterns? *Mouth shut, Sophie. You'll wake Mommy.*

She turns and runs through the crowd, out through the tent flaps and over the cobbles, faster than she's ever run. Through the tunnel, the brambles and the nettles, finding one foothold then another between the stones in the wall, their secret route to the castle gardens.

She runs over the immaculate lawn that sweeps up to the castle, past the lights of the orange grove, over the gate by the bridge, and into the woods. Her feet pound on fallen leaves, sorrel, wet mud, wherever they find solid ground. Thorns prick, branches claw. Her jacket catches in a tree and she wriggles free of it, like a floundering butterfly.

Behind her she hears Hannah shouting, "Stop, Sophie, *stop*!" But she will never stop, she will run this filthy body of hers into the ground, until she collapses, living or dead, from shame and sorrow. Her shoes come loose; she kicks them off and runs on barefoot. She breathes in the muddy scent of the woods: foul and fresh at the same time. The wild, pure air.

She climbs over barbed wire and her white dress catches. She pulls hard and steel barbs rip through the shiny fabric. She pulls and pulls again until it is free. Hannah is closer now, close enough for their eyes to meet among the bare branches. Hannah, a drunken nymph, whose hair has fallen in matted tangles around her face, who lets out a wail.

"What the *hell* has gotten into you, Sophie?"

"What did you tell them?"

"The truth! I told them the truth."

"Oh Hannah . . . what have you done?" Sophie hides her head in her hands. Twigs crack among the shadows. "You wanted it too, Hannah. Every single time. You wanted it too."

"It was wrong, Sophie. I sinned against God and everyone. My own father won't even look at me . . . do you know how that feels? And all because of you, Sophie. All because of you."

Sophie shakes her head and starts to back away. *All because of you, Sophie. You and your filthy desires. You can try to believe in your own innocence but you're a monster just like him.* Her feet sink into the mud. *You wanted it, didn't you? You lured him to your room. It was you all along, don't you see?*

"Why do you have to wreck everything?" Hannah cries. "You keep on pushing and pushing. Look at you standing there. What the hell are you doing with that knife?"

Here it comes, the frenzy, the hysterics she has seen so many times before.

"Do you want to cut me? Is that it? Slice me open, drag me down with you? Is *that* what you want?"

Here they come, the pounding fists. She flicks open the blade and thrusts the knife out in front of her. A knife, when no one will listen. "That's enough. I mean it. Not one step closer."

Something moves among the branches. Damiaan's face appears. He leaps over the barbed wire and pulls Hannah toward him.

"Stop it, Sophie. You're out of your mind."

Damiaan to the rescue. *If only she knew.*

"Do you want the truth, Hannah? What your darling boyfriend did with me, the day of the White March? Remember, when we disappeared? We were *together*, Hannah. And it was wonderful and he kissed me, long and hard. He kissed me. Me, me, me."

Hannah laughs. Of course he didn't. Her beautiful boy and this crazy little girl. Why the hell would he? She looks at Damiaan, sees him hesitate, and the ground beneath her falls away. She knows enough. In a flash, in a rage, she runs for Sophie, hands clawing the air, pink skirt flying up behind her. A scream.

"Do you want to know how it feels?"

Damiaan shouts, "Hannah, no!"

A claw tears at the white dress.

"This is how it feels!"

In the woods a girl stands naked. Muddied and pale, with a prom dress at her ankles and a knife in her hand.

The cold night air gnaws at her flesh but Sophie feels nothing at all. Not the first drops of rain running down her shoulders, not the thorns digging into her foot. A limp arm with a useless knife hangs heavy beside her body. She looks at Damiaan, the shock and confusion in his stare. *Here I stand, naked before you.*

A moment's silence. Then he begins to laugh. Hannah laughs too, uncontrollably, a heartless sound. Rain streaks her body but Sophie is already gone. High she flutters, up among the treetops, higher still on quick, bright wings through an endless sky.

Look, down there, a girl with a knife. Stripped to the bone. And two drunken shadows closing in.

HOME

BACHTE-MARIA-LEERNE, 1996

SHE CYCLES HOME AS FAST AS SHE CAN, HEAD POUNDING. WHEN she sees her house in the distance she feels her stomach turn, flings her bike down beside the road, throws up among the bushes. I can't let anyone see me, she thinks, I have to push on. Steer clear of lampposts. Be invisible. But there is no one on the streets. Everyone is sleeping.

Soon she will sleep too. Soon. The thought comforts her. Once she's crept inside the house, dried her feet on the towel in the kitchen. Once she's taken off her dress and stuffed it under the bed. Once she's showered, quiet as can be, and it has all been washed away.

Her dress, heavy with water, dirt, blood. Should she burn it in the garden? Maybe bury it somewhere on the way to school? Yes, that's better: a shallow grave for a soiled party dress. A dress that promised so much and now is only tainted, tainted. There's only one option now: Say nothing to no one, ever again. One word and she'll lose everything. From now on, there will only be silence.

She wipes her wet cheeks, props her bike against a tree, and walks up to the door. It can't be hard to say nothing when you have the perfect reason why. When you do it to protect forever the one you love the most. Day by day, it will get easier. Week by week, what happened will feel more unreal. In ten years' time, she will have shaken off the memory of that chalk-white face.

Not one word about the night, the woods, the silence when it was all over. How he stood, fists clenched, neck tight, panting like an animal. A hunted predator. Unrecognizable.

My God, what have we done?

III

VIRGINIA

HAPPY BIRTHDAY, WILLIAM!

NOANK, 2014

M OVE OVER, KNIGHTS." IN A SPACE THAT'S TEN-BY-TEN, FIVE elves battle their way past a bunch of straggling shield-bearers who missed their exit cue. King Lear takes another swig of Dutch courage before entering the stage, while Ben, swathed in a tablecloth, gives the electric fan a quick test run ahead of the grand finale.

Opening night of the big Noank Shakespeare medley is in full swing and the adrenaline is pumping. The spartan theater has been decorated with a generous layer of frosting, every inch festooned with streamers and twinkling in pink, silver, and gold. It's Elizabethans, on acid. Down at the front, a bunch of kids are gazing up at the stage, spellbound, while the grown-ups fill the rows of folding chairs behind them. The audience is cheering, the actors are on fire.

Ben lumbers over the boards like a stray circus bear. Between the lines, Irminia does her best to spur him on: *You can do it, honest you can*. What those two mean to each other Hannah has never quite understood. The image of the dainty New York starlet and the rugged handyman thrashing away between the sheets continues to defy her imagination. But it runs deeper than just friendship. Ben has always been there, for every blocked drainpipe, every leaky faucet. For every difficult decision and every setback. Hannah was always happy to see his rusty yellow van pull into the driveway, the beaten-up Ford Transit with that legendary slogan emblazoned in white: *YOU NAME IT, WE FIX IT!*

She knows nothing of his past, except that he served two jail terms, one of a few weeks and one of twelve months. Fraud of some kind. It's not something they talk about, light-years removed from the Ben she knows.

The Ben mangling iambic pentameter on the local stage is a friendly giant, ill served by the white linen draped unflatteringly around his beer belly. The sprigs of shrubbery someone stuck to his head have him scratching behind his ears and the prompt card tucked in his palm is growing sweatier by the minute. More or less on cue he stutters: "The course of true love never did run smooth."

Hannah closes her eyes. Shakespeare's words slice through the stupid glitter and move her. She thinks of Boy, the man who would have done anything for her. His faithful eyes, the tender hands that would touch her wherever she wanted, that lingered appreciatively wherever she desired, indulging her every whim, unconditionally.

How she had loved him back, answering his caresses with a

similar infatuation. She had admired him, desired him. Together they were a match made in heaven, the perfect team until, one day, she quit. No, she didn't quit. *Something in her quit.* For she can still recall everything about her love for Boy, even on this Shakespearian folding chair she remembers it with astonishing precision. A giant, wondrous thing that she can almost reach, but is unable to feel. A passion she can recall, but not evoke.

Love is madness, the Bard famously wrote. If that is true, then she is cured.

She peers over her shoulder. Cross-legged, on the floor by the exit, a pale girl sits and waits, picking impatiently at her white dress. The ghost girl follows her everywhere now, a cloud in her eye, a strange flaw on the fringes of her vision. Now you see her, now you don't. Now there is a sulky little girl by the door; look again and there will only be a conifer.

King Lear finally staggers offstage, cheeks an alarming shade of red, to be replaced by the mayor wielding a pointed stick. He strides up to an enormous balloon that has been bobbing above the stage for the entire performance. In the wings, Ben flicks a switch and the electric fan starts to whir noisily. Struggling to be heard above the din, the mayor bellows, "And so ladies and gentlemen, please join me in saying a hearty *Happy Birthday, William!*"

As the actors troop in from the wings, the pointy stick pops the balloon to release a flurry of brightly colored paper that is propelled into the audience on the stiff breeze whipped up by Ben's fan. The assembled players take a bow and thunderous applause erupts from the hall. A disco anthem comes belting from the sound system: *We Are Family.*

Is that what we are? Hannah wonders. Family? Are these

really my people? There was a time when I woke up every morning in the blue house. This was my world back then: Old folks whiling away their days by the shore, youngsters too green to long for someplace else, thirty- and forty-somethings who had missed their chance of escape, flamboyant Irminia, reformed Ben. How different it all feels, like looking at the same people from a distance. A haven has vanished. When a place has grown so strange, how can it still feel safe?

HALF AN HOUR LATER THE THEATER LOOKS MORE LIKE A JAMBOREE. Hannah helps out, filling big bowls with cheap potato chips and setting out plastic beakers for the special beer concocted by Morgan, a retired lawyer with a passion for home-brew. A large sign proclaims in proud letters: *FREE SHAKESBEER!*

Ben has swapped his tablecloth and laurel wreath for his civvies and is standing at the bar chatting. He waves and she wanders over. He throws his big arms around her, a blanket of warm flesh, the kind of hug only a bear can give. He looks relieved.

"Okay Hannah, time to get the *real* party started!"

She laughs and helps herself to a beer.

"Have you seen Mina?"

She shakes her head and takes a cautious sip. Morgan's brew tastes sour and heavy. From across the room a smile with open arms is homing in on her.

"Hannah, how *are* you?"

It's Ellen, a friend of Irminia's, sporting a floral kaftan and ridiculously long earrings, and packing a hysterical laugh.

"Fine."

"I hear you're writing a book. Exciting! Almost ready to hit the shelves?"

One step along from the dreaded "How's it going?" Loaded
with the implication that a proper writer would have put this baby
to bed long ago. The earrings whip through the air, distracting
her. Hannah knows the type: human lapdogs, all innocence while
they lay claim to your very soul with their pathological devotion.
Down, girl!

"Yes, getting there."

"And how's the single life in New York?"

Hmm, let's see. Thirty, no job, no book, no man.

"Just great." And she cranks up the tall-tale machine one
more time, churning out fabrications about her fabulous pad,
rattling typewriter, parties, friends, lovers. Her very own New
York spectacular. Hannah hits Broadway. One success after another. Ellen listens breathlessly.

"Why that's just wonderful! Doesn't surprise me one bit. We
always knew you'd go places." A pat on the back. "From the very
first moment you landed here."

Landed. As if she'd fallen from the sky. *Once upon a time.*
Quite by accident. A leafy glade she had happened upon during a
walk in the woods. Nothing like the reality of it: panic, urgency,
desperation.

"But oh my, isn't it awful news about Irminia? It must be a
terrible blow for you too." Head tilted, eyes shining with com-
passion. Princess Diana has a lot to answer for. The ghost girl
was right to sulk by the exit. Hannah wants nothing more than
to leave this minute, back to her room by the cove with its sweet
memories. *If they're still around, that is.* She excuses herself and
goes in search of Irminia.

She looks everywhere: in the foyer, in the toilets, on the
stairs, by the front door. Irminia is nowhere to be found. She puts

her beer down on a table, climbs onto the stage, and goes down the steps into the wings. There in the dark, narrow passage behind the stage she sees Irminia with Ben leaning over her. She smiles: *the old rascal!* She turns to go but Ben's voice stops her in her tracks. "Hannah, come here." She makes her way through the shadows to find Irminia slumped against a table, her face pale even in the gloom. Wig cast aside, bare skull exposed, gaze far away, cut adrift.

"Help her, Hannah," Ben says and she hears his ragged breathing, sees the sweat beading on his forehead. A shock of realization: The bear is scared.

"What's wrong, Mina?"

She shakes her head, looks at Hannah, panic. "My legs . . . I can't . . . They've gone."

Hannah reaches for the limbs under the long skirt, two lifeless lumps of flesh. Irminia's elven heels wobble. She buckles and collapses on the floor.

The faintest whisper. "Take me home."

SPOTLESS MIND

NEW YORK, 2014

IRMINIA FELL. SUCH A TRIVIAL, INNOCENT INCIDENT, HARDLY EVEN worth mentioning—but not to her. With Irminia's collapse something in Hannah fell apart: Reality is now a place she can no longer trust. Nothing is for granted in a universe that threatens to take Irminia away. Such a universe is treacherous, it's evil and it's vile and by no means a place where Hannah would ever want to exist.

"Go back to New York," Irminia had told her after two days. "Go home. Don't let me ruin your writing." She listened and now she's here, walking the early Manhattan streets, lost in some kind of lucid dream. The buzz of city life feels distant, rippling around her like water down a mountain stream. Agatha, Barbara, they are gone. Vanished in thin air. The voicemail messages of her publisher have shifted from gentle reminders to subtle threats. *If you don't deliver right away, Hannah, we will need to reconsider everything.*

She feels her laptop weighing down in the backpack on her shoulders, blaming her nonstop: *You're not writing, Hannah. You're letting it all slip away.* At St. Martin's she always forgot to bring the right books with her to school. There was so much to think of every day and she just happened to focus on all the wrong things. One day, Mrs. Goos of geography decided to teach her a lesson and made her carry six atlases around in her backpack all week long. She nearly strained her back carrying that enormous weight up the stairs, through the hallways, and back down again.

But the burden of the atlases is nothing compared to the contemptuous gravity of this laptop in her bag. Today she will obey Irminia and, yes, she will write. She's made a start by picking up a book at Michael's store and now she makes herself walk all the way from the Upper East Side along the fringe of Central Park to the subway at Union Square. Walking clears her head. The book, an old biography of Virginia Woolf, is clamped under her arm. A gentle rain is falling. Cool drizzle tingles on her cheeks. The air is thin.

Slowly it dawns that she is walking in the direction of her old neighborhood, a part of town she has avoided ever since Bee's circus party, her ignominious fling with the Observer, and her last glimpse of Boy. But today her feet take her right up to the sign she knows so well: *Cornelia St.* How many times had she looked up at those white letters and thought, who wouldn't want to live on a street with such a perfectly sweet name?

She remembers summer evenings, drinking wine on the cramped fire escape, children playing with water down on the sidewalk. Boy and their friends talking intently about life, as if they understood what it was all about. She thinks of late nights, being dropped at the door and the taxi driver waiting patiently while she wrestled herself out of the cab as elegantly as her spinning head and complicated dress would allow, how her skirt would sweep across the sidewalk and how she glided through the glass door, this blessed Cinderella. It was a fairy tale, all right. And fairy tales only last so long.

The plane trees still line both sides of the street, the nameplates still gleam beside the door. Only now hers is missing. Instead there is an empty space where Boy chipped away her name in a fit of anger.

It all looks the same, but nothing is as it was. She's a stranger, an intruder now; every step feels like a violation. She half expects an overzealous cop to grab her by the collar and march her to the end of the street, shaking his head in disbelief. *Young lady, this is not yours anymore. You made a choice, remember? The wrong choice. Too bad, but there's no way back.*

In the Cornelia Street Café the same people are sitting at the white linen-clad tables, munching on their *Kale! Caesar Salad*. She stops to look inside. Shiny happy people, dabbing the corners of lipsticked lips with crisp, starched napkins. She gazes up at the windows of her old apartment. The silhouette of a vase of flowers, a pile of towels, the back of a photo frame. No sign of Boy.

She lingers for a moment, then shifts her look from the windows to the book in her hand: Hermione Lee's study of Virginia Woolf. What would it be like, fifty years on, to read your life rendered by someone who never knew you or your friends, who only understood the time in which you lived from books, withered photographs, and questionable films?

I want to tell *stories*, she had said, standing in Stella's office for the first time. *Stories*. As if that were so special. Stories are incompetent; she knows that now. By their very nature they are so different from life itself. Traitors, that's what they are, hypocrites, taking all kinds of liberties. No one acts, no one lives with the benefit of hindsight.

She stares at the image of Virginia, her contemplative gaze, her porcelain skin, a girl of nineteen straight out of a doll's house. That Virginia is not Virginia. This Hannah is not Hannah. Worn sneakers, a jacket covered in stains: *How could this ever be Hannah?*

For the first time she feels with painful certainty: Her writers are not doing what she wishes them to do. They are not helping at all. They are sabotaging her, dragging her back to places she needs to forget. All the way back to Bachte and she doesn't want to go back to Bachte. *Can you learn how to forget?*

Hannah presses Virginia's biography firmly to her chest. She marches herself to the end of the street and doesn't look up until she sees the steps leading down to the subway. She descends, to the trains that sigh and rattle underground. The trains that rush underwater and take her back to another so-called home. She finds herself a seat and leans against a murky window. She takes her phone and notices there's a message waiting. A text message from Boy.

Hannah! did I just see you walking down our street?😊

VISITING VIRGINIA

LONDON, 1912

VIRGINIA LEANS AGAINST THE SIDE OF THE CHINA CABINET IN THE kitchen and looks him straight in the eye, something she only really accomplishes with Leonard.

"I feel no physical attraction in you," she says.

He does not answer. These words come as no surprise.

"But I can imagine that our marriage would be *a tremendous living thing that is always alive*."

He stares at her, stunned, overcome. She has rehearsed this announcement, of course. It had to be delivered seamlessly and above all stylishly. After all, one only has the opportunity to say such a thing once in a lifetime. She wanted it to be a beautiful sentence, one her mother would have been proud of if she could have heard it.

She feels him glow. Virginia, that brilliant creature who had her choice of suitors, has chosen him, a fledgling writer, the tenant who rents her attic room, a penniless Jew. Had he been predisposed to physical displays of emotion, he would undoubtedly have launched his bony frame the length of the cramped kitchen, grabbed her by the hips, and planted a fierce kiss on her insolent mouth. But Leonard does not leap, does not grab. He says, "Yes, Virginia, it would."

Her choice is not born of passion, but of conviction. She knows that he will devote himself to her, that he will make her happy. Leonard's eyes swear allegiance, speak of a long and stable life together. He will partake in her every emotion, follow wherever she goes. Such is the depth of his love. And no, the depth of a love is not difficult to fathom. Virginia has little patience with her friends and their endless doubts about the feelings of their intended. Women who confuse fact and hope all too eagerly, a cowardly pursuit. If one dares to know, love is easily measured.

NOW THAT SHE IS NO LONGER MISS VIRGINIA STEPHEN, BUT Mrs. Virginia Woolf, new duties lie ahead. During a ten-week course in Good Housekeeping on Kensington Street, she is put through her paces by a sturdy woman in a pink-frilled apron. The Apron strides up and down between the tables at which fourteen ladies toil, surrounded by bowls containing the requisite quantities of flour, butter, yeast, and salt. The fact that the course is one elaborate excuse for not having to put pen to paper is something Virginia denies for as long as is humanly possible.

Her long hands knead the firm dough. Lesson 3: Our Daily Bread. Slender fingers force their way into the unyielding lump. I will never eat bread again, she thinks, now that she knows how intimately other people's hands have handled this food. Her lump is smaller than her neighbor's, and a good deal harder by the look of things. Perhaps it is because her hands are always cold to the touch, impart too little warmth.

The Apron casts a glance at Virginia's table and gives a subtle shake of the head, a minuscule movement taut with disdain. Virginia presses her fingers even harder into the pale, unappetizing substance. What on earth does she think she's doing? She was made to string words together, damn it, not pummel dough.

Her first novel, *The Voyage Out*, is lying half-written on the shelf. She is convinced that Leonard will not think it good enough. She will disappoint him. Her writing is lacking, just like this stupid loaf.

The ovens are opened. Virginia carves a *V* into her dough. Now she can only wait for it to rise and listen to even more banal tips from the Apron. Followed by some friendly chitchat with her classmates. She loves a good gossip, albeit of a certain standard. She revels in the encounters in her sitting room on Gordon Square, where some of London's keenest minds gather to discuss everything under the sun. Where every evening the air sizzles with revolutionary thoughts. Where nothing is taken for granted, because there is no recipe.

She rinses out her bowls in the kitchen sink. Her brain is not yet ripe. That is the reason. She sounds it out every day, but it is not yet ready to construct accomplished sentences, to harvest the right words. She scrapes the flour from the table, making thick stripes as the white powder slowly disappears.

Only then does she notice. Her heart stands still. She drops the tea towel and holds both hands out in front of her. On her right, a long, elegant ringless finger. *It's gone*. She looks everywhere: on the table, in the sink, among the spatters on the floor. Her neighbor looks across and sees a wild creature down on her knees, crawling over the tiles. She asks if everything is all right. Virginia calms down, regains control, assures her there is nothing wrong. She doesn't dare say the words out loud.

What kind of wife loses her wedding ring within weeks of her marriage? Keep calm, Virginia. Deep breaths. All things considered there is only one place it can be. She turns around and peers into the hot oven at her half-risen loaf behind the tinted glass.

ONE HOUR LATER, VIRGINIA IS WALKING PAST THE FENCE OF KENsington Park. The sky above the city is growing dark and she hears her low heels click in the empty street. A few stray locks blow across her face. Smiling, she brushes them aside. The air is crisp, invigorating. Her fingers feel naked. She is a free woman once again, without the certainty of a marriage, without the shelter of her husband. Suddenly she senses that anything is possible. That every step she takes is her own. A glorious sensation. Virginia Stephen is still alive and well and walking the streets of London. In one hand she carries a handbag full of recipes, in the other a married lump of bread.

I DON'T KNOW WHAT I CAN SAVE YOU FROM

NEW YORK, 2014

Boy strolls in wearing a gray jacket that fits his lean torso like a glove. His thick blond hair swept back, quasi-casual, impeccably tousled.

"Looking good," Hannah says.

The words don't reach him. He fumbles to remove the two little buds from his ears, the shades from his eyes. Hear no evil, see no evil. Boy as the embodiment of the new urban creed.

"Sorry, what did you say?"

"Nothing."

He slips his iPhone into the tailored pocket of his fake leather bag, tucks away his eco-friendly Chinese Moso bamboo frames, looks her up and down and pulls a face.

"What on earth are you wearing, Han?"

Same black skinny jeans she's been wearing for days, a baggy T-shirt, her sneakers with the flap-away edges.

"Are you getting enough to eat?"

She parries his question with a frown. Why the hell did she ever agree to this meeting? He called her at a moment of weakness: *Hannah, I've got to see you.* She had run out of excuses.

They order coffee and wait in silence. A little old woman traipses through the café with a dog in her arms, a small, hairless rodent that trembles like an alarm clock in her manicured hands. "And who do we have here? *Coo-eee*," she blares at a lady friend. Or at the dog, who's to say? Hannah looks away, repulsed as always by dog people babying their docile little darlings.

"Han, I can see there's something going on. You can't lie to me."

She shrugs and looks back to see the little rat being slid into a satin pouch. A designer pouch for a vibrating pooch. There's no end to the madness. No switch. If only there were a switch. One for him, one for her. *Fuck on/off.*

"Talk to me," he says. "The last thing I want is to be one of your *yeah-yeah-I'm-fine buddies.*"

Two coffees hit the table. Boy fishes a Stevia dispenser from his bag: good for your blood pressure, downers in your uppers, the new urban creed. Amen and hallelujah.

He looks at her, gauging her mood. "I miss you, Hannah."

Where has she heard that before? She doesn't miss him, no way. She is relieved to have escaped his claims, his insatiable urge for warmth, love, hope. The way he extracted promises from her. *Do we have a future? Is everything okay between us?* Questions that suffocated her on a daily basis. That begged for a single answer. An answer like . . .

"I love you."

She stares at the rough brick wall, the crooked lines of mortar. A sketch of a palm tree, a picture of a couple talking on the phone with crossed wires. In her mind she pulls the lines between the red bricks straight. They're too crooked, all wrong. Someone has to make them better.

"Did you hear me, Han? I love you."

She hears him. But every time *she* said the words, they hurt. Because she always knew her love was limited, she knew they could only go so far and then she'd have to fend him off. There's a past she can't talk to him about. Secrets in a cardboard box. A truth so deep and dark that it would suck all the love out of any relationship. No, she can't tell him the truth. And she won't be his lie.

"Nothing has changed, Boy."

He stirs his coffee and his smile brings out the soft dimples she knows so well.

"We're Robert Redford and Meryl Streep, you and I," he says.

"Huh?"

"You look a bit like Streep, I look like Redford. The two of them had a thing going."

"Those two never had a *thing*, Boy. It was a movie. They were acting."

"What does it matter?"

"Besides, you look nothing like Redford. He was red-haired, you're blond."

"You won't even try to understand."

"No, I don't understand and I'm *not* Meryl Streep."

She thinks of the movie, of Redford's plane crashing in Africa. *S'il te plaît, apprivoise-moi, dit-il.* Please tame me. In the years when they were together, when Boy was away on a trip, she sometimes secretly hoped that his plane would crash. She never mentioned it, but that was when she knew something had snapped. Yet here they are again. Starring in another sequel of their movie, not necessarily the best. He leans forward and takes her hands in his, more earnest than she has ever seen him.

"Hannah, will you marry me?"

What did you just say?

"I'll take you back. Tell me what you want, I know I can give it to you."

For God's sake stop crawling! What kind of parasite are you?

"I know I can make you happy."

No you can't.

Her head spins and she pulls her hands away. *What you want is to own me*, to lure me into a web, saddle me with a bunch of kids and before you know it I'll be mashing up baby food day in, day out, one of those women who are the reason there are too few women in the highest ranks because they would have to be dragged screaming from their offspring first.

"You have no idea what I need, Boy. You have no idea who I am."

"Babe, I know you better than you do."

"Well, that's a fucking arrogant thing to say."

"But baby, it's true."

"I don't want this, Boy. So you can cut out the *baby-baby-baby routine.*"

They fall silent again. June Carter in *Walk the Line. Baby,*

baby, baby. Only he's June, she's Johnny Cash, and their tragedy is built on more than drink and drugs alone. Of course she wants to tell him everything. Of course she wants to let it out. *There was blood, Boy. So much blood, I couldn't stop the flow. No way to stop it. Everything turned red: the lace, the leaves, the earth, the night.*

But she cannot say it. He would never understand.

Boy lowers his eyes and clears his throat.

"Do you remember Christmas last year? We were so cozy around that tiny Christmas tree. We had turkey, remember? We talked for hours and even danced. Can we at least do that again this year?"

She looks at him, thinks of that pathetic little Christmas tree, so very brittle, faint. He's like the tree, she thinks, aching to be so much more than this half-forgotten friend, this cheap ornament banished to a corner of a room. She looks him straight in the eye, something she only ever does with Boy. He smiles at her, warmly, gently. And all at once she glows. She doesn't like where this is going, but in her heart she knows. She's already there.

MEMORY FOAM

NEW YORK, 2014

WHEN IT COMES TO LOVE, SHE HAS THE BACKBONE OF A JELLY-fish. Even a lapdog like Boy can break down her defenses. After one drink too many she went back with him to Cornelia Street. They didn't have sex, it was much worse than that. Bodies entwined, they fell asleep on the bed that had borne witness to it all: the conversations deep into the night, the tame best-friend sex, the cuddles and pillow fights, the scratchy Sunday breakfast crumbs.

She looks at the alarm clock: four a.m. Parched, gets up and goes to the bathroom for a drink of water. Her glass is standing where it always stood, on the left of the washbasin. She drinks and looks at the freestanding bath with its lion paws. Her shampoo and shower milk are still there. Did he use them up himself and buy new ones? His love runs that deep.

She turns on the faucet and water gushes into the bathtub.

She balances on the edge. The room is spotless, the black-and-white tiles gleam, bath mats all fluffy and soft. Everything is just as it was.

Suddenly she sees Hannah, the Hannah she used to be, wandering in through the bathroom door, brushing her teeth, rubbing on her creams, the daily ablutions. Hannah with the beautiful, round breasts she used to have, not these teabags hanging loosely from her chest. Her stomach is empty, her thighs have wasted away. Everything is just as it was, yet she is nothing like herself.

She fumbles open a crumpled plastic wrapper and sniffs the little powder that's left. Virginia was skinny too. She wanted to be like her mother, a muse to famous Victorian artists. But no one wanted to paint the daughter, even though she wore wide dresses that painstakingly veiled her imperfections. She felt ugly in her giant's body that would never be elegant or delicate enough, however little she ate. Even an icon like Virginia had a body once, and was a woman once, perched on the edge of a bathtub, fretful and insecure, fighting her own flesh.

Virginia sits in a corner, leaning against the rounded pipes of the towel warmer. Knees bent, cold hands buried among the folds of her skin. She is afraid. Of the dark. Of the plummeting descent and the agonizing recovery. The doctors have no idea what is wrong with her. They have no words for her condition, only a litany of symptoms: insomnia, headache, lethargy, anorexia, hyperactivity, hallucinations.

To be thirty years old and to see your dead mother everywhere you look. To hear the birds chirruping in Greek. If only she could escape. She had three of her teeth pulled. A pioneering treatment from America: The bacteria from the roots were injected under her skin. It was painful. It didn't help.

No one can help her. An illness without a name is carved into her skin. For they will never go away: the half-brothers with their games, their sickening games that filled her with a fury that will never fade. No one can turn back the hours. No one can bring Virginia's dead mother back to life. Or Clara, Agatha's dear Clara. A traitor in a raincoat. The woods, a knife, a stone, feet covered in blood. *Forget, forget, forget.*

Why can no one see that she is lost?

Hannah rubs her eyes. No, she is not lost. She just has to get out of here. Now. Not another second in this naked writers' den. She stands up, turns off the faucet, tiptoes back into the bedroom. She gathers her clothes and stares at Boy, still sound asleep. The pale streetlight shines in on his face. He sleeps silently, as always. Naked, a stranger.

STOWAWAY

NEW YORK, 2014

Don't mind me. THE BLUE TRACK JACKET WITH THE FELT LET-ters is hanging in a dark corner of the apartment. Hannah walks over, presses it to her face, breathes in. The smell is different now, musty. She takes it over to the mirror and holds it up in front of her. Not as small as you might think. *Fuck it.* She pulls it on.

It feels soft, a little tight around the shoulders but it just about fits. Something heavy digs into her side. She reaches into the pocket, takes out the knife, and puts it down on a box. Wearing the jacket makes her feel reckless and strong. She looks at a feisty Hannah in the mirror and nods. It's time.

Through the biting December cold, Hannah hurries to the subway station. A pale child hobbles along behind her. The ghost girl is a constant presence. She doesn't even have to check, walking the child the way she would a dog. She is never alone anymore. Together they wait for the next L train.

The doors slide open and they step into a packed subway car full of parcel-laden passengers hurriedly checking off festive shopping lists on the latest Xmas app. There is a smell of warm apple fritters and the crush feels strangely cozy. Only at Christmas do things tingle this way. Santa Claus beams down from posters, euphoric kiddy-faces hover above luminous gifts. Old-fashioned sentiments such as *May your days be merry and bright* worm their way like a mantra into New York's collective subconscious. People seem that little bit more human. *Merry and bright*. We can do this. A couple of days a year.

She transfers to a 4 train at Union Square, gets off at Grand Central, and walks down Madison Avenue, past an enormous Christmas tree ripe with red balls. A quartet of carolers stands in its shadow, juggling sheet music and beakers of steaming coffee in their thick mittens. She turns the corner onto Forty-Second Street where the stately entrance to New York Public Library looms with its faux-Corinthian pillars and the two stone lions standing guard.

The monumental entrance hall is deserted and the wooden counter looks smaller than usual. A slender woman is bustling around behind a yuletide arrangement of stiff holly twigs, shriveled berries, and a pricker with a jolly Santa. Plastic never dies. She sees Hannah and smiles, asks her if she'd like a cup of hot chocolate. Just this once, our little secret, a treat for the true diehards working right up to Christmas.

Hannah feels a pang of shame. The few fragments she has scraped together for her book are hardly the work of a diehard, but she nods and takes a mug into the almost empty reading room with her. In one corner, a Japanese student is feverishly typing away. At another desk, two girls are whispering over open books. No, she's not here to work, but she's here to do the hardest job that she has ever done. She sits down at a computer, takes a pill from her jeans pocket, and swallows. She drinks her hot chocolate and waits for it to kick in.

Here it comes, the clarity, that glorious rush, a brain sharpening, a blunt pencil drilling into a pointed tunnel. The kick is here. Now the real work can begin. The real thinking. *The knowing.*

She types her name. Sees photographs of smiling girls with hockey sticks, a woman posing in her rumba outfit, a businesswoman in a tailored suit, flashing a whitened smile. People she could have been. Same-name strangers she would never have seen if not for the Internet. She refines her search. That's more like it. The newspapers. Belgium. *Het Laatste Nieuws. De Morgen.* Sunday, November 17. She has never come this close before.

No time to catch her breath. Before she can blink, a row of screaming headlines pops up on the screen:

MYSTERIOUS DISAPPEARANCE IN BACHTE
ANOTHER MARC DUTROUX?
BACHTE ONE MONTH LATER: STILL NO ANSWERS

She scrolls through time. As the weeks go by, the articles get shorter. From a thousand words: *As the situation in Belgium grows more explosive by the day, this new case threatens to bring the judiciary to its knees.* To sixty: *The authorities are no closer to solving the Bachte case.*

Her eyes dart across the screen, hungry for more. She clicks one of the articles at random, starts reading in the middle of the page, sucking the words into her head.

> . . . the Public Prosecutor continues to insist that the Bachte missing persons case has nothing to do with the Marc Dutroux affair. Even so, a modest White March took place in Bachte yesterday to protest the lack of progress in the investigation. Dozens gathered on the village square carrying white balloons and banners, demanding that the authorities continue their inquiries.

She stops. Clicks. Reads as fast as she can. Craving more. Click. Read. On and on:

> Dora B., the mother of Sophie B., says she has nothing left to live for. She is devastated by the sudden decision to bring the police investigation to a close. "They should leave no stone unturned," she tells this newspaper in an exclusive interview. "How are we supposed to go on with our lives when none of this has been resolved?"

Hannah gasps for breath but the air escapes her. Her lungs feel small and tight, the lungs of a little girl.

> Dora B., the mother of Sophie B., says she has nothing left to live for.

She clicks again, another headline. One that smothers all her senses. Her heart pounds mercilessly and she clasps her hands to her chest to calm it down. Glancing around the room, she feels it spin. Fear strikes. The others, where are all the others?

She heaves herself to standing and staggers out into the hall, to the slender librarian and her hot chocolate. From the corner, leaning against the stone wall, she watches the woman working away calmly, opening and closing drawers, writing cards for the presents she will soon be placing under the tree. Safe and sound, merry and bright. It's going to be all right. This is here and this is now. Hannah will live to fight another day.

Slowly the air returns, her lungs open, and her heart finds its rhythm again. Not this, never again. No more digging in the past. It's over. *Over.* But can she ever forget the words she read? The one screaming headline that won't go away:

LOCAL TEENAGER'S BODY FOUND IN MOAT
NEAR BACHTE

LET US PRAY

BACHTE-MARIA-LEERNE, 1996

ON CHRISTMAS EVE THE CHURCH IS FULL OF UNBELIEVERS. They only turn up because the service is part of the festive package, a sermon to go with the turkey and the tree. Father Remmelt, the parish priest, looks out over the sea of faces, infallibly separating the goats from the sheep. He hears them miss their cues, fluff their lines, and mumble their way through the hymns. But when Mass is over they will be the first to come up and shake him by the hand, as if looking him in the eye warrants a papal dispensation for the rest of the year.

The Good Lord frowns on hypocrisy but the community of Bachte needs Him now more than ever. Only He can bring peace to this traumatized village. It is the first Christmas since the horrific events. The Gospel readings and the sermon have been carefully selected to reflect the situation. Father Remmelt has rehearsed for hours to get the tone just right: solemn yet soothing, authoritarian yet humble. "And in particular we pray, Lord, for our own Hannah Delvaux. Sustain her at this time of loss and in the challenging times ahead. We beseech thee, O Lord, give her the strength to carry this cross."

Hannah prays for the floor to open up and swallow her whole. She practically crawls inside her hymnbook, hoping no one is looking at her. But of course everyone is looking. Eyes full of pity, looks of sympathy she does not deserve. Father Remmelt gives her a compassionate nod. The same man who heard her first confession when she was only six. It had been cold that day in the little church of St. Martin. All of the children in first grade were waiting in the pews. She remembers looking up at the Stations of the Cross, at the suffering of Jesus. A foot covered in blood. A chalk-white face. A cave. A new life.

When her turn came, she was trembling like a leaf. She straightened up her pleated skirt and walked up to the oaken door. Behind it the priest sat waiting in a darkened room, hands folded in his lap, his long white skirts flowing over the stone floor.

"Come in, child," he said. There was a chair across from him. She went over and sat on it because it looked like that's what she was supposed to do. The gloom frightened her. She peered around the room and could barely make out the shelves of books, two empty glass bowls on a round table covered by a woolen cloth, a washbasin, a white shirt hanging from a hook. A stale smell of sweat and lentil soup.

He raised one hand in the air and made a sign of the cross.

"May the Lord be in your heart and on your lips, that you may confess your sins in perfect contrition."

"Amen," she said, usually a safe bet.

The priest sat silently, head bowed. She knew the time had come to tell her sins and she cast around desperately for a crime committed in the course of her six-year-old life. She had not been mean to anyone, she hadn't told any fibs, she had always done her homework, maybe not all that well but she did try. What does the Lord want from her? Father Remmelt waited, unmoving.

"I stole sweets from the candy jar," she said. "The one on top of the cupboard."

He nods.

"Marshmallows and lollies and Mars minis."

A hint of a smile on his moist lower lip. "Is that all?"

Should there be more?

"Yes, Father."

He raised his jowly chin, told her to say seven Hail Marys, held his hands above her head and murmured, "I absolve you from your sins in the name of the Father and of the Son and of the Holy Ghost."

"Amen."

She got up, opened the heavy door, and returned to her spot in the pew. Fourteen faces looked up at her. She said her Hail Marys. Not for stealing candy, but for the lie she had just told for the sake of something to say.

Clean, she will never be clean again. Hannah looks around at the festive worshippers in the packed church and knows that it is true. There are no more confessions at school, though now she would have something to tell the priest, a sin no amount of Hail Marys can erase. But she could never bring herself to confide in Father Remmelt with his moist lower lip.

A hum of activity, everyone gets to their feet for communion. *Take, eat. This is my body, which is given up for you . . .*

There was a body, small and frail. She saw the fire engines that stopped on the cobbled square, police cars by the moat. The castle looked desolate in the headlights. It was evening, already dark. No one saw the girl and her bike in the shadow of a tree, watching as something was lifted from the water.

On the stretcher between the claws of the crane lay a pitch-black shadow. The strands of hair hanging down turned the shadow into a body. Then the contour of a foot, so small and child-like in the glare. A foot of flesh and blood, a foot she had touched, kissed. She gagged, threw up beside the tree, climbed back on her bike, and cycled home as fast as she could.

A white tent remained at the water's edge for weeks. The whole area was sealed off and combed for clues. The world's press camped out by the moat. Hannah went back every day to look at the stretch of water with its little island, but there was nothing more to see. Eventually the foreign journalists left, taking their satellite trucks with them, and only a huddle of local hacks were left behind. The tent came down. The water was silent.

Father Remmelt brings the service to an end. He speaks of tribulation and forgiveness. *Go in peace.* Suddenly she feels a hand on her shoulder, the weight of her father's palm. The touch she has been praying for all this time. She looks up at him. He smiles and for a second she almost believes that somehow things will be all right.

BLOOD FEAST

NEW YORK, 2014

H E CALLS HER HA. SHE LETS HIM, AS LONG AS HE KEEPS THE little bags of white powder coming.

Drugs were always around, at the photo shoots and fashion events. Models who popped a pill amid the salted snacks behind the scenes to make sure they didn't wobble when it mattered most. Party animals who couldn't set foot in a club without the buzz from their drug of choice. Hannah had never cared much for all that. Until the Catcher came along.

He looked like such a righteous guy, his puppy-dog eyes gazing into hers on the dance floor at the Boom Boom Room, her sweet revenge on Bashful. It started with a suggestion. "It's pure organic, baby. Believe me, everyone who's anyone lives to be a hundred on this stuff." Gradually she began to see just how far into horticulture the Catcher was. How celebrated and select the customers who never paid a dime because it's good for business if you're the guy who keeps them high. Who slipped Williams his coke, hands Corpus J. his speed. *Pacino loves this stuff.*

Every evening with the Catcher is an exhilarating relay race, one freaky party after another. Nights full of outré outfits, unfettered bodies, boundless fantasy. Everything's pure expression, though no one's sure what of. Night after night they whirl through Manhattan and dive deep into the underbelly of Brooklyn. *Travis, my friend!* People light up when they see the Catcher. And if not, he has a little something to kindle the fire.

It's New Year's Eve and the Sylvester Blood Feast is in full swing in a vacant penthouse in Bushwick, property turned hot by the rumor that Ed Sheeran nearly snapped it up. *Blood is the New Black*, it said on the invitations. The place is heaving with patients with their insides hanging out. Mangled faces leer above glittering tuxedos. Sadistic doctors in silk jackets wield cruel medical instruments and androgynous nurses strut by on masochistic heels. Terminal cases sway to the beat with a mobile intravenous drip at their side. The music pounds and pounds. A caged contortionist throws disturbing shapes to the rhythm. A warning is pinned to the bars: *Do not feed the drug child!*

Hannah is standing at the bar, flirting with a corpse. Without his chalk-white makeup and the black rings under his eyes he might be a looker. His name is Shy. Because she can't help herself or hasn't had enough to drink yet, she is talking about her book and what she has now christened her writer's block.

He nods, claims to have started writing a novel himself once upon a blue moon.

"When faced with a difficult situation," he says, gazing into the metaphysical void at the far end of the bar, "I always ask myself: *What would The Muppets do?*"

Postmodern phronesis. Kermit as a moral compass in a world that already has one foot in fantasy.

"Is it really that simple, Shy?" she bawls above the music.

The corpse punches her shoulder. "Fuck yeah, baby."

She laughs, throws her arms around him, and presses his wiry body firmly against hers, just because it feels right. He grabs her ass cheeks, pulls her to him, and she feels his hard dick.

"You're gay, Shy. Remember?"

He cocks an eyebrow and flings a dead arm in the air. "Sexuality is fluid, baby."

She winks and slips away into the pulsing crowd. She needs to pee and squeezes her way through the dancing sick bay to the toilet from hell. There's a good reason why partygoers end up pissing in doorways and alleyways: anything to avoid the designated shithole where everything is damp and dripping, clumps of used toilet paper stink up the place, and brown spatters decorate the floor.

One hand pressed against the wall, she pees hovering above the seat. She half misses, but what's a girl to do? Add her scent to the others; it's as much her territory as anyone's. The bowl reduces us to dogs. Gods on two legs. Shitting bodies. Stop thinking, Hannah! Get out of here now.

She pauses in front of the rusty mirror beside the toilet door. Ruffles her blond hair. Yes, she's looking gorgeous. A drunken surgeon wanders up to her, red hair, dreamy eyes. She returns his gaze. He kisses her, tongue teasing. An instant later he's gone and she's back on the pounding floor where everything is radiant and the world is water cascading from her shoulders. The Catcher beckons.

"Let's go. I have to pay Greenpoint a call."

"I think I'll stay here awhile," she says.

"Okay. You still good?"

By which he means *You still got enough?*

She nods. He kisses her and smiles. She has no idea how much he uses himself. He always seems collected and calm. Everything she is not.

Walking over to a corner of the dance floor, she sits down on a speaker, closes her eyes, and lets the deep bass line pump into her. How would Virginia have felt here? Perched on this black box in her long rustling dress? *Boom, boom, boom.*

She thinks of Belgium, how she longed for something to spirit her away, abduct her, take her hostage. Anything to escape the ice-cold, small-town desolation.

Boom, boom, boom.

The heart of the world is beating. Here she sits, surrounded by bloody monsters packing pills that can kill you in seconds, that can take you higher just as easily.

Virginia was thirty when her demons found her again. Thirty, my age now, Hannah thinks. But if Virginia had been a twenty-first-century New York City girl, the Catcher would surely have found a little pill to cure her ills. Something to dampen down the doom, to still the voices, the incessant twittering that urged her on to wild, stupid excesses. A sniff of something to rein in what she called her *hairy black devils*. To keep her in the here and now, the only thing that really matters.

Moments of being. This is what Virginia meant, this moment here, on this speaker. Sublime happiness, here and now. The beat pounds on and on, space shimmers through her head, and suddenly she is there. She can almost feel it, smell it, see it clearly, out of nowhere: a shop window on Fourth Avenue filled with stacks of her book. From society scribbler to the latest literary sensation. Her words in the hands of strangers. A bolt of self-confidence shoots up her spine. Yes, this is how talent feels. *It's pure organic, baby.* She can do it, she really can!

SWIMMER

SUSSEX, 1927

Dear Dolphin,

I cannot begin to tell you how happy I am that To the Lighthouse *pleased you so! You ask why I attach so much importance to what you think, far more than what the critics have to say. It is because you are my own dear sister, Vanessa, and an exceptionally talented artist besides.*

You view my books as a painter's canvas, you oversee the novel as a work of art, a single whole. That makes your opinion more valuable to me than that of all my literary friends put together.

The heat today is oppressive, even indoors. I am sitting at my writing table with its view of the fens and the hills, and a glimpse of Leonard's pond where we delight in our fish. Four goldfish and a carp swim in the water but it is rare to see them all at once. Yet I can assure you that the fish are more important to Leonard and to me than everything being said in Westminster today.

In recent weeks, I have written myself breathless— thirty thousand words in two months! Now I wish only to dive for cover and to lose myself in the work of others. I read and read and have hatched a plan to write a book for the Hogarth Press that will center on six novels. Focusing on half a dozen masterpieces I want to try and say everything that can be said about literature in a span of one hundred and fifty pages. Is it not a splendid idea?

I am reading Balzac and Tolstoy. Almost every scene from Anna Karenina is etched into my memory, though it has been fifteen years since I last read it. What have those writers done to us? What more is there to say about sex and realism after Tolstoy? How can we write plays more poetic than Shakespeare's? Literature is one giant brain that cries out for change. But are we capable of supplying it?

I want to write beautiful books, but now and again I find myself wondering why. Perhaps because Mother felt we had it in us. She knew that you, Nessa, would be a great artist and I a successful writer. And so do we not have an obligation to do our very utmost to prove her right?

I am feeling a little better. The headaches come and go. I try to imagine that the pain too has a reason—it is an idle fancy.

But I digress and feel sure I bore you with my words.

One more thing I wanted to tell you: I now have my costume ready for Angelica's party: two long ears and two furry paws (remember the March Hare?).

Write to me, my dearest Dolphin. You are beautiful, loving, pure. I am none of these things.

Your Virginia

ONE TRICK PONY

NEW YORK, 2015

"LET ME TELL YOU, HAN, IT WAS NOT A PRETTY SIGHT." BEE BITES into a cracker and wanders through the kitchen in her satin negligee. She lifts the percolator from the stove and pours pitch-black coffee into two large mugs. Hannah is sitting on a stool, slumped against the wall. Her body feels like it's run a double marathon before being thrown under a subway train.

She brings the mug to her lips and winces. The sting of a body having its revenge. Damn right, too. There was a time when she trained to run actual marathons, when pain still held the promise of progress, a body growing stronger by the day. Christ, she used to be healthy.

Used to be. Last night Bee found her sprawled facedown on the dance floor, the Blood Feast in full flow all around her. A patient to beat all patients. Shame doesn't begin to cover it.

Hannah looks down, speechless. Scenes flash by: Bee holding

her hair back as she vomited in the taxi all the way to her house, Bee's gentle hands tucking her in under the sheets of the sofa bed, blankets under her trembling chin, as if she were a child, or worse, a troubled, irresponsible adult. *Who is she becoming?* She closes her eyes and covers her face with both hands. When she was little she used to think that covering your eyes and seeing nothing promptly made you disappear. The hard-wired logic of a three-year-old: if you don't see, you can't be seen. If only.

"Oh, give over, Hannah. Do you seriously think you're the first person I've scraped off the floor and shoveled into a taxi? So you took something you couldn't handle. Shit happens. On with the show."

She lets the old Ethel Merman motto sink in: *On with the show.* It doesn't quite fit. A lot of things don't fit right now. Like what she's wearing, a shirt she's never seen before in her life.

"Whose shirt is this?" She tugs at the white cotton she woke up in.

"Beats me. Were you out on your own?"

Hannah shakes her head. Even that hurts.

"Ah . . . Travis, right? He's bad news, Han. Ditch him, the sooner the better."

Bee sits down on the stool opposite and looks at her. Hannah wants to crawl away in shame, sink into the floor or at the very least make a run for it. But with these leaden legs she knows she won't even make the front door. Come on then, she thinks, read me the riot act.

"You're skin and bone, Hannah. You look tired and you look . . . what's the word I'm looking for?" She plays with her mug, squeezes her eyes shut, searching. "Tormented."

Hannah moans. "Tormented? Seriously, Bee?"

"You know what I mean, darling. And what's with the fuck-you aesthetic? You're walking around like some howling junkie. Where are your designer shoes and those adorable Hannah dresses?"

Cornelia Street, where else? *Happy Street* with the *happy wardrobe* and the *happy memories*. Somewhere among the dresses on the rack her old life is dangling. She swallows a mouthful of coffee, gazes out of the window at the yellowish trail of traffic trickling its way through Manhattan.

"Are you even writing?"

At last, a straightforward question. Gone are the days of the subtle *and-how's-your-book-coming-along*s. No more veiled inquiries. The time has come for unadorned skepticism bordering on impatience. *Are you even writing?*

She shrugs. "I'm kind of in a research phase. Virginia Woolf."

"Ah, the famous writer. Isn't she the one who walked into the sea?"

Yes Bee, *that one*. Only it wasn't the sea, but an oversized creek just around the corner from her home. The Ouse, a river no one's ever heard of. The sixth longest river in England. The sad old sixth. A short stroll from Virginia's country house, a practical, familiar way to go. And as she walked into the water there was no coat with pockets full of stones, as everybody seems to think. There was a single large pebble. One stone was enough to keep her body down and make it gone for good. Pale skin slowly disappearing in the underwater void. Blurring lines, disintegrating just beneath the surface. Sinking, sinking. Never to surface again. To find her gone. Forever.

"It was a river," Hannah snaps.

But it was big enough to make Virginia a legend, because the words she wrote were so strong and beautiful they stood the test of time. Stronger than Hannah's words will ever be. How would it feel? she wonders. To be brimming over with the writing talent that she so clearly lacks? Sure, she can earn her daily bread pounding out throwaway copy for the glossies, words to read while you eat, letters lighter than crumbs. But the real deal: Crafting sentences that will live on forever is something she cannot do. In a heartbeat, the thought forces its way up her throat and out through her lips.

"I can't do it, Bee. I just can't."

She sobs.

"I thought the writers would be on my side, but they are traitors, Bee, they try to draw me in, to take me back to where I don't want to go. They betrayed me, Bee, the monsters, and I don't know what to do without them. They were my heroes, not my demons. I tried, Bee, I really did, but I can't do it. I can't."

She cries, her shoulders shaking of failure, loss. Bee stares at her. Then she slams her palm down on the tabletop, so hard the mugs jump.

"Bullshit! Of course you can!"

"No, Bee, you don't have to pretend . . ."

"I'm not the one pretending, Hannah! Look at the mess you're in. You're not looking after yourself. How can a body that neglected create something meaningful? When did you last wash your hair? When was your last meal? When I pulled that shirt over your head I could count your ribs. No, you can't write, Hannah. Not in this state you can't."

"You don't understand," Hannah says. "There are ghosts, people from the past. Children. Games, stupid little games."

"You're rambling, Hannah. You're not making any sense."

Bee gets up, marches over to the kitchen counter. Seconds later two crackers smeared with thick layers of peanut butter are thrust under Hannah's nose.

"Now *eat!*"

Hannah wipes away her tears and tries to smile. *Come on, eat something, babe.* She takes a bite and feels the nutty dry texture stick to her sore gums. Bee waits and watches as Hannah eats, two hands locked at her waist, a matriarch in a negligee.

"And steer clear of Travis, Han, he's a dealer. You know you can't trust those guys."

Hannah chews and nods.

"No more Travis! Deal?"

She shakes her head obediently. What time is it? Will Travis be awake by now? Where could he be? And how can she coax him into giving her more shit for free? Did they have a fight last night? She needs to call him, fast. Make sure they're still okay. But first she has to get out of here. Travis isn't the problem. Bee doesn't know a thing. Soon, nobody will know. She can't let that happen. No.

She looks up at her friend, tries to smile, then does what she's supposed to do, what she does to survive:

"Yes, Bee. You're right. No more Travis."

She lies.

THE ACCIDENTAL TOURIST

NEW YORK, 2015

I T'S THREE IN THE AFTERNOON BY THE TIME HANNAH TRUDGES UP the warehouse stairs with her bag of groceries. As the door to her apartment swings open she thinks she must be dreaming. But no, there she sits. On the dirty mattress, handbag on one side, bunch of keys on the other, a book on her lap and red-framed reading glasses perched on her nose.

Irminia looks up. Hannah remembers the spare key she handed over shortly after she moved in. In case of an emergency. Today is not an emergency, not even close. Hannah curses, blurts out angry words. But she's not angry, she's panicking.

"When I gave you that key, it wasn't an invitation to turn up out of the blue!"

She looks around edgily, scanning the room for traces of anything unfit for Irminia's inspection. Her eyes shoot from the shriveled plant to the stinking rubbish bin to the powder-specked ziplock bags on the windowsill, then settle on the tangle of sex-soiled sheets on which her unwanted guest is sitting.

It's no use. Nothing about this place is fit for Irminia. The bare room she had prettified during their talks on the porch, inventing a writing table, a sofa piled with cushions, a double bed and a downy quilt you can get lost in. The kind of room where books get written.

"I haven't heard a word from you. It's been a month now. I've been worried. You don't reply to my messages. You never pick up the phone."

Hannah raises her eyebrows demonstratively.

"Oh, I see. And that's my duty? To man the phone lines at all times just in case you start to worry?"

She turns and heads for the fridge, determined not to meet Irminia's gaze. What's wrong with a few white lies? Making things more appealing than they really are. Virginia did it too, after all. *I want to appear a success even to myself.*

More appealing, Hannah thinks, not like this sad sack of a human being on my mattress. After the Shakespeare debacle, Hannah had refused to think of Noank. She only wanted to call if there was a chance things might get better, not in the certain knowledge they could only get worse. But here she is, the Irminia she's been so desperate to avoid, a dim echo of the woman she once was, the woman Hannah misses. She lowers her eyes.

"Sorry, Mina. You gave me a fright. I was out of line."

Irminia doesn't say a word.

"Would you like something to drink?"

She nods. "What have you got?"

"Water."

"Water's fine."

Hannah turns on the faucet, which splutters and growls as usual. "They're working on the pipes again," she says. "Sometimes it's dark brown but today it's not so bad. Here you go."

Irminia takes the mug, peers into it for a moment, then quietly puts it down next to the mattress. Hannah sits beside her, troubled for the first time by the sour smell of the bedclothes.

"Mina, why didn't you tell me you were coming?"

"Because I wanted to see it for myself," Irminia says with a wave of her right hand. "I wanted to see all this."

This apartment without furniture, where the fridge is always empty and the water is barely drinkable. Where the air stinks of stale rubbish bags, the windows are filthy, and the windowsill is strewn with the remains of free coke samples.

"Why, Hannah?" She points to the windowsill.

"It's occasional, helps the writing."

"Can I read a section?"

"No."

"You're too skinny, Han."

"Yeah, yeah." *You too*.

"But *you're* not dying."

Silence.

"I didn't come here to fight," Irminia mumbles. "I'm not that strong."

"Mina, listen . . ."

"No, Hannah, it's your turn to listen." Her bony fist slams a puff of stale air out of the mattress. "There's one thing keeping me awake at night, and that's you. There's nothing to keep me here, apart from you. The idea that something might happen to you, that everything we've been through was all for nothing, that there was no point to it all. *That*, Hannah, is what I cannot bear." Her voice cracks, tears flow. "You will not destroy our memories. I won't stand for it. Do you hear me? *I forbid it.*"

"Mina, how on earth can I destroy *your* memories?" She looks at Irminia for an answer that she already knows.

"By destroying yourself, Hannah."

The faucet drips, a truck rumbles down in the street.

"Things aren't so bad."

"Not so bad? Not so bad? You're still breathing, still talking. What does that mean? How the hell am I supposed to die knowing that I'm leaving you here like this?" Her eyes open wide. "I can't, Hannah, *I just can't.*"

Her veiny hands fall into her lap. Powerless hands. She fumbles for a tissue in her designer bag, tries to dab her tears away but ends up smearing her thick mascara every which way. A white face with black, hollow eyes. Hannah thinks of Shy.

"I'm sorry, Mina. I don't know what it is." She licks her thumb and gently rubs the trails of mascara on Irminia's face away. "I'm afraid that I'll forget. Without you, Mina, there's no truth. There's nothing real to hold on to. Don't you see? It's impossible for me to go on. Nothing will be real ever again. I don't want to forget anymore. I've already forgotten so much."

Memories hidden among memories, like leaves in a wood. And no one ever found out. Who would have thought? To the authorities it was just another missing person case in a country gone mad. *End the cover-up!*

Hannah bends forward and they hold each other. But who's comforting who? Suddenly she feels Irminia's body stiffen.

"What is that?"

Irminia points at the backpack in the corner, the blue track jacket, the penknife lying on a box.

Hannah shrugs. Irminia's pale cheeks flush red. Her big eyes flash with fury.

"What the hell do you think you are doing, Hannah?" She lashes out and her knuckles hit the wall. "For Christ's sake! I am not going to let you destroy everything. I won't do it, I won't. Throw these things away, Hannah. Burn them. You owe me that much."

Burn everything, Archie had said. But she doesn't want to.

"Mina, let me be."

"No, I will not let you be!" She struggles to her feet, grabs the jacket and the knife, and walks over to one of the rubbish bags.

"Mina, don't!"

Hannah rushes toward her. They tussle above a mess of hair clippings, stale pizza, and rotting fruit. Hannah is stronger. She clasps the jacket to her chest and stalks off into a corner of the room, holds up a palm to Irminia. *Stop! That's enough!*

In fury, they stand face-to-face, savage with incomprehension. Irminia, her pale face smudged with black, shaking on her frail legs. Hannah with one hand raised and in the other a kid's jacket, clenched to her chest. Strangers for the first time. Centuries of silence.

Irminia closes her eyes and waves a hand in resignation. "Have it your way."

Please just go now, Hannah thinks. But Irminia isn't going anywhere. She walks over to the kitchen and starts unpacking a plastic shopper: sponges, bottles, spray, a bucket. She fills it with brown water and sloshes suds over the concrete floor.

Hannah remains in her corner till it starts to feel embarrassing, then puts down the blue jacket, slides the knife into her jeans pocket, and rolls up her sleeves.

Two hours later the rubbish bags are outside, the mugs have been rinsed, the sheets have been hung up to dry. The fridge has been sponged and the air has been cleared. It's a new year and the windows are gleaming—if only on the inside.

FROZEN

BACHTE-MARIA-LEERNE, 1997

SOMETHING'S WRONG, EVERYONE CAN SEE. SHE BARELY SPEAKS, cannot concentrate. In desperation, her parents have resorted to the school psychologist. They always used to put their trust in the Lord, but now Hannah seems to be beyond even His help.

She hardly eats, refuses to listen or do any homework. Whenever there's a test she fills page after page with lines and circles, an endlessly repeating pattern of twigs and leaves. When a teacher asked her about it, she started screaming hysterically at the top of her voice. No one has dared say anything since. Nothing about Hannah recalls the happy child she used to be. Before whatever it was that happened happened.

After Christ comes Freud. Hannah walks down the school corridors to the psychologist's office. She sits down on the purple chair because she thinks that's what she is supposed to do. The wall is hung with paintings, colored splotches for people to fill in for themselves: a wounded bull, a bird in flight, a puddle.

As expected, the psychologist greets her with the friendliest of faces. She is wearing a neat white blouse and a bunch of bracelets that clatter annoyingly on the tabletop.

"My name's Elsa."

Blah blah blah. Hold it together, Hannah. Don't give anything away. Elsa is the enemy.

The windowsill plants are standing in pots painted by children. White net curtains shield the windows that look out onto the schoolyard. The pupils playing outside look like ghosts. The room is warm. Elsa opens a folder and pretends to read—as if she doesn't already know what's written there—and then looks up.

"You've had a difficult year, Hannah." Correct.

"Your parents are worried about you." Silence.

"They think it would help if you talk about what you're going through." Silence.

"Hannah, I think so too."

Hannah clamps her hands around the edge of the seat. She feels the rough fabric stretched tight over the steel frame. Her lips are sealed.

"Hannah, if you experience something that troubles you, Hannah, and you never speak about it, the secret nestles in your body and it can grow and grow till it takes over everything. Think of it as a balloon that doesn't shrivel up as time goes by, but gets bigger and bigger."

That's that, then. The price she has to pay, her penance for their sin. If they hadn't done it, she would be free. But apparently there's a balloon inside her now, growing and growing.

The woman says *balloon*, but she means *tumor*. A malignant force growing, spreading through her body, like the throat cancer that killed her grandma. This tumor will never go away either, not if she keeps her mouth shut.

"I'm here to listen, you know. How do you feel, Hannah?"

She shrugs.

"Are you sad?"

Of course I'm sad.

"Are you angry?"

That too.

Elsa waits.

"I understand that this is difficult, Hannah."

Why does she keep repeating her name? It must be a trick. Hannah looks at the ghostly shapes out in the playground, skipping, jumping over elastic bands. It's a game she's good at, or used to be. Playtime is over now, for good.

Elsa slaps her folder shut and removes her reading glasses. She leans forward on her elbows as if to say *just between you and me*.

"Okay then, let's talk about something else. What have you been doing lately, Hannah? What's the last thing you did that made you feel happy?"

Happy? A word from another time. A time when festivals and smoking on the sly made her smile. When she got a kick out of showing off her new clothes and hanging around at The Sloop. What's she got in common with the Sloop crowd these days? They all treat her like a leper. Shoot her looks of pity that make her skin crawl. No, The Sloop's no place for her anymore. There is nothing to be happy about. It's only when she's asleep that things are okay. But no, wait. There is something.

"I swam in the lake."

Elsa looks startled, finds her friendly face again. "You went swimming? When?"

"Last week, after school. In the little lake at the back of our house."

In the middle of the lake is their island. A clump of earth in the water, bristling with thistles, not much bigger than a kiddies' playground. Thistles and a single tree.

Peals of laughter from the children outside. Elsa leans back in her chair.

"Hannah, it's February. Wasn't it very cold?"

She shakes her head. "It felt good."

The icy water gnawed into her skin, made every inch of her feel alive.

"All I really want to do is swim."

"How do you mean?"

"All I want to do is swim."

There is nothing more to say.

MAGNIFICENT

NEW YORK, 2015

S HE'S ALREADY TIPSY WHEN SHE MEETS HIM AT THE DOOR OF 17 East Sixty-Ninth Street, a dignified townhouse that once belonged to muppeteer Jim Henson. It's been ten years since Muppet Mansion was sold to an investor who hardly ever puts in an appearance, but is happy to rent it out for *special occasions*.

The basement workshop was once the place where Kermits were stitched together. Nowadays, the legendary home of the world's most famous puppet family has a permanent FOR SALE sign in the garden.

The Catcher is standing by the sign, waiting for Hannah. He waves when he sees her, looking suddenly like a boy of twelve. His palms are fiery red. It's his trademark: For the best shit in town call Travis, the guy in the red gloves, the Michael Jackson of the drug scene. He pulls her close, kisses her long and strong on the mouth.

"No mask, Ha?"

She plucks a cardboard cat face from her bag. He winks, takes the ribbon in both hands, and knots it at the back of her head, careful not to mess her upswept hair. Tonight she has made an effort for him and this so-called exclusive party at Henson's house.

Someone beckons. "Gotta go," the Catcher whispers. "I'll come find you."

She saunters up to the entrance alone and passes two door-men, grinning as they let in a group of blond Miss Piggies. Stilet-toed dollies in sleek dresses that will hit the floor as soon as they are inside. The males are suited and booted and will remain so. This might be the twenty-first century, but the words "nude" and "female" are still the default combination.

Age seven, Hannah remembers watching an episode of *Dynasty*. The theme tune alone filled her with excitement, a mix of bold brass and seductive strings. A receptionist whispering in a guest's ear: There's a surprise waiting for you in your room, a *very special surprise*. The camera floating along behind the guest as the door to his room swung wide, at which point her mother let out a yelp and slapped a hand in front of her eyes.

"Don't look! You're much too young! *That woman is naked!*"

She obeyed, of course. Eyes shut tight in the face of corrup-tion. *My body is a weapon.*

Henson's hall is dimly lit, a white marble floor, a chandelier flickering with actual candles, a host of Muppets immortalized above a dresser. Two stiffly corseted women exchange a friendly hug. Little pats on the back. Tentative lipstick kisses. A super-market greeting in a sex paradise.

Hannah unzips her little black dress and feels it slide from her body. She hangs it up among a crush of dresses, skirts, and blouses.

Someone holds a tray of champagne flutes under her nose and unthinkingly she takes one. She sips, walks on, feeling radiant and light. Bashful can kiss it goodbye. Her life has taken a new turn, one that's so much more exciting. *Whatever happened to fulfilling?*

A grand staircase sweeps up from the hall: mahogany balustrade and richly carpeted steps. Wood paneling on the walls, intricately carved with flowers, leaves, and nudes of the female persuasion.

Hannah ascends, a few steps behind a pair of long, strutting legs in high heels and garters. In the flickering glow of a hundred candles, it looks good enough to eat: creamy skin and a tight, silky ass. All the girls here have an ass like it, slim hips, taut faces. Masks upon masks.

Upstairs the warmth envelops her. Wood fires are crackling and every room is strewn with cushions and mattresses. A sluggish beat is pounding. Outside every door, a fishbowl of condoms, glinting in silvery packaging. Beside them a stack of leaflets listing risks no one here wants to dwell upon.

The old floorboards creak with every step, a sound that pricks through Hannah's drunken haze. And what is that smell? A penetrating scent. Sweat? Yes, but mixed with something else . . . The scent of lilies, spilling from a huge vase in the middle of the room. Behind them stands a man with glistening eyes and a bird mask. The house is a film set, theme park, and all-you-can-eat buffet rolled into one.

Someone screams and she decides not to hear. Something

trips her up and she hits the floor. She looks around to see a dwarf writhing on the carpet, naked but for a garish tie. *A hundred bucks apiece extra and you get them naked*. "Sorry," she says. He gets up, smooths his tie, and sticks a bowl of pink bonbons under her nose. She nods, takes one, and her teeth sink into what tastes like marzipan, sweet but with a bitter edge. What it is, God only knows.

A hand caresses her shoulder. She looks up to see the glistening eyes of the birdman. He smiles. She thinks of pigeons bickering on the roof of a Bushwick loft: *grubby, filthy creatures*. She shakes herself free and her head spins.

The lazy beat goes on, slowing and drifting further away. She is sweating, everything goes slow-mo, a hazy déjà vu. Perhaps her corset is laced too tight? She squeezes a hand between the boning, feels for the lace at the back and loosens the bow. Dwarves are hobbling around everywhere, silver trays partly obscuring their swinging cocks. Expensive, A-list dwarves. What was in that marzipan? And since when does she eat things without knowing what they are? Irminia is right: She is letting herself go. But who is she letting go?

She climbs the stairs to the next floor, where the rooms are smaller. It's more crowded but Hannah no longer feels people's eyes on her. It's almost as if she is alone in this endless house. Suddenly she finds herself in a long hallway that seems deserted. At the very end something slips out of view—a pale and skittish creature. It flits to and fro, too quick to be seen. Hannah walks toward it. So small, it must be one of the dwarves. No, not a dwarf—it is a child. A little girl, stark naked, her hair in braids. The girl stops and turns around. *Here I stand, naked before you*.

Hannah screams, runs into a crowded room, full of people who will help her, protect her, who can tell her what is real and what is not. No, not these people, these writhing bodies by the crackling fire. Not these lumps of flesh folding around and disappearing into one another, thrusting, kneading, licking. Sticky hands jerking themselves to climax. No one here can tell her anything. These are hardly people at all. They are mindless, pounding sacks of sawdust. Pill-popping Muppets.

In a corner she spots the Catcher, lounging against the wall. At least she thinks it's him. A white mask shields his face. He is flanked by two female nudes, their hands everywhere. A red hand glides over their pale skin, a flagrant admission. Off to the side she hears sounds of running, cooing, spanking.

Kicking off her heels, she curls up on a Chesterfield. The leather feels cold. Two arms enfold her and she relaxes, pressing herself deep into warm feathers. The birdman.

Go on, do me. He undresses her, carefully unfastening the clips of her stockings. *My body is a weapon.*

He presses a hand to her thigh, fingers his way into her panties. She feels him glide on, press deep. Suddenly the Catcher's face appears next to hers. *Where did you come from?* she wants to ask. *Is this what you want? Is this what I want?* He kisses her mouth, her eyes, her neck, clamps a fiery red hand tight around her throat.

Cardboard is ripped from her nose, her eyes, the mask of a cat. No, the mask of a fresh start. *This is the way. A mask called Virginia. A mask called Barbara, Agatha.*

She stares up and a chandelier of icicles rains down. The walls crowd in, her breath leaves her. *No air.* She feels teeth biting, blood on her lower lip. She presses her fingertips to the blood that runs fresh and bright. *No air.* She is choking.

Is she giving in? Giving up? There is no difference. Her whole world moves and heaves. Sickening, shimmering. She is a head that is singing, singing fit to burst. And it feels good, *so fucking good*.

JUST A JACKET

NEW YORK, 2015

I T HAS DISAPPEARED. IT'S NOT UNDER THE SHEETS, NOT BEHIND THE fridge, not in any of the boxes. Hannah charges through the apartment. *The fucking thing is nowhere to be found.*

"It'll turn up, Ha. You'll see."

The Catcher is loitering impatiently by the door. "It's just a jacket, babe."

They ate together, the empty plates are still lying on the mattress. And as she squeezed into her outfit for tonight's party, Hannah suddenly felt the urge to put on the track jacket.

"Just shut up, will you? You don't understand. This is fucking important."

"Get a grip, Ha. Come on, here's something to help you relax."

"I don't need any of your shit. You can go without me. I'm going to stay here and keep looking."

"Look where, Ha? I mean seriously, the apartment is just about empty as it is. Where do you expect to find it?"

He's right of course. There's nothing to find in a place like this.

"It's time to go, now get dressed."

"I'm not your fucking child!"

"We're leaving. I've got people waiting."

Yeah, the people who *really* matter. A bunch of hungry animals with more dollars than sense, craving their next fix.

"Your people can go fuck themselves!" she screams.

Quick as lightning he grabs her arm, pulls her to him, presses a pill on her tongue and clamps her mouth shut. She flinches. She slaps. She swallows.

He cups his hand to her fiery cheek. She raises a finger.

"Don't you ever do that to me again, Travis."

But it's too late for fighting. The calm has arrived and is already enveloping her brittle body. A warm wash, a gentle ocean swell. She finishes dressing and together they stroll down to the waiting taxi. He in his black tuxedo, she in her sparkling dress. The ghost girl tramps down the stairs behind them.

Just as they are about to get into the cab, her phone rings. She ignores his look of irritation, walks a short distance, and picks up.

"Hannah? It's Ben. How soon can you get here?"

SECRETS AND LIES

NOANK, 2015

H E's WAITING NEXT TO HIS RUSTY YELLOW VAN AND WAVES WHEN
he sees her. *YOU NAME IT, WE FIX IT!* She crosses over
from the station to the parking lot of the Henny Penny conve-
nience store. The back window of his van sports a row of stickers
with the Noank emblem: a black anchor set in a red-rimmed circle with a line through it. He greets her with a nod and holds her
tight.

"I'm glad you could make it this quick."

Without another word, they drive to the blue house. A calm
February evening, bare trees line the road, thin trails of cloud
above Beebe Cove. Just before they arrive she asks, "How is
she? Be straight with me."

He says nothing, a silence that can only mean *it's worse than
you think*. She curses, stares out through the window. ~~Silence
should shut the fuck up.~~

The front door opens as they roll onto the driveway. Irminia smiling in a bathrobe and pink slippers. Hannah has never seen those fluffy, frumpy things on her feet before. Irminia in slippers. *That's* how bad it is.

"You're here!" She spreads her arms wide and does her best to shine. She is not wearing a scarf and Hannah is shocked by her baldness, a pale scalp dotted with tufts of gray. A caricature of cancer.

"Would you like something to eat?"

They walk through the living room, Irminia leading the way with an odd gait, as if she is biting back pain with every step. Her once elegant frame is listing to the left. It's painful to watch but Hannah is determined not to cry.

"Well girls, I have a job to finish. I'll be back in a bit." Ben turns and waves an awkward farewell. He knows when he's surplus to requirements. A job at eleven in the evening, *yeah right*.

Since a smell of decay has replaced the aroma of freshly baked bread, Hannah suggests they sit out on the porch as always, where the Christmas lights are still twinkling. Irminia nods enthusiastically. Wrapped in blankets and warming their palms on steaming mugs of herbal tea, they gaze out over the dark garden at the little stretch of cove caught among the bare branches of the cherry tree. Winter has been kind and the first crocuses are already peeping up among the grass, far too early. The ghost girl runs over and stares at them with wide eyes.

"It was sweet of Ben to call me," Hannah says.

"Well, it wasn't my idea, you know." A hesitation. "But I'm glad. So glad you're here." She smiles and folds her pale hands around her mug.

"Mina, what's the deal with you and Ben?"

"What do you mean?"

"I mean, like, do the pair of you have wild, passionate sex?"

"Wild? Sex? Now?" She laughs and shakes her head. "But in the past? Yes, we sure did. We've been through a lot together. Ben is a very special guy."

"Was he your lover when I was living here?"

"We never really found a word for it. Neither of us needed a label. There's a difference between a relationship and flat-pack furniture, you know that yourself now. Folks around here were all too eager to slap a name on it but we refused. We have our own kind of love and that's good enough for us."

Hannah nods.

"And he has done so much for us. More than you will ever know."

The foghorn sounds, just like it used to.

"But Mina, I want to know."

"Knowing doesn't always make things better."

"I don't believe that."

"No?"

"I don't believe in secrets." A sudden flutter among the trees.

"In your case I can understand that."

My case. The Mysterious Affair of Hannah. She feels a restlessness inside, feels control slipping away. She remembers the savage fury in their eyes as they faced each other in her empty apartment only weeks ago. Today the savages are tucked up in blankets, sipping tea on the porch. But nothing else has changed.

Irminia fishes a pack of cigarettes from the pocket of her

bathrobe, ignores Hannah's look of disapproval, lights up, and inhales.

"What if I were to tell you that I did it for you?"

Words wrapped in warm smoke. "Gave up the love of my life, my successful career, everything. For you. Would knowing that make you happy?"

She turns her bare head, looks Hannah in the eye, hammers home the question.

"Or is that something you'd rather forget?"

Hannah is aghast, lost for words.

"I gave it all up, Hannah, and you were the reason."

Irminia stubs out her cigarette, levers herself out of the chair, and shuffles her crooked body into the house. She returns with a manila envelope and places it on the stool between them, the stool that used to hold their red wine. She sits down and points.

"Open it whenever you feel ready."

They stare out at the water glistening between the trees. A breeze is stirring, the air feels colder. The ghost girl wants to go indoors.

"What am I supposed to do with this, Mina?"

"Open it. If you want to."

"Now?"

"Whenever you want."

Hannah looks down at the blank, brown surface. What if Irminia is right and the truth is nothing but a mousetrap? *Agatha's best kept secret.* You cannot choose to know and then choose to forget. You can only know or not know. Start the car and disappear into the night. Walk into the River Ouse. Or not.

The ghost girl is standing by the stool, staring at her with a slow, creepy shake of the head. *Don't do it, Hannah. Don't.* She closes her dead eyes. Stupid little girl.

Hannah puts down her mug and picks up the envelope. Irminia stretches out her arm and tea spills on the ground. "You don't have to, Hannah. There are certain things you just can't talk about."

Bullshit! You can talk about anything. And *yes* she does have to. The secrets and the lies are tearing at the seams. Shaking, she rips open the envelope. It slips from her hands and as it falls, a torrent of smaller envelopes spills out. Hannah stops breathing.

Not Irminia. Not the woman who has always been so good to her, her guardian angel. She wants to scream, kick, lash out. *Why, Mina, why?* But the silence holds, all words are stifled. Irminia was right. The truth spread at her feet is unspeakable. This says it all.

SUICIDE IS PAINLESS

SUSSEX, 1940

VIRGINIA WANTS TO DIE READING SHAKESPEARE. IN THEIR garage, with the Singer growling and spewing fumes, she wants to disappear slowly but steadily into the words of the Immortal Bard. *Fade far away and quite forget.*

Every day they hear the hellish roar of the fighter planes, a desperate, hollow noise that drowns out every sound and blasts the countryside. The floors tremble, the china rattles in its cabinet. The threat looms ever closer.

Since the Blitz destroyed their home in London, they have been exiled to their house in the country. They wait for the invasion the way patients wait for the doctor. *Our turn is coming.* And when the Nazis come, a Jew will not stand a chance. Their GP paid them a call and Leonard pleaded with him for morphine pills, which he says is the least painful way. They regularly discuss what they call their *suicide pact*. Leonard believes a euphoric ending is best. Virginia does not believe in euphoria, but in sedation. Chloral hydrate calms her when the roaring of the planes begins.

She drags a cast-iron table through the garden and sets it next to a stone wall under a large elm tree. The warm light of late summer ripples through the leaves. She smiles; things seem to be improving. The Hawkers are fighting back. She takes hope from the distant boom of the bombs, the wailing sirens, the searchlights raking the night sky above the marshes, in search of German planes. We have not yet been defeated.

A white tablecloth and fine china. Today she is trying to bring a festive note to afternoon tea. She places a vase with freshly plucked flowers on the table. Leonard is sitting reading in his deck chair, but she knows very well that he is keeping an eye on her. Always keeping one eye on her. He too can feel the darkness coming on again, the weight descending, the mist reaching out for her. He knows that the next fall will be one she cannot bear.

"Virginia!"

Her sister comes strolling through the garden gate, as she does every Sunday: radiant smile, arms wide, hands flecked with paint, and a couple of neighborhood children skipping along behind her. Children love Vanessa, and think Virginia is a queer old bat. This she knows. When she passes they stare at her walking stick and the big straw hat that casts a shadow on her gaunt face. The children hear her muttering to herself and they whisper: *Maybe the lady writer is a witch.*

"Can we have some cake now?"

They swarm around the table. Virginia nods. The children

devour the cake, a rare treat in wartime. She goes and sits on the round chair next to her sister. She pours the tea. Something doesn't feel right. Vanessa places a hand upon her thigh. *He's had a word with her*, she thinks.

"How are you, Virginia?"

The tone of the question makes any answer superfluous.

She attempts a cheery "I'm fine, Ness."

"I hear from Leonard that things are . . . difficult."

"Things are difficult for everyone."

Virginia straightens up the suede bows on her blouse.

"Are you taking care of yourself? Not working too hard?"

She sees the neighborhood children running across the lawn. Tumbling and laughing, turning cartwheels in the grass. How much do they understand about the war? Perhaps more than she does. If only she were a child. If only she *had* a child. But the doctors thought it ill advised. She is unfit to be a mother.

"Last time, shortly before your attack, you were pushing yourself hard too. Leave off writing for a while, give yourself a chance to rest. My God, Virginia, if anybody has earned one . . ."

An attack, is that the word for it? Illness as invasion. Is that why the bombs lift her spirits? Are the Hawkers battling against her own darkness too? *We have not yet been defeated.*

"Are you listening, Virginia?"

She doesn't answer, only stares at the tablecloth and aligns her teaspoon with the edge of her napkin. This conversation does not belong to a day like today. No, today things were better.

"Leonard says that you're scrubbing the floors again."

A shrug. "It helps if I keep moving."

She scrubs the floors, polishes the silver, takes long walks on the paths nearby, along the banks of the Ouse where the rushing water helps her forget the roar of the enemy.

"Leonard is afraid, Virginia."

She squeezes Virginia's arm tightly with her painter's hands.

"No more writing. Take some rest."

"I am sixty years old, Ness. I can decide for myself what's best for me."

WHEN THE CHILDREN ARE GONE AND THE BOMBERS ARE SILENT, SHE goes to her room and sits at her cluttered desk. The surface is strewn with dusty notebooks, salvaged at the last minute. Their bombed-out home on Mecklenburgh Square in London looked more like a doll's house than anything. The walls had fallen away and you could look straight into every room at the crippled sofas and the cheerless hearth. Flags of torn bedclothes flapped in the wind. Wearing her best boots, she had stumbled through deep piles of rubble, in search of one thing only: her diaries, hidden away in the drawer of an old dresser. They were still there.

Virginia runs the flat of her hand over the front of a notebook, holds a blackened palm up to her face, sees the pink lines like cracks in the soot. She presses her palm to a blank page. The lines are printed there, shooting off in all directions, a snarl of twigs.

This is Virginia. Every fiber will be committed to paper, every day, every hour, every afternoon tea, every walk. Her diaries fill twenty-three volumes. These words are her strength, her medicine, buckshot to keep the birds at bay. Singed at the edges, they are still here. She is still here. *My death is the one experience I shall never describe.*

OH BOY

NEW YORK, 2015

There's a knock at the door. There's never a knock at the door.

Hannah gets up, grabs a T-shirt from the floor and peers through the peephole. Out in the hall stands a real-life cartoon: Boy with his bleached, toothy grin holding both hands in the air. Paper bag in one, cardboard tray with two steaming cups of coffee in the other.

"Croissant, Han?" he shouts.

She laughs at this image from another planet, from a decent life where good things come in paper bags. How is he to know she snorts her breakfast nowadays?

"Just a sec."

She pulls on a pair of jeans and slips a mini ziplock bag into her back pocket. Why is she insisting on getting dressed for a guy who knows every inch of her body? Who has made love to her so many times, in so many places? How quickly intimacy evaporates. How easily familiarity fades and embarrassment returns. Fully clothed, she opens the door.

She registers the inevitable shock in his eyes and sees him conceal it as best he can. He casts around for a lightness of tone, the levity of a Woody Allen movie. *My girl has let herself go but hey, that's life for you. I mean, it's not like she's dead—love could still be just around the corner.* Cue strains of Benny Goodman.

He glances around. "Cool place. Where did you hide the furniture?"

"Very funny, Boy."

"Is this it?"

"Yes."

Saying it makes her strangely proud. This is it, all I need to get by. This is who I am, what I am inside. With you I was an illusion, here I really exist. Empty, isn't it? Ugly. Do you still want me now?

"Sorry, just give me a minute." She locks herself in the toilet, takes the ziplock from her back pocket, and tries to lay out a line on the flat of her hand. She inhales it as quietly as possible. *Can you hear someone snort through a toilet door?*

She flushes, reappears, walks over to the kitchen, and feels that fantastic punch behind the eyes. Better. Awake. Alive again. She takes two clean plates from the pile that has materialized since Irminia's visit and throws two cushions on the floor.

"No butter."

"No worries, Han."

They sit down to their Parisian-takeout breakfast. Oddly enough, she's famished and wolfs down her croissant with thick blobs of the jam Boy thoughtfully provided. He asks about her book and she waffles enthusiastically about how it's beginning to come together. How things are looking up. The words come so easily she starts to believe it herself. She talks and talks and talks.

He looks at her the way he used to when she was still up on her pedestal. Full of love and admiration. At first she had wallowed in that gaze: head tipped a little to one side, pupils preposterously dilated. But then it slowly, gradually started to drive her mad. He can't help it; his adoration makes her livid.

"Why didn't things work out between us?"

Aha. There it is: the question that came with the croissants.

"Boy, there are millions of women in the city. This is New York. Everybody's kind of single. You'll find someone else. Someone younger, a new and improved model. You'll see." She winks and mops up the last of the crumbs.

He stares at the mattress, so dirty he could never bring himself to sleep on it. This place disgusts him, of that she is sure. He wants to take her with him, reinstall her among his furniture, his decor, his doll's house.

"It's just so tragic, Han."

"What's tragic?"

"When something of value hits an obstacle."

He minored in philosophy.

"Tragedy is a waste of time," she sighs.

"Not if you think that . . ."

"Come off it, Boy! It didn't work out. It's over. Chin up and move on."

"You call this moving on?" He looks around the room.

"Thanks for that."

"Hannah, there was nothing I wouldn't have given you." He spreads his arms, palms up, helpless. "Please, tell me, what did I miss?"

She looks away. Why is it so hard for him to see? "You didn't miss a thing, Boy. I had everything and it was too much to take. I didn't deserve it."

He laughs. "What the hell do you mean? *Deserve?* Is this fucking shithole what you *deserve?* This place looks like a prison, Hannah. I'm sorry, but it does. Like some fucking kidnapper's den. This is not you, Hannah. You shouldn't live like this!"

And suddenly it dawns on her to ask. How does he know where I live? She never told him. A deliberate strategy, aimed at avoiding encounters like this. She can think of only one answer.

"Did Bee put you up to this? Give you my address?"

He says nothing, looks startled, a deer in the headlights.

"I thought you two couldn't stand one another. So what's going on? All of a sudden you're reconciled in your concern for hopeless Hannah?"

"Irminia," he mumbles.

"What did you say?"

"Irminia called me."

Irminia. Of course. Hannah can write the script: a long, dramatic monologue down the phone. You have to keep an eye on Hannah. This could all end very badly. Playing the guardian angel to the bitter end. Not a word about her stash of envelopes. And Boy lapping it up, delighted to have the perfect pretext, a noble cause to underscore the breakfast-time offensive he had dreamt up weeks ago.

"She only wanted me to look out for you, that's all. She's worried."

Worry appears to be contagious.

"I am thirty years old, Boy. I can decide for myself what's best for me."

GREAT EXPECTATIONS

NEW YORK, 2015

EVERY MURDERER IS SOMEBODY'S OLD FRIEND. AN OBSERVATION of Agatha's that Hannah loves: Murderers are people too. She saw him standing there in front of the MegaMedia, on the corner of Seventh Avenue and West Twenty-Third Street. A prosaic place to meet again but somehow fitting. He was looking at hi-tech televisions and super cameras as she caught his reflection in the storefront window. The blue eyes, the soft curls—it could only be him. Damiaan.

She approached him cautiously, as if stalking a wild animal you are afraid will bolt and run for cover. A creature you want to stroke, timid and fearful. She sidled up beside him, feigning an interest in the latest flat-screen technology. He turned away.

In a nanosecond he must have registered her presence and in that same nanosecond turned his gaze away. The way you glance at something that means nothing at all to you. Something flickering on the outer reaches of your existence. The shadow of a shadow.

Damiaan walked on. She gasped for breath, knowing it could not be him. What is there left to believe in now that she can no longer trust her own eyes? What is there to be true to when the truth unravels in a string of failures, falsehoods, and cruel twists?

Hannah collides with a fat man as Damiaan strides on without a backward glance. I am invisible, she thinks. She walks on, clutching a blue-green folder that smells of the paper she covered her schoolbooks in as a little girl. A rubbery smell of expectation, the excitement of a new school year. Who will be my teacher? Which classroom will be mine? Cactuses on the windowsill. A car blasts its horn, someone barks an obscenity. She jumps back onto the sidewalk, blinks, shakes her head. *Here and now, Hannah. Focus.* Across the street is the stately building that houses her publisher's offices. This is her moment.

She passes through the revolving door and has the baby-faced receptionist announce her presence. The girl asks her name and Hannah stares at her in disbelief. *Can't you see who I am?* Even her own publishers don't recognize her anymore. The girl nods, makes a note, and points her toward the elevator.

Max's door is locked. Hannah sinks to the floor and sits outside his office with her back against the wall. Ten minutes later he comes strolling down the corridor. He jumps when he sees her.

"Hannah?" It sounds like a genuine question. Unrecognizable, wherever she goes.

"Come in," Max says. "What a surprise."

Clearly baby-face's message hasn't reached him in time. He opens the door and turns to greet her but she has already passed him, heading straight for the empty chair opposite his desk. He takes a seat and leans back, pressing his fingertips together.

"You clearly have something on your mind."

Such powers of observation. Hannah nods. Cactuses on the windowsill. She knows what she is about to say.

"I quit."

"Sorry?"

"I'm done."

He closes his eyes, shakes his head.

"Hannah, you've not come here to tell me that you're abandoning the book?"

She places the folder in front of him.

"Here's the contract. Do whatever's needed to dissolve it."

Strange word, "dissolve." Like a marriage. Like sugar in coffee. Decompose would be more accurate. *In the end your body eats itself.*

"No."

"What do you mean, *no*?"

He pushes the folder back across the table at her. "This isn't you, Hannah. This is not what you want."

"Max, spare me the Messiah routine. Do what you have to do. Then I can walk out of here and you will never have to lay eyes on me again or expect anything else from me. Exit Hannah. One less problem for you to worry about."

His jaw slackens. She laughs. At least, she pretends to laugh, because there's something rummaging around beneath her words, something nasty. A filthy little beetle eating away at her decision, denying her the relief she expected to feel.

"Hannah, may I say something? As a friend . . ."

You are not my friend.

"Take a good look at yourself. You're falling apart. You're not taking care of yourself. You barely even look like the Hannah I used to know."

Used to. Past tense. Way to go, Mr. Pep-Talk.

"Look, I don't know what's going on, but . . . Here, let me give you a number."

He opens a drawer and takes a card from the top of a pile, an ample supply for his pool of lost and lonely scribes.

"I know this guy personally. He's the best at what he does."

The last thing she needs: a therapist to break her fall. How hard is it to see that this, all of this, is her choice? That she is ready to take the consequences.

Max, my dear, you just don't get it. I'm not falling because I fell, I'm falling because I jumped.

EVER AFTER

NEW YORK / HASSELT, 2015

TOLD YOU NEVER TO CALL THIS NUMBER. EVER."

At first he pretends not to recognize her voice. Then he hears the urgency, a ragged undertone, and his mask falls away.

"I had no choice."

Among the hundreds of Verhoevens in Belgium, she finally found the right one. No longer in Bachte, but in Hasselt, the other side of the country.

"I can't go on like this."

"I am going to put down the phone. You know there's nothing else I can possibly do. I have nothing to offer you. Nothing."

He's whispering in a tight voice, almost hissing, as if to keep a predator at bay. All at once she can picture the scene: Mr. Verhoeven, older and wiser, in his baggy jacket. A neat terraced house in Hasselt. Wife, two kids, a south-facing garden. What time is it there? Eight o'clock, they have just finished breakfast. The children are hopping on their bikes and heading off to school. He is about to leave for work. And she can destroy it all, just like that.

"I can hardly remember anything. I don't know what it was like anymore."

"Hannah, it doesn't matter what it was like."

"Irminia is dying."

Silence at the other end of the line.

"I'm sorry to hear it."

Hollow words. Hannah recalls her last sight of Irminia that evening, as she left the blue house with an envelope full of envelopes tucked under her arm. A crooked body in the doorway, her anxious expression as Ben drove Hannah down to catch the last train back to the city.

Irminia stood there alone and did not wave. To wave would have been absurd. Her bald head, a chalk-white hand clamped around the doorknob. Steeling herself for a backlog of pain. The past catching up.

I am this man's past.

"I keep thinking what we did was wrong."

"Hannah, we didn't *do* anything."

"It was wrong."

He falls silent. She hears rough material rubbing against the receiver, restless lips, the thumping of her own heart. And then he speaks, sternly.

"I want you to be happy, Hannah. Forget everything. It's the only way. Do you hear me?"

The only way. A chapter less at every step. Further and further, back in time, emptying the pages. Erasing, wiping out the past. Until no one can recall that cold November night.

"I wish you all the best, Hannah. Honestly I do. Goodbye."

And he hangs up. As if you can ever hang up on the past.

THIS WAS MY BODY

NOANK, 2015

THEY TALK IN MUTED VOICES BECAUSE THAT IS THE WAY OF THINGS. Nothing but respect when death is near. Keep quiet in the face of the one thing no words can change.

As a child she was given a doctor's set to play with, a yellow plastic case with strips of fake bandage and scissors so soft you could bend them. The stethoscope was the only thing that impressed her, because she loved what happened when you spoke into the disc.

Speaking through the membrane with the earpiece in her ears, she heard a familiar sound that reverberated close as can be. When she felt lonely, the hum of the words comforted her. A warm, fuzzy voice that always had a story to tell.

Irminia lies propped up on a mountain of pillows, eyes closed. Ben is standing by her side. A nurse looms out of a dark corner of the room. White apron, orthopedic sandals, a long, forbidding face, the kind of woman Irminia would have shown the door under any other circumstances.

Hannah puts down her bag, swears, and marches over to the bed. Supporting Irminia's head with one hand, she pulls three pillows out from under her with the other.

"Whose bright idea was that?"

She throws them on the floor, lumpen sacks of feathers. Ben and the nurse look on in shock.

"Mina doesn't like pillows. Didn't anyone think to ask her?"

"Shhh!"

The nurse presses a stiff finger to her lips. *Don't scream, Hannah, don't scream. This has to be undone. What we did has to be undone.*

"She's asleep at last."

What's with the baby talk? *The little dear has finally nodded off. Cried for hours but finally we can all have a bit of peace and quiet. Whatever you do, don't wake her up.* But Hannah wants her to wake up. Now, tomorrow, the day after, always.

"Mina," she says.

The nurse tuts and storms out.

"Dear Mina."

Slowly, Irminia opens her eyes. Hannah smiles through the tears.

"You're here," she says softly.

"Of course I'm here, Mina. Come on, let's get you out of this place. I'll make a bed for you out on the porch. The three of us can carry you."

Her head rolls from side to side. "I'm fine right here."

A punch to the gut. Hannah struggles to catch her breath.

"No, Mina. Let's go to the porch. It's no trouble, honest."

She signals to Ben and begins to pull back the bedclothes. A limp body on a damp undersheet. A thin plastic tube where no tube should be. A sheath snaking out of the body into a jar of piss. Everything in her wants to scream. What have you done to her? *This is not her body.*

Irminia speaks slowly. "It's all right, sweetheart."

Hannah shudders and stamps.

"No!" *It's not all right! I don't want this!*

Ben looks at her in admonition and regret kicks in at once. Stamping her feet like a child, a rebellious toddler. *Death is part of life, little girl. Haven't you heard?*

He tucks the bedclothes back under Irminia's chin. Hannah stands silently by the bed. A frail hand softly stroking hers, so terribly cold.

TWO HOURS LATER, THE NURSE RETURNS. HANNAH ASKS IF IT'S A matter of days or hours. Irminia has stopped eating, stopped drinking. This cannot go on much longer. *Terminal dehydration* is the phrase. Your insides dry out, like a dead plant. Like the flowers on the walls of Barbara's study: rose and lavender, white butterbur and wood anemone. Drying out is for flowers, not people. Least of all the people you love most. Hannah takes a cloth, dips it in a glass of water, and brings it to Irminia's chapped lips. Irminia turns her head away.

BEN SITS DOWN BESIDE HER.

"She loved you like her own daughter."

"Loves."

"You were so important to her."

"Are, Ben, are."

"Did you know that Irminia couldn't have children of her own?"

SHE PADS ACROSS THE WOODEN FLOOR THAT GROANS AT EVERY STEP, gazes down at Irminia's listless body resting on the bed. She leans in, close as can be, strokes her bare head, and hopes she is still listening.

"It doesn't matter, Mina, that you didn't send them."

Her fingers feel their way over soft tufts of gray.

"I understand. It's better this way. You mean more to me than she ever did."

She says nothing. She breathes.

A little while, Mina. Just a little while longer.

THE LIGHT COMES SLOWLY. HANNAH LIES DOWN NEXT TO HER waxen body. Holds her tight and then lets go. Slowly she lets go.

A voice whispers.

"What did you say, Mina?"

She brings her ear close to her lips.

"The best part of me," a paper-thin breath, "is that I got to be your Mina."

She closes her eyes.

Not for a moment. Forever.

HANNAH LIES BESIDE THE BODY. HOURS GO BY. OR ARE THEY MIN-utes? She hears bumping at the door and two poker-faced women roll in a couple of large cases. They are wearing neatly pressed suits and murmur empty words of condolence. Ben helps Hannah from the bed. She lets him, but refuses to leave the room. Ben steps outside. She stays.

After removing their jackets, the women set out their tools. A narrow metal plank waits against the wall, glinting cold in the light of morning. The women ask Hannah to kindly leave the room. Hannah refuses. Are you family of the deceased? She nods.

The women draw back the bedclothes, wrestle with a body that refuses to give itself over to the metal plank. It catches on the edge. The women's hands tug at the shoulders and torso. When one hip is on the plank, they force the rest under with short, fierce thrusts until the whole body is lying on the silvery surface. A body on a platter. Is this still Irminia? When does a body become a corpse? When is it really over? The women go in search of a socket.

They wait in silence until the plank has cooled. The metal surface hums. They open the windows and let in the chill air. The morning sun shines on Irminia's pale skin and her long white nightdress. The suits remove more items from their cases: knives, scissors, little boxes, jars of cream.

One of them fires a questioning glance in Hannah's direction. *No, I'm staying.*

They rub their strangers' hands over her dead face. Hannah gags, cannot bear their indifferent touch on Mina's delicate skin. She stands up, lurches for the door, hears a strange noise: a compressed click, like a button being pressed, or a staple gun. She turns to see one of the women place a device against Irminia's skull, pull back a fold of skin, and staple it in place behind the ear. A postmortem face-lift.

"What the fuck are you doing?" Hannah lunges at the woman and knocks the machine from her hands. "What the fuck are you doing to her face?"

Ben rushes in.

"This is exactly why we would rather not have anyone in the room. It can be a distressing process for the next of kin. Now please, take her with you."

"Ben, *look what they're doing!*" Hannah screams.

"This is standard procedure," says one of the women.

"*Stop them*, Ben! Please . . ."

But the colorless staples have already been planted in the skin and Irminia's face looks peaceful, on the lifted side.

BRAMBLER

NOANK, 2006

Dear Mom,

Things are going well here in America. Fall has come to New England and the wild leaves are turning all shades of red, orange, and brown. It's like nothing you've ever seen! I often walk through the woods here and sometimes through the back gardens, which run together seamlessly and where the grass is so neatly mown. I see the plants showing off their flowers, how the apple tree drops its apples, the brambler its brambles. Is that even a word: brambler? It seems like it should be.

I am writing columns for a magazine you used to read. Can you guess which one? They send me off to parties and ask me to report on what I see. I get to chat to the rich and famous, for a little while at least. You won't believe who I saw last week—Richard Gere! Wasn't he one of your favorites? He was at the other end of the room and he was surrounded by bodyguards, so I only caught a glimpse, but it was him all right. It made me think of you. He looks much older than he does in the movies, by the way. After a few weeks you start to realize that the most interesting thing of all is the façade itself. The make-up artists, the stylists, the image consultants, and the agents: They are the real stars.

Even though I go to a lot of parties, I'm working hard and steering clear of drink and drugs. I don't even feel the urge to try them. It probably helps that I get to see how they turn people into animals, drowning their sorrows and snorting away their fears. I would really prefer to write about that side of things, but it's not the side the readers of your favorite magazine want to know about. I'll spill the beans one of these days though, tell the world everything I've seen. It will make an amazing book.

How's everything with you? It would be lovely to hear your news sometime, though I understand it must be hard. Perhaps you don't even want to write me. But I hope you read my letters and that they will keep you company till you realize you miss me.

Lots and lots and lots and lots of love

KICK

NEW YORK, 2015

NOTHING FEELS LIKE IT DID. NOTHING *FEELS* AT ALL. SINCE SHE left the blue house in Noank and that broken, stone-cold body, everything in her has stopped. Hannah walks numbly through the subway station, the ghost girl with the braids silently tagging along behind her.

Irminia is gone. The fifteen thousand words she has written about the writers: also gone. She deleted them, just like that. She pressed one key and let the cursor consume every word. A single key. *A single stone.* It wasn't hard to do. They were nothing more than hollow talk, anyway, scraps and snippets of dead women she will never know.

She hoped that with the words the stupid child would have disappeared. But she remains, dogging her every step. In every packed square or busy mall she hopes to shake her off, only to glance over her shoulder and find her there once again. The more she tries to ignore the ghost girl, the closer she seems to come.

Hannah's stomach rumbles, it's been too long since she has eaten. She wanders into a Starbucks and peers through misted glass at the cakes and sandwiches, and the little calorie labels she used to read. Everything looks disgusting. She grabs a bag of potato chips from a basket. The ghost girl shakes her head. Something snaps.

"Get lost."

She looks the girl straight in the eye. "I've had enough of you. Now go."

The girl stares back.

"I mean it, Barbara."

The girl stands motionless.

"I deleted you. Now, fuck off."

The girl shakes her head. Perhaps it isn't Barbara, but Agatha or Virginia when they were much younger. People look up from their laptops and lattes.

Hannah sinks to her knees, jabs a finger at the child. "Whatever your name is, I want nothing to do with you," she hisses. "You're just somebody whose words I happened to read. Who helped me through lonely nights, who eased the pain. So why are you torturing me? I want you to go, forever. Do you hear me? Go!"

She rises to her feet and turns around. A barista who can't be more than seventeen gawps at her from behind the counter. Hannah smiles, tries to put on a cheerful face. She understands how strange it must be to see a customer down on her knees hissing at thin air. She understands that no one else can see her tormentor. The ghost girl tugs at her T-shirt.

"No!" She shakes her off. The child falls. Before she has time to think she has lashed out with her foot, a kick to the stomach. The girl curls up, does not cry out. Hannah kicks again. And again and again. There is blood, somewhere under her dress it's bleeding. She stamps, drives her heel into the fallen child's face. Again and harder, harder still. What she's doing disgusts her. The horror is unbearable, but it feels so good.

"Go!" she screams. "I told you to go!"

White noise, a walkie-talkie. Two cops run into the store, right past her. The barista points. Hannah sees the bleeding, broken child slumped against a rack of New York mugs.

"I'm sorry," Hannah groans suddenly. "I'm sorry, little girl. I didn't mean to. I'm so sorry."

"Accompany us outside please, miss," says one of the cops. "Stay calm and there will be nothing to worry about. We'll take you outside and you can go your way." She looks up. It feels as if she is dreaming, as if there's an ocean between her and the policeman's stern expression.

The girl is still lying there, curled up on the floor.

"But can I just leave her behind like this?"

LIKE A VIRGIN

NEW YORK, 2015

THE CLUB IS WASHED OUT, THE PARTY IS OVER. MOST OF THE clubbers have gone, the only ones left are long gone too. The acrid stink of piss reaches her from the toilets at the back.

"Are you okay?" asks the Catcher, as if he cares. He knows that Irminia is dead and he is keeping her doped up with his supplies, the only consolation he has to offer. He disgusts her, everyone disgusts her.

"Take another little something, Ha."

She nods and looks at the ghost girl, curled up under a stool. The girl is whole again, but keeping very still. All she seems to do is sleep. Someone coughs and Hannah looks around.

"Shh!" No ugly noises. But the coughing goes on, just like those sickening beats.

The white powder she's been snorting isn't doing it for her anymore. She needs something better. She pushes her way in among the slow-mo remnants on the dance floor, dripping faces swaying numbly to the music.

Someone holds out what looks like a postage stamp. She sticks out her tongue to receive it, stiff as plaster. *This is my body.*

"What is it?" she asks for the sake of saying something. The boy's eyes flash and fluttering his hands like a manic Mickey Mouse he yells, *"Magic!"*

It melts but nothing happens. Nothing is doing anything tonight. She swallows and snorts like a demon but zero effect. No high, no kick. Even the drugs have given up on her.

She presses her back to the cold wall and slowly slides to the floor. Knees against her mouth, smaller than small, all but gone. Still wearing the clothes she wore when she stood by the bed, beside the face-lifted corpse that looked nothing like the woman she loved. What is missing can't possibly be stapled back into place.

It's better this way. Cut adrift from Mina, her final anchor, she's free to float in any direction. There's nothing to hold her down. She shivers. It's cold here and it's time to leave. She stumbles through a narrow hallway with smelly, sweaty walls.

She sees familiar faces on the wall: Agatha, Barbara, Virginia. They smile at her as she walks by: "Write about us," they beg in unison. Their faces bulging out of the swelling, gritty wall. Then they roll their eyes: "But you're not writing about *us*, are you?" Hannah turns. The faces come too close, howling, screeching: "It's never really about *us*, is it?" "Shut up," she screams, smacks her hands on the wall and begins to wipe her smug writers off. Stupid writers. Slowly they sink back into the wall. *There.* She steps outside.

Into the dark where beetles big as people scuttle. Why the fuck are the streets of New York crawling with beetles? Giant beetles with thick shells, smelling musty like the age-old classrooms of St. Martin's. She remembers a poem the nuns taught her. She knew it backward and forward, this poem by Guido Gezelle, a priest who wrote about some beetle squiggling in the water.

You write and the water keeps nothing seen / The written is out and gone.

The air feels thin, too thin. She smells the Hudson, feels her pocket. One more pill.

The Christians don't grip what it does mean / O writer, what did you work on?

Faster she walks down to the water through beetle-infested streets, insects monitoring her every move. No place safe, nowhere to crawl or hide. The child that hid inside her belly, that little child of Boy's.

Her head is spinning, thinking of the tiny girl who never got to be. Babies don't get to choose. They are born fragile and scared. Victims. But not her. She came to the world, fists clenched, ready to fight. *Hannah, we can save ourselves. We mustn't give up. Help me, please.*

Straight to the water she runs. That's all she ever does, she runs. Don't try to save me, you're not fast enough, you can't run like I run. You'll arrive too late, desperately look around and.

Find me gone.

MORNING AFTER

NEW YORK, 2015

MORNING GLARE. CHILDREN CAW. CROW CHILDREN. SHE SEES but feels nothing. Flat out on the sidewalk, cheek pressed to a filthy flagstone. Chalk letters on the ground. She looks up and sees the face of Garibaldi in the clouds. Somewhere close a fountain clatters. Cramp in her stomach, spit in her mouth. She wants to get up but she cannot move. Her body wants no further part in this.

Cruddy pigeons coo among the crumbs, won't so much as look at her. *So in the end your body eats itself.*

Sneakers jog past. No one tries to help her. This is how it feels to be invisible, eyed by passers-by wary of breaking what is already broken.

Wheels squeak to a halt. A scooter stops beside her. A red helmet, a small surprised face staring out from under it. The boy must be seven at most; she forces a reassuring smile. *Life isn't as ugly as it looks, honest.* I'm only resting here awhile. *Soon I'll get up and go about my grown-up business.*

The smile capsizes. Two little eyes flare in shock and the red-helmet swims out of view. She feels something foaming in her mouth. Let go, don't let go, let go. *Write, little writer, write.* Until you can write no more, until the words no longer come, down where words no longer reach. Where everything is gone.

Far away a crow child caws.

"Mommeeee, over here!"

THERE

NEW YORK, 2015

THE SNEAKERS OF A NURSE CALLED LEA SQUEAK DOWN THE COR-
ridor. The room smells nice, of sterile substances and the
colorless roses on the bedside cabinet. Hospitals aren't bad at all,
they ease her mind. What's wrong with waking up between white
sheets in a house where the hall light is always on, where there are
always voices?

She wriggles out of the nightdress and pulls on her clothes.
It is time.

"Are you sure, Hannah?" Bee looks worried, leaning against
the bare white wall. Red coat, lipsticked to excess, hair swept up
in a wild Winehouse bun—a misplaced exclamation mark. "You
can stay longer, you know. The doctor said so."

"No, I want to go."

She rubs the angry spots where minutes ago the drip entered
her arm. Shocked, bruised skin. The nuns used to ask her why

she had so many bruises. That was as far as their pseudo-saintly concern ever went.

She picks up her backpack and heads for the door. Bee squeezes her arm gently as she passes.

"Hannah, I know it's not my place to be issuing warnings but . . ." She frowns. "You nearly didn't make it this time."

She pushes Bee's hand away. "There won't be a next time."

"And you know this because?"

"Because I know what I want."

They walk down a labyrinth of corridors and out into the open where a sports car is humming on the tarmac, Boy at the wheel. He pops his head out of the window and looks at her with an irritating mix of relief and trepidation.

She strolls right past him.

"Thanks guys, but I'd rather walk. I need some fresh air. See you later."

"Hannah!" Bee's voice is on the verge of cracking.

"No. I'm not a child, I'm not sick, and I've been walking the streets of New York for years. Go on home. I'll call you both. I promise."

Hannah turns and crosses the Mount Sinai garages. Out past the traffic barriers and back into her city.

THIS IS THE WAY. THERE IS NO OTHER. A BENCH BY THE HUDSON, home to a bag lady who walks in her shoes. The noonday sun beats down, the man-sized beetles have made way for dawdling tourists. A helmeted teenager zips past on a racing bike. Ferries chug, yachts glide across the water. How far can the eye see? The horizon is flat; in theory she should be able to see the outer reaches of Europe. And further still, to a Belgian village where for years no one has been waiting for her.

A simple act, so trivial. An everyday deed that means nothing at all in the grand scheme of things, but everything in the frame of a single human life. There is no doubt. There are only words, a single sentence that says the impossible. That says she is not dead. That she is still alive. No, *that she has come back to life*.

Her trembling fingers balance on the little keys. How often has she dreamed about this? Dreamed she could not do it, that her fumbling fingers could not find the keys. She knows the number well, knows she never moved.

The connection is made in a moment or two. The phone begins to ring. Five times, then six. Someone picks up.

"Hello?"

Her voice, *it's her voice*. The world lurches and tilts. She swallows.

"Hello, this is Hannah speaking," says the voice at the other end of the line. In the background she hears a child crying. A child in a Belgian house.

"Hello, this is Hannah. Is anybody there?"

One sentence. Begin again. "Hannah, it's me."

She holds on tight to the bench, squeezes her eyes shut, and forces the name from her lips. A name she has not spoken for eighteen years, the name of a girl who disappeared without a trace.

"It's me, Sophie."

IV

SOPHIE

BACHTE-MARIA-LEERNE, 2015

I N A RENTAL Mini WITH GPS, I AM DRIVING THROUGH A VILLAGE I know like the back of my hand. Bachte, four o'clock on a Tuesday afternoon, spring is in the air. I pull into one of the empty parking spaces by the church.

As I step out of the car, I don a pair of sunglasses and pull up the collar on my gray raincoat. As if anyone would recognize me after all these years. I walk through the narrow streets, feel the windows and walls crowding in on me. I am not afraid. I'm scared as hell.

My heels click on the cobbles, I walk toward the village pub, down the long street that winds its way up to the castle. Café Gaston. Tentatively I push open the door and hear the familiar ding-a-ling of a bell so often heard but never seen.

There is always an air of gloom about Gaston's. Smoke-stained net curtains obscure the windows, thick drapes block out half the light. Everything smells brown, everything is brown: the bar, the paintings on the walls, the ashtrays on the tables, the tarnished mirror above the hearth.

Behind the bar stands a grouch with a massive beer belly, braces stretched to breaking point. He greets me with an absent-minded nod and taps another couple of beers. A couple is sitting at the window, squabbling over a map. The radio is belting out one pathos-ridden Belgian ballad after another. An old woman in stocking feet appears in the doorway behind the bar and clatters a handful of doggy treats into a plastic bowl. A flabby brown dachshund snuffles its way toward her. In a tiny cage on the bar a parakeet is screeching.

Something is clawing at my insides. I want to scream till the glasses burst, the woman in socks faints, and the dachshund chokes on its dinner. Welcome to the place I never wanted to come back to. The place that nearly destroyed me. And yet here I am. A Jacques Brel song: *Sophie est revenue.*

As casually as possible, I make my way past the beer belly and over the threadbare carpet. A glimpse in the mirror marks me out as a jittery interloper in a redundant raincoat. The thought of seeing her again. *Hannah, dear Hannah.* We will hug and our embrace will feel strange yet warm as ever. I remember a quiet corner at the far end of the bar, where the radio's blare is muted, where the girls who dared used to sneak a beer with their older boyfriends. The corner is still there. So is she.

Hannah's hands are clasped around a glass of tonic. Her blond hair is brown now, dyed and crimped. She was always so tall and slender, I had never seen anyone so graceful. But the woman clutching her tonic is weighed down, sagging, as if whacked on the head with a mallet. She is wearing a pink V-neck sweater over a white blouse. On the collar there's a yellowish streak of baby drool.

I raise my eyebrows and fling open my arms, feigning instant recognition. Anything less would be offensive. Somewhere inside there's a glimmer of hope that I might be mistaken, that the real Hannah will wander in any second, as beautiful as ever, radiant and light.

"Hannah," I exclaim. And it feels all wrong. Her name. My name.

The woman at the table smiles and gives a halfhearted wave.

"Sorry I'm late. The flight was delayed. Something to do with the jet stream."

I smile nervously. Dented Hannah does not get up. I sit down opposite her at the little table. The soft leather seating has grown tougher with the years, cracked and full of holes. We say nothing, our thoughts are miles away and just around the corner. Eighteen years ago, a dark November night.

RUNNING DOWN THE ROAD, RAIN BETWEEN THE COBBLES. THROUGH the tunnel. A heel breaks, my ankle twists, I clamber up the wall I've climbed so often, but never this alone. Feet slip on moss, my white dress streaked with black. Where am I running to? Running away, that's all I know. Away.

Voices in the distance, the click of other heels. She's coming after me. I run furiously, legs pumping, farther and faster than ever. Past the castle, over the barbed-wire fence. Keep out! Into the deep, dark woods where they will never find me. Twigs and branches in my face, wet leaves on the ground. I trip on a stone and fall. My knee hits a tree stump. It bleeds. I feel nothing at all.

"I THOUGHT YOU WERE DEAD," SHE SAYS.

Just like that, out of nowhere. A slap in the face, the twist of a knife. You should be dead. *You shouldn't be alive.*

"But here you are, Sophie."

I nod, a pointless confirmation. Even that feels wrong. I am Sophie, but then again I am not.

"Looking good," she almost snarls.

"You too, Hannah." I smile.

She shakes her crimped curls.

"No need to lie, Sophie. I know I look like a worn-out door-mat."

I shiver. It's the irony. For years there has been every need to lie. Our lies, exactly as we agreed to them that night. Premeditated lies.

I whisper, "You're right."

IN THE WOODS A GIRL STANDS NAKED. MUDDIED AND PALE, WITH A prom dress at her ankles and a knife in her hand. Two drunken shadows closing in. What do they want from me? What will they take from me? Everything. Everything I do not want to give. I smell booze on his breath.

"THREE KIDS?"

"Eight, six, and one. The youngest is a girl."

Hannah talks about her failed attempts to find a job as a dental assistant, about marrying the man who wanted her most. About how he grew tired of her, two children into the marriage, and how they found each other again in this new baby girl. About forgiving him his infidelity.

"We made it through," she says.

"What does he do?"

"Landscaping. Paving, terraces, flower beds, that kind of thing."

I nod and yearn for the gin I ordered.

"I Googled you, of course. You did good, Sophie. Journalist in New York, your own column. I'm impressed."

"Life always looks better online."

"Well, at least you're not living on the Kortrijkse Steenweg with three kids."

"It hasn't been easy."

Hannah looks up, icily. "Really, Sophie? It that right?"

Here it comes. The undercurrent breaks the surface. The tone set by that first limp wave of the hand. Hannah's eyes are mocking, burning.

"*You've* not had it easy?"

I feel it all slipping away. The poignant script, the heartrending scenes I had imagined: childhood friends reunited, sobbing in each other's arms. *Dear Hannah, I've missed you so.* An endless embrace, sighs of relief, voices that won't stop talking until every memory is rekindled. But here in the gloom of Gaston's, the whole script has imploded, a vacuum has sucked the past dry and left nothing but a distance, thick as walls. And something else, something darker.

"Well, fuck you. I thought you were dead."

Blame.

"We were supposed to be in this together, Sophie. *Together.*"

Black rims around her eyes. She has been crying. I am lost for words. The barman saunters up, puts a glass down on the table, and wipes his damp hands on the apron in the shadow of his belly. He eyes us suspiciously. I smile a sweet, fake smile, hardly a smile at all. The urge to make a dash for the door grows stronger but for now at least there's gin. I drink it in one gulp.

Lies to the police. Time and time again, Hannah told them the story of what did not happen. *Yes, Officer, we settled our differences outside the tent and then we cycled home, all three of us. Yes, Damiaan too. Yes, Sophie too.* Monstrous lies. No one went home that night. Their ways parted in the Bachte woods and none of them ever came home again.

Two drunken shadows. My hands shake, the knife pounds in my grip. My mind has flown, my body remains. This body, the filthy imprint of a drunken father's hands. Don't touch me! Don't fucking touch me! My fists want to lash out. His shadow touches me and they let fly.

A reflex. Steel pierces flesh. It's that simple. I am that strong. Not powerless at all, but strong. Hannah screams. Damiaan is silent, clutching at his side. The blood comes now, a thick red line spilling down his leg. He staggers back. He shuffles. "Fuck," he gasps. "Fuck."

Hannah lunges at me in fury, pulls the knife from my hand. She cries in panic, her arms flail, hysterics. "What have you done?" Damiaan tries to calm her. She shoves him away and again she wails. "What have you done?" He stumbles, reels, falls to the ground as only the wounded fall: meek, heavy, hard. An awful sound. Something cracks, something snaps. A boy lies broken, his head on a stone. Blood pours from his temple. Face unmoving, eyes wide open, lips frozen in a surprised "O." As if in that last instant he knew his fate. A stone. A stupid stone.

"THE WHOLE COUNTRY HAD LOST ITS MIND. IT WAS SO SOON AFTER Marc Dutroux. People saw monsters, pedophile conspiracies around every corner. Two more innocent victims. It was all over the news for weeks. Then they found him in the water. His body, Sophie. I saw them pull his body from the water. Do you know how that felt?"

She stares at me, leans across the table.

"I loved him, Sophie."

I look down.

"And all this time you were living it up in New York. I thought you were dead. But no, you were over there making a name for yourself. My name, Sophie, *my name*. And now you drop by to tell me *you've* not had it easy?"

A cord pulls tight around my throat. I can't breathe.

"One phone call, Sophie. Was that too much to ask? One lousy phone call."

I hunch over, fighting for air. She doesn't notice, keeps on talking.

"*My* name! What was all that about? Some kind of twisted tribute? What did you expect, Sophie? That you could come waltzing in here like the Queen of fucking Sheba and grant me the honor of playing along with your catharsis?"

I watch Hannah's lips spitting out sickening words.

"Well, don't think you can just turn up out of nowhere and destroy my life all over again, everything I've struggled to build up these past eighteen years."

But that's exactly what I think and what I am about to do. *I am Sophie, the truth is mine.* The crime is ours and we will pay for it together. *Enough.*

"You don't have the right, Sophie. You took one life from me, I won't let you take another."

Enough. I dive across the table, and even as I do it I know that it's wrong. In a heartbeat I grab Hannah's collar, clamp my hand over her ranting mouth.

"Shhh!"

THE BLOOD IS EVERYWHERE. I GRAB A HANDFUL OF LEAVES AND TRY to stop the flow. His eyes are vacant. Damiaan is gone. I press my ear to his mouth. There is no breath. Press my hand to his bloody throat. No pulse. Everything is motionless. I let go, stumble backward. Hannah cries out. Instinctively, I turn and clamp my hand over her mouth.

"Shh!"

Her stare is blank. She is a rag doll. I am not. We have to be smart. This has to be undone. I want it to be undone.

"Hannah, this was an accident." I search for understanding in her gaze. "There's nothing we can do for him."

She trembles, shakes. I tell her what I have always believed, what has always helped me through: Don't give up, keep going, it will be all right.

I take hold of a foot, a shiny black shoe. I try to drag him along. I can't. His limp body is too heavy.

"Hannah, we can save ourselves. We mustn't give up. Help me, please."

Raggedy Hannah takes hold of the other foot in her fumbling hands. Together we manage to drag his body back through the woods. Two girls and a corpse. Hannah doesn't look down, sees nothing through her tears. I pull with all my might, search for water among the trees. The lake around our island. A place where the boy can sink. Large stones in his pockets. How many stones? How long does a body stay afloat?

Soon we will forget. Forget this, forget him. The water will stay silent and I will be Hannah's once again.

"DON'T FUCKING TOUCH ME!" HANNAH JUMPS UP, STABS A TREM-bling finger at me. "I'm warning you, Sophie, keep your mouth shut. This is my life. Don't you dare say a word. You will do what you've done so magnificently all these years. You will shut up and disappear."

Her voice falters, cracks. "And don't ever come back here again."

She turns and walks away. The bell at the door tinkles.

The barman polishes his glasses and pretends to have heard nothing. The squabbling hikers have departed. The dachshund yawns and stretches. Hannah has left and the truth has left with her, just like that. The end.

Outside, crows swoop and squawk. *No, this is not the end.*

I grab my coat, toss some coins on the table, and run after Hannah. I see her striding off in the direction of the castle. Her shoulders are shuddering.

"Hannah, wait!"

"No, I'm done waiting," she screams, she sobs. "I've waited eighteen years of my life for you."

My pointed heels slow me down, keep catching on the cobbles. I kick them off and tuck them under my arm with my raincoat. My sunglasses clatter to the ground and smash. I run barefoot along the winding path that Hannah has taken, walking blindly toward the castle wall.

The lush green of the gardens heaves into view, an over-wrought oasis, a misplaced vision. Perfect sloping lawns under a clear blue sky. Elegant metal benches, a trimmed box hedge, hollyhocks, begonias, fuchsias in the bud. Everything as it has always been. A wretched Wonderland. Alice. Suddenly I'm Alice, at the wrong end of the rabbit hole.

"Stop!"

A tall woman in blue dungarees, reading glasses perched on her nose, comes hobbling over waving her arms. "Stop!" she pants, cheeks flushed and red blotches breaking out on her neck.

"Garden or castle?"

"Sorry?"

She looks miffed. "Are you visiting the castle or only the gardens?"

The red blotches multiply. I am lost for words.

"The gardens," says Hannah, because someone has to say something.

"That'll be two euros each."

I fumble in my coat pocket for a five-euro note. The woman hands me back a coin and fiddles with a roll of tickets. She tears off two blue strips.

"Here you are. And here is the leaflet. It's open house next weekend. You can see the castle for free then."

She presses a flyer into my hand. A photo of the castle with the Belgian flag flying high.

LOSE YOUR HEART TO OOIDONK CASTLE

ITS FABULOUS FAIRY-TALE GARDENS

AND THE GLASS MENAGERIE

WHERE TIME STANDS STILL . . .

Not a word about the body of a boy fished from the castle lake all those years ago. The violence in those peaceful woods beyond the barbed-wire fence. *Private property. Keep out!* We have broken every law, flouted every commandment and here we are, tourists in our own history. Killers with tickets.

OUR DRESSES ARE STAINED. WATER, EARTH, BLOOD. I TRY TO FOCUS but I cannot think. A moment ago it all seemed so clear.

Hannah looks at me in despair. "You have to go home," I say. "Cycle as fast as you can. Make sure no one sees you." She pulls at the skirts of her blood-soaked dress.

"Exactly, so no one sees the blood. Go straight to your room. Tomorrow, tell everyone you went straight home. We quarreled and settled our differences and then you went home. So did I. So did Damiaan."

Raggedy Hannah looks lost and alone. I grab her by the shoulders and stare into her eyes. "Are you listening, Hannah? Let's pretend we're in a movie, a thriller, and we're the leading actresses. We can do this. If we stick to the same story, no one can touch us. Ever."

As I say the words, I feel that we are one again. Closer than ever. Blood sisters.

"And you?"

"I'll head back through the woods. I'll be fine. We'll be fine, do you hear me?"

Hannah nods and turns around. Slowly she disappears among the bushes.

My head starts spinning, I sit down. The earth feels wet, unsteady. I am scared to death. This is not a movie. What have we done? I cannot make myself think.

Should I stay here till they find me at last? Girl turned killer.

Girl turned monster. The scratches on my skin, the blood. Traces everywhere and no one to help. Never anyone to help. No, wait, there is someone.

I know what I have to do.

Back on my feet, I run through the woods as fast as I can to a little house where the door is always open. The cinders on the path tear at my bare soles. My feet tingle with pain. I step inside and call his name.

Stumbling overhead, floorboards creaking, feet on the stairs. In the dark hallway, Mr. Verhoeven appears in his boxer shorts. He stares at me in horror. At the girl standing by his fridge, her white dress soaked in blood. A girl with a knife, pleading for help.

"My God, Sophie, what happened?"

I am trembling from head to foot. I hear the knife hit the floor. He picks it up, drags me into the hall, and closes the door. He asks me nothing, holds me close. I feel his warmth. Not a dangerous, treacherous warmth but one that will protect and save me. Someone to save me. At last someone to save me. Slowly I disappear.

"Two days later it snowed, remember? It was like the snow came to cover our tracks."

We are sitting on the edge of the lake, our lake. I look up at her through my tears.

"What about Damiaan's bike?" she asks.

"Yes, Damiaan's bike, our shoes, my jacket caught in the trees. There were so many tracks to cover." And no, it wasn't the snow.

"He cleared it all away. I think he may even have found Damiaan. We never spoke about it. He told me to forget everything, promised that things would get better for me. He told me he had a plan."

A plan, an arrangement, an impossible promise: Never look back. The only escape route, he said, was to leave my life behind, sever every tie. The idea was crystal clear. A life for a life. A fresh start, a new name.

For me, there was only one name. The only name I ever wanted. Hannah.

Four days later we drove to the port of Zeebrugge, where the belly of a big cargo ship was waiting in the early morning mist. The boat that would take me to the other side. The wide ocean, waves that rolled me into the eager arms of a complete stranger, a woman who desperately wanted a child.

Just before I went on board he stroked my cheek. *"Have a good life, Sophie,"* he whispered. I don't know why, maybe it was the look in his eyes, so frenzied, desperate. All at once, I understood that he chose to save me as much as he chose to save himself. My escape was his revenge. *We have more in common than you think, Sophie.* He'd been there, he too knew the fitful sleep, the hidden anguish, the imprint of two filthy hands. I was his solace, his secret master plan. A life for a life.

"I wrote to my mother, Hannah. Mr. Verhoeven said he would tell her where I was."

"She didn't have a clue."

"I know that now. He never told her. They never sent the letters I wrote."

They had never intended to. For there had been another part of the plan, another unspoken deal: a mother for a mother. A woman in Bachte who did not know how to be a mother, who would sink like a stone and drink herself to death. And a woman in Noank who wanted nothing more, who protected me, loved me as her own child, and hid all my letters in a deep, dark drawer. *Children don't get to choose. But who would you have chosen, had the choice been yours?*

"Do you believe in fate?"

Hannah shrugs.

I pick up my raincoat. "I believe in choices."

I slip my hand into the pocket and pull out the knife. Our pen-knife with the bloodstained antelope. Shock flares in Hannah's eyes.

"What are you going to do with that?"

I click the blade open. One more track to cover. The last, conclusive piece of evidence. The final trace of what we have done. Grounds enough for a confession, a court case, the punishment we deserve.

Hannah reaches out, stumbles over her words.

"This is a village, Sophie. If you tell the truth, I will lose everything. My world is a small world. Bachte is not New York."

Lose everything. What's *everything*? An old house on the Kortrijkse Steenweg, a dreary job as a dental assistant, a marriage on its last legs. I flick the blade open and shut.

Hannah tilts her head, a *pretty please* that lost its power long ago. She presses her palms together, just like we did on the day of our first holy communion.

"I have three kids, Sophie. What are they going to do without me? I'm begging you, let's leave this behind us."

Burn everything. Why should I? I returned to be Sophie once again, to tell the whole truth and nothing but the truth. To finally see the real story hit the headlines: MISSING GIRL FOUND, POLICE BLUNDERED. THE LIE THAT KILLED A DES-PERATE MOTHER. BACHTE CASE: NO LINK WITH MARC DUTROUX.

My White March. My bid for justice. Tell the truth and to hell with the consequences. I have my name: *Sophie*. Nothing else matters now.

I say nothing, turn my face away.

A sudden scream. Hannah lunges at me and wrenches the knife from my hand. Her fist closes around the handle and she holds the blade out in front of her.

"I have a life here, Sophie. It's not much, but it's *mine*."

A shiver runs through me. *I am Sophie and that life is mine.* The world tilts and spins. Here we stand, an echo of that long, cold night when two girls exchanged lives in a deep, dark wood.

I run at Hannah, make a grab for the knife. We push, pull, drag each other to the ground. I slam her arm aside; she kicks me full in the stomach. The knife makes wild scratches on her skin, my skin. It falls.

Chests heaving, we scramble away from one another. Hannah fixes me with an ice-cold stare.

"Do you know how much I've hated you all these years?" Her voice is bitter, fierce. "I never understood you, Sophie. You live in another world."

"And you, Hannah, have no idea what my world was like. I would have died if no one had helped me. I got a chance and took it. I damned well took it. Of course you don't understand. Your father was a saint. My father was a monster. Do you understand? A *monster*."

Hannah stares at me, bewildered. In a country forever haunted by the memory of Marc Dutroux, everybody knows what monsters do.

She stammers: "I had no idea."

I bury my face in my hands. "How could you?"

She struggles to her feet, brushes the dirt from her jacket, with feeble strokes, tears well up in her tired eyes.

"Go on then, Sophie. Do whatever you want."

She wipes the tears, shakes her head.

"You always have."

I watch her disappear among the bushes. My dear friend. My Hannah. The same bushes as that night, when raggedy Hannah jumped on her bike, cycled home through the dark, and fell apart in her room, never to be patched up again.

Not all wounds are binding. Not all mistakes will heal. Most of them fester on, spewing sour and bitter consequences a whole life long.

I stand by the lake as darkness falls. I stare at our little island, at the tree that has witnessed it all. In the twilight across the water, a little girl appears, the ghost girl I have been for so long. She stands by the tree and stares back at me. Her eyes challenging, yearning.

I get up and walk toward her, up to the water's edge and then beyond. My wet knees disappear into the cold lake. My body still remembers how it was, the weight of the water. How I held him down with all my might, trembling with cold and fear. How we crawled from the lake in our soaking dresses, thin fabric clinging to Hannah's porcelain skin. A luminous water nymph.

The knife throbs in my fist. *I love you, Hannah.* Even with your dark-rimmed eyes and your angry words, your shaking shoulders and the stain on the collar of your blouse. That little yellowish streak of baby drool. *How many lives can I take?* I raise my arm, grit my teeth, and hurl the knife as far from me as I can.

It hits the surface of the silent water. The mirror breaks, the knife sinks. Deeper, deeper still.

There goes Sophie. *Sophie is gone.*

Not for a moment. Forever.

I stare at the circles on the lake. Watch the broken surface become smooth once more. I look up at the island, where the little girl has disappeared.

BAREFOOT, I WALK TOWARD THE ENTRANCE TO THE CASTLE GAR-dens. The gate is locked; the woman in the blue dungarees has gone home. I turn back and find our secret route. Out through the rabbit hole.

Halfway down the winding, cobbled road, I remember my shoes and put them back on.

Dim lights are shining behind the thick curtains at Gaston's.

I think of school, counting the days, holding your breath until life begins, longing for the chance to make something of yourself.

My fingers press the keys. It must be afternoon in New York.

He picks up, I listen to his name.

"I'm coming home," I whisper and hear a brittle smile at the other end of the line.

My cheeks are glowing, my fingers playful and free in the empty pockets of my raincoat. Today life begins, I think. And this time I know for certain. It begins.

AUTHOR'S NOTE

AGATHA, BARBARA, VIRGINIA

On December 3, 1926, Agatha Christie disappeared. On December 14 she was found in a tired and confused state at a spa hotel in Harrogate. She never spoke about her disappearance.

On December 7, 1939, Barbara Newhall Follett disappeared. Early in the evening she left her house in Brookline and was never seen again.

On March 28, 1941, Virginia Woolf disappeared. Her body was found three weeks later on the banks of the River Ouse, several miles from her Sussex home.

When researching this novel, I immersed myself in the lives of these three remarkable writers, through biographies, articles, diaries, and letters. The events of their lives narrated in this novel actually took place.

However, it is important to bear in mind that each scene is described through Hannah's eyes. Any elements that do not chime with the strictly biographical are Hannah's interpretation. In New York, she draws on the lives of these writers to bring her closer to her own truth.

And that truth is, of course, entirely fictional.

ACKNOWLEDGMENTS

This story owes a big warm thank-you to:

JASPER HENDERSON—for your incredibly keen eye, your patience, and knowing how to nurture a writer's mind.

LAURA BROWN—for your smart and sharp approach to the story; it's been inspiring and a feast to work with you on every aspect of the book.

CECILE BARENDSMA—for your warmth, your relentless energy, and clever, creative ways in getting the book noticed.

ERIC LANGE—for bearing with this writer's crazy moods and needs, for inspiring me and making life a loving and adventurous journey.

Thank you Eric de Vroedt, Emily Griffin, Mary Sasso, Theresa Dooley, and the entire Harper Perennial team, Willemijn Barelds, Lars Anderson, Lea Schnek, Tatjana Brinkman, Anje Roosjen, Marjanne de Jong, and Bea Leinders for delivering every little big piece that added significantly to *Find Me Gone*.

Last but not least: thank you, OSCAR VAN GELDEREN and every dude and dudess at Lebowski for "bowling" my book fabulously.

ABOUT THE AUTHOR

SARAH MEULEMAN is a Belgian writer and journalist. She was co-creator and host of the television show *Sarah's Savages*. Sarah is a *Vogue* columnist and has written many interviews with international artists, politicians, and celebrities. She studied Germanic philology (University of Ghent) and literature (University of Amsterdam, cum laude). *Find Me Gone* is her debut novel, which has already been published in Dutch and was nominated for the Bronzen Uil for best literary debut.